614

Power is Never Gentle

A Novel

Zo Ramey

For myself.
I earned this.

I did it, Mom

.

Table of Contents

CHAPTER ONE

614 - Elia

I hate moving. I don't know if it's the boxes, the heaviness, or the reminder that starting over always costs more than you expect. Maybe it's all of it. People love to romanticize fresh starts—new apartment, new city, new life—but when you're standing in an empty penthouse with nothing but echoes and exhaustion, it feels less like a fresh start and more like recovery. A slow exhale you've been holding for years.

The space looks untouched, museum-level quiet. Wide glass windows, cold air drifting in, floors too polished to feel lived in. Even the echo feels unfamiliar, like the building is waiting to decide whether it accepts me or not.

What bothers me most isn't the silence. It's what isn't in it.

No cologne hanging in the air.
No footsteps pacing behind me.
No schedule taped to the fridge.
No voice correcting my tone before interviews.

Just me. Just peace.

And peace feels strange when chaos has been your baseline.

I come from a ten-year marriage that felt more like a sentence than a union, and every day I thank God there were no children caught between us. Kids deserve stability. What we had was a performance—camera-ready on the outside, cracked right down the middle behind closed doors.

Let me clear something up before Hollywood spins its narratives. I'm not Halle, Angela, or Viola. I don't pretend to touch their league. But I can hold my own. I've headlined films, held my weight in ensemble casts, and made my mark on enough scripts that assistants whisper my name before I walk into a room.

But every "win" out here has a price—privacy, sleep, pieces of yourself you don't get back.

That's how I ended up in this empty penthouse, sleeping on a blanket like a runaway.

My soon-to-be ex wasn't just my husband—he was my manager, my handler, my everything-but-God.

He curated my image. Dictated what I wore, what I said, who I talked to, how I ate.

He called it protection.

I called it survival.

Eventually, I stopped calling it anything. I just lived inside it because living outside it felt impossible.

But there comes a moment in every woman's life when she looks around and realizes she's become a guest star in her own damn story. The cameras stop, the makeup wipes off, and you don't recognize the person staring back.

Hollywood doesn't help. There are no real friends here. They love you when you're hot, avoid you when you're lukewarm, and disappear when you cool off. I watched it happen over and over.

A co-star I'd defended for years stopped answering my messages the minute Anthony got booked on a podcast that could "elevate her brand."

A director who once swore I was his "creative soulmate" stopped inviting me to his rooftop gatherings when my last film opened soft.

Another actress—someone I introduced to half her current contacts—was suddenly "too busy" for brunch meetings once my marriage rumors started leaking.

You learn quickly: loyalty here has a contract, an NDA, and an expiration date.

Anthony wasn't always the villain.

He was the man who saw me when I couldn't see myself.

He was the one who told me to stop playing small.

He pushed me when no one else believed I deserved a seat at any table.

And the truth is—I needed that once.

But you can outgrow the version of yourself that loved someone.

We didn't meet in some romantic whirlwind. It was embarrassing, actually.

I was on a date with a man who "lost his wallet" at bill time—thirty-five years old and disappearing like a teenager when the check hit the table.

He muttered something about going to the bathroom after I advised there would be no night cap and vanished for fifteen minutes.

I knew he wasn't coming back.

I knew the waitress knew he wasn't coming back.

And the pity in her eyes irritated me more than his disappearing act.

I ordered another glass of wine out of pure spite.

That's when Anthony walked up.

"Excuse me, ma'am," he said, "but I couldn't help noticing, two glasses of wine, but you're alone and... your date hopped in a Lyft ten minutes ago."

I forced a smile even though my dignity was somewhere in the alley with that man's excuses.

"Well," I said, "dates don't always work out. But I'm not wasting a perfectly good glass of wine because a grown man felt like acting twelve."

He smirked. "My mother didn't raise me to overlook a woman in need. I'm obligated to bore you with stories about stocks and bonds for the rest of the evening."

The man was dressed.

Black Louboutins, charcoal Armani suit, black-on-black Submariner Rolex—clean, neat, controlled.

Chocolate skin like Morris Chestnut with that LL confidence in the shoulders.

He looked like success.

He looked like he knew it, too.

But I wasn't anybody's damsel.

"I appreciate it," I said, "but the 'my mama raised me right' line isn't going to work. I'll cover my check and go home."

He didn't flinch. He just took the bill from the table, ripped it clean, and handed it to the waitress.

"I'll have the Barclay Prime cheesesteak—medium," he said. "And she'll have your finest. Do you have Petrus Pomerol 1998?"

The waitress nodded and left.

Anthony crossed his legs, adjusted his jacket, and placed the napkin across his lap like he owned the entire situation.

I should've walked out.

But my Uber was still ten minutes away.

And his arrogance was—annoyingly—entertaining.

"So," I said, "are you actually going to bore me with "Stocks" while I kill time?"

"No," he replied calmly. "I thought I'd enjoy my meal while staring into the ocean of the deepest reflections of the stars."

I blinked. Slowly.

"That makes absolutely no sense."

He shrugged. "Maybe not. But I get forty-five seconds of bliss looking into your eyes. The other fifteen are wasted on your blinks."

"That was so corny" I replied giving him a 5 second blank stare.

It was stupid.

It was corny.

But it worked.

We laughed—real, belly-deep, unguarded laughter.

That moment cracked open a door I'd kept locked for years.

"I'm Elia," I told him. "Like 'E-LEE-uh,' in case you try to remix it."

"I like that," he said, checking his phone. "Anthony Bennett. Do you have a last name, Ms. Elia? Or should I loan you mine?"

"Elia Girard," I said. "And I'll be keeping it."

"Noted."

We talked until closing.

If love lived only on memories, we would still be married.

He wanted to wait until marriage.

We didn't, not completely, but we waited enough to make the tension dangerous.

We got married six months later—not because it was perfect, but because it felt like the right kind of chaos.

Rio was our honeymoon.

And let's be clear: we never saw Rio.

We saw each other.

He woke things in me I didn't know existed. I was mid-twenties, he was mid-thirties, and I was still learning my own body, still learning the kind of woman I could become. Back then, he felt like the answer to questions I never knew how to ask."

Then business crept in.

Then business took over.

Then business replaced everything else.

He left Wall Street, moved to California, and poured himself into managing my career.

He was brilliant at it.

At twenty-five, I was everywhere—scripts, premieres, magazine spreads.

Then came the shift.

There was the time he corrected my red carpet pose—through clenched teeth—because my shoulder angle didn't match the "brand mood board."

The night he canceled my mother's flight because "family complicates the narrative."

The morning he left mid-argument because one of his clients texted him—"real money comes first."

And the silent treatment he'd give me if a director complimented me too much.

Little things that grew into big things.

Big things that became the end.

And once — just once — I learned how quiet a room can get after a door closes too hard.

We became strangers in designer clothes.

One morning I woke up, looked at him, and didn't feel anything.

Not love.

Not hate.

Just... absence.

So I left, filed for separation, packed a few essentials, and moved out before he could talk me into staying.

I didn't plan for the consequences.

I just needed out.

Now I'm in an empty penthouse sleeping on a blanket that feels thinner every night.

But even with the cold floors and stiff necks, this emptiness feels better than that marriage ever did.

The espresso machine hisses behind me as I rinse my face.

My phone vibrates on the counter.

Movers. Finally.

"Hello?" I answer, wiping mouthwash from my lips.

"Yes, ma'am. Confirming delivery address for your furniture. Our team is in the area."

"1744 N. Wyllcoax Blvd, Los Angeles, 90028," I say.

"Penthouse number, ma'am?"

I let out a long breath.

"Suite *614*."

And just like that, my new life finally starts to take shape.

CHAPTER TWO

616 - Shai

"Another person moving into the building?" I ask Pete as I step into the lobby and immediately regret not wearing steel-toe boots. The whole place looks like someone dropped a department store from the ceiling. Boxes stacked to the vents, rolled-up rugs leaning like drunks, an elliptical blocking half the walkway, and a lamp shaped like a jellyfish staring at me like *try it.*

I hand Pete his Starbucks — caramel macchiato, extra drizzle — his unofficial bribe for keeping the building civil and keeping an eye out for me. Never know what kind of stalkers are lurking.

"Thank you, ma'am. Always a pleasure," he says, already sipping.

I raise an eyebrow. "Ma'am?".

"—Shai," he corrects quickly, grinning.

"Much better."

"Yeah," he continues, nodding toward the hall, "looks like you've got yourself a new neighbor. Moving into 614. Actress. Or influencer. Or something. Pretty, though. Sweet. And if I wasn't married..." He gives me that old-man shrug.

I squint at him. "Pete. Behave." I say, stepping into the elevator.

The doors close before he can say anything else. My floor is chaos. Straight chaos. It looks like a tornado with an Amazon Prime membership came through. A mover is trying to wedge a triangular dresser through a square doorway like geometry is optional. Someone dropped a box labeled "Kitchen Fragile" and whatever's inside is clicking ominously like it's filing a complaint.

"Good luck with that," I tell him, unlocking my door and sliding inside.

Silence. My kind of quiet.

The penthouse smells like cedar and espresso — home and work. My sanctuary. My command center. The place where my brain actually shuts up long enough to form solutions. The only space in the world where I don't have to translate myself for anyone.

People call me a techie, but that word is too small. I'm the CEO and founder of Intel-Ligent — the baby I started with nothing but instinct, spite, and a chip on my shoulder big enough to power the Eastern seaboard.

We've got offices in three cities.
Global contracts.
Patents that would make your favorite billionaire sweat.
A board that doesn't breathe unless I say so.

Antoine handles the interviews, photo ops, red carpets, charity galas, political mixers — the whole PR-diplomat-corporate sweetheart thing. He's built for it. Clean smiles. Good suits. Talks like he came out the box prepped for a press conference.

Me?
I prefer anonymity.
Control over attention.
Results over applause.

The world sees Antoine, but Intel-Ligent runs off my mind, my strategy, my innovation. You can't misinterpret hierarchy when I walk into a room. Not because I yell. Because power doesn't announce itself. It arrives.

Still, even power comes from somewhere, and mine didn't come from anything pretty.

Jersey raised me.
The real Jersey, not that TV version with tans and tantrums.
My mother died when I was twelve. Father? A rumor with a pulse.

After the funeral, relatives tried to step in, but sympathy never solved anything. Survival did.

I bounced. Couch to couch. Stairwell to stairwell. Shelters some nights. Libraries others — the ones that stayed open late enough for homework and early enough for warmth. I remember the hum of vending machines more than I remember anybody's bedtime stories.

You learn a lot about yourself when life strips you down to instinct.

You learn that if the world doesn't make room for you, you carve your own place.

You learn discipline no parent ever taught you.

You learn never to depend on anybody's "good intention."

Antoine was the one person who didn't treat me like baggage. His father died around the same time I lost my mother, and grief glued us together. I was at their house so much his mother started looking at both of us sideways. Strict woman — Bible-thick beliefs, household rules etched in stone.

She didn't like me staying over.

Didn't care that I wasn't into her son.

Didn't care that we were just kids trying to survive something bigger than us.

But Antoine saw me.

Not as a burden.

Not as a threat.

Just as Shiloh — the kid with the attitude, the busted sneakers, and a stubborn streak that could bend steel.

We studied together, ate together, kept each other in line. He called me out when I did stupid shit. I kept him off the block when half the guys we knew were drifting into gangs or getting swallowed by street politics and street pharmaceuticals.

We promised each other we'd do more in life.
And somehow, we did.

I got accepted into Columbia at sixteen — full academic track, honors, accelerated courses. Antoine got into Rutgers the year after. We were convinced we were destined for greatness.

College was easy. Too easy. The questions were predictable, the professors fascinated that someone my age was keeping up, the material something I could devour without blinking. I took pride in being the outlier, but outliers get bored fast.

I dropped out at eighteen with a 4.0 and a hole in my chest big enough for a new obsession.

Tech. The raw kind.
Not the polished Silicon Valley fantasy — the messy, brilliant chaos beneath it. The logic, the code, the puzzle of systems that judged nobody except your brain.

I lived in labs and libraries.
Borrowed textbooks.
Snuck into Princeton's tech lounges through connections who were barely older than me but twice as brilliant.
We debated everything — encryption, binary structure, systems theory, ethics.
One night, a debate about binary compression got so heated someone threw a coffee cup.

And that's when it hit me.
Not the cup — the future.

A program.
A system.
An idea that refused to leave my head.

I called Antoine.
Told him I was building something.
Told him I didn't know what it was yet, but it was going to be big.

He didn't ask if I was sure.
He asked what we needed.

We gathered every sharp, brilliant misfit we knew — hackers, coders, engineers, creatives — the ones who didn't ask permission because they knew no one would give it anyway.

Our first board meeting was in a cramped apartment with mismatched chairs, lukewarm pizza, and code scribbled across a whiteboard so old the marker stains were permanent.

We argued for hours.
Argued code architecture.
Argued about whether the world was ready for what we were building.
Argued about who would sleep and who would finish debugging a subsystem by sunrise.

Six months later, we had a stable program without a bug in sight. A year later, we bought our first tiny office — six desks, two borrowed laptops, three broken chairs, and a lease we celebrated like a wedding.

After that, it was a blur.
Funding rounds.
Partnerships.
Patents.
Scaling.
Hiring.
Sleepless nights that turned into empires.

Twenty years later, Intel-Ligent stands shoulder-to-shoulder with Apple, IBM, Microsoft — giants who don't scare me, because competing with giants is fun. Easy battles bore me.

Antoine became our public face.
He looks good on camera.
He sounds good in meetings.
Investors love him.

I move in silence - show up when I have to, especially when the loudest people in the room want the power without the spotlight.

Walk into the office in matte-black slacks, a tailored jacket, and polished Chelsea boots — the kind of fit that whispers money without ever raising its voice.

My presence does the talking.

Antoine jokes that he wishes he had my privacy.

I tell him privacy is expensive, and he wouldn't survive without an audience.

He laughs because he knows it's true.

I pour myself a glass of orange juice, grab a water, and settle at my desk. Three monitors glow at me — judgmental, bright, ready to ruin my morning.

Mikey — our Security Director, our resident genius, our government-adjacent wildcard — sent me a "training exercise."

Subject line: Training Day.

The message reads:

"New code.

Crack it in five minutes and you get your next lesson.

Script changes each attempt.

Screen goes dark on click.

Good luck, grasshopper.

- MK"

Dramatic as always.

I click the link.

Screen goes black.

Binary rains down.

Password loops, encrypted blocks, dummy firewalls — his usual showmanship.

I dive in.

Fingers moving, brain switching gears.

Four minutes and thirty-seven seconds — I'm in.

Before I can enjoy it, Mikey pings me again:

"Bottom right link."

I click.

"Open the embedded script."

I do.

LAPD's internal database fills my screen.

"Mikey... what am I looking at?" I type.

"Search Antoine."

I type Antoine Joseph.

There it is.

Drunk and disorderly.

Mugshot that looks like a man fighting gravity and losing.

I breathe out slow.

There's annoyance, sure — but underneath it, that familiar protective instinct. Antoine is brilliant, loyal, necessary... and chronically allergic to staying out of trouble.

"You couldn't have just TOLD me this?" I send.

"Where's the fun?

He's in the tank. It was done quietly, luckily no media involved.

They'll release him when you get there.

Told them to let him sleep.

Lol."

"Tell them, I'm on the way. Have him outside waiting please."

I shut everything down, grab my keys, and head out.

The drive is quick. When I pull up to the station, Antoine is sitting on the steps looking like a rejected action figure — shirt wrinkled, expression confused, hair fighting for its life.

"Antoine," I say, crossing my arms, "what the hell were you doing last night?"

He grins lazily. "Sky Bar. Lakers cheerleaders. Shots. Spontaneous concert. Star-Spangled Banner. Shirt off. Crowd loved it. Ten out of ten, would do again."

I pinch the bridge of my nose. "You are the COO of a multi-billion-dollar tech company. You cannot be out here acting like a TikTok cautionary tale."

He laughs. "They were pretty."

"Did you at least get a number?" I ask.

He perks up. "Of course. Look at me."

Which means he bought all the drinks and they disappeared before dessert. Classic Antoine.

"Where's your car?" I ask.

"Still by the bar. I hope."

"Breakfast first," he says, groaning. "Jail food doesn't sit right with my spirit."

"Fine," I say, unlocking the car. "You're paying."

As we pull off, I put on Lauryn Hill — real Lauryn, not appearances and features. Her voice fills the space like memory.

"She ever drops a real comeback album," I say, "the industry's done."

Antoine hums "Ex-Factor", dramatic and off-key.

Two Jersey kids in L.A.

Built something out of nothing.

Still keeping each other alive.

CHAPTER THREE

614 - Elia

Thank goodness the move went smoothly. The movers only managed to break a vase I picked up in Italy a few years back, so I can deal with that. The rest? Boxes. Too many boxes. And every single one of them is sitting here judging me.

But wine first.

"Alexa, connect to speaker," I say.

A soft chime.

"Now play SZA, SOS."

Her voice fills the apartment—warm, moody, perfect for a day like this. I let myself sway, just a little two-step between boxes, letting the stress roll off. I reach for one of the smaller boxes labeled KITCHEN??, trying to convince myself I actually labeled things correctly during the rush.

Then my phone rings.

Of course.

And of course it's my mother.

I already feel my soul leave my body. She has *no idea* I moved out of the house I shared with Anthony, so this will be fun.

"Hello, Mother," I say, trying not to sound like I'm holding back a groan.

"Hello, Elia! I was sitting here and wondering why my daughter, my only daughter, has neglected to tell me that she was leaving her husband?"

"Mother, I told you months ago that things were not working out between Anthony and me," I say while digging through a second box, now irritated because I cannot find my wine opener.

"Well, you know the Lord has blessed that marriage. You need to go on down to the Ebenezer First Baptist Episcopal Church of Christ and talk to the bishop. You know he counsels married couples and helps them get through the tough times. I would hate for your souls to be condemned for all eternity just because you hit a rough patch. The Bible says all things are possible through Christ and Christ alone... Elia, are you listening to me?"

"Yes!"

Actually, no.

I'm tearing through packing paper like a raccoon in the night.

"I *am* listening, and we tried counseling. Right now we need some time apart."

"Ok, baby, well you know I will be praying for you."

"Ok, Mom, well I have to finish unpacking. I will call you tomorrow. Make sure you take your medicine and call me if you need me," I say, trying not to make it obvious that I'm rushing her off the phone. The Good Book says honor thy mother. It does not say I have to be sober doing it.

"I will, Elia. Call me tomorrow, and do not forget to say your prayers. Sometimes it feels as though He is not listening, but He is always there on time."

"Yes, Mom. Goodnight."

I hang up quickly—before she decides to hit Part Two of the sermon.

I love her, truly.

But she is the saint of all saints. She's the woman who prays over the mail. And right now? I don't need a scripture. I need a corkscrew.

I scan the room again—boxes stacked everywhere. I *could* run down to the store, but honestly? No. I own a wine opener. Pete—the doorman—mentioned earlier that my neighbor across the hall seemed "cool." And frankly, after the day I've had, I will happily knock on a stranger's door for one tiny piece of metal salvation.

I slide on my slippers and head across the hall. The hallway is spotless, quiet, smelling faintly of whatever expensive neutral scent luxury buildings pump through vents to feel rich. I knock lightly.

Nothing.

Of course.

I knock again, louder this time.

"Coming!" someone calls. Locks rattle. Then the door cracks open. "Yeah?"

And okay... not what I imagined.

Standing in front of me is someone who is absolutely mid-workout. Sweat still on their shoulders, tank top clinging a little, basketball shorts sitting just right, Nike trainers. Mocha skin, short natural curls, clean lineup, tattoos with meaning—not for show. Solid build, confident posture. And teeth so white they practically sparkle.

"Hi," I say, adjusting quickly. "I'm Elia. I moved across the hall the other day. I'm still unpacking, and I was wondering if I could borrow a wine opener?"

"Yeah, sure," Shiloh says, easy and unbothered. "You can come in while I grab it if you want."

And here I go ruining it.

"No, I'm fine here. Thanks!"

Way too fast.

Way too defensive.

Immediately, I regret it. Because now it's going to seem weird—like I'm uncomfortable or judging or cautious. I don't need those rumors floating in a penthouse building. I really do not need to be the straight actress who's "weird with the gay neighbor." That headline would live on the internet forever.

"Suit yourself," she says, and closes the door. Not rude. Just done.

I stand there like an idiot.

Did I offend her? Probably.

Is this how neighbor wars begin? Most likely.

I debate going back home and pretending this never happened. But just as I turn to leave, her door opens again.

She hands me the wine opener.

"You know," she says with a smirk, "you shouldn't give up so easily on something you want so badly."

Her smile is sharper this time. Controlled. A little mischievous. And that dimple in her right cheek? Yes, I noticed. Details matter. Clean nails, bright teeth—no pests migrating from that unit into mine. Priorities.

"Thank you so much," I say, genuinely relieved. "I'll bring it back in a few—"

"No, keep it. I've got more. That's the crappy one anyway." She steps back toward her apartment.

"I'm sorry—I didn't catch your name," I call before she disappears again.

"That's probably because I didn't throw it," she says, and shuts the door.

Well then.

Not rude.

Just... dry. Sarcastic. Direct.

Probably very East Coast.

I shrug, glance at the opener, and head back inside.

I've got SZA playing, finally have a way to open my wine, and a mountain of boxes waiting for me.

"Thank you, 616," I whisper as I close the door behind me.

CHAPTER FOUR

616 - Shai

New neighbors. Perfect. Right when I finally hit the cool-down portion of a HIIT workout that nearly folded me in half. Instagram makes it look easy, but hold a plank for a minute and a half and your quads start filing for emancipation. My tank is drenched, sneakers still on from the circuit, trying to breathe through the last sequence when I hear the faint thump of boxes dropping in the hallway.

So much for zen.

I grab my towel, wipe the sweat off my face, and stretch my shoulders as I walk to the kitchen. I love this building because it's usually quiet—adults, moneyed people, no TikTok kids screaming into ring lights. But today the universe said, "Here, Shai. Have some chaos."

Pete, the doorman, mentioned someone new was moving into 614. Some actress. There are a few industry people on the top floors already, but they're usually discreet. Then again, "discreet" in Hollywood means the paparazzi only show up twice a week.

I grab a bottle of water, down half of it, and lean against the counter as I think about what Pete said. She seemed "sweet," according to him. Pete calls everybody sweet, unless he hates them. Then they're "characters." So I don't know what that means. But something about the way he said it... I don't know. Maybe it was the way he almost choked on his own spit trying not to gush about her.

I shrug it off. Neighbors are neighbors. I keep to myself anyway.

Still, when I opened the door earlier, she surprised me. Big doe eyes, caramel complexion, delicate features, maybe five-three on a tall day. Hair pulled back into a ponytail with light brown highlights I could tell were her natural shade. Petite frame, fitted tee, sweats, slippers. Relaxed, simple, but you can tell when someone is used to being looked at. She had that quiet awareness, like she knows her face works.

Actors and musicians are always short. Napoleon complex, Hollywood edition.

I wasn't prepared for her to be standing there asking for a wine opener. I had just finished cooling down, still in workout mode, hair curled from the sweat. She looked... startled. Not scared, just... surprised that her neighbor was me.

Happens a lot. You walk out expecting a safe, predictable silhouette and end up face-to-face with someone who doesn't fit neatly into the categories your mind prepared. That micro-pause before people reset their expectations gives everything away.

But she was polite. Nervous. Over explaining. It was almost cute.

Almost.

Anyway, she has her wine opener now. I gave her the worst one because people who don't return things love to keep the expensive ones. She can keep it. I've got four more.

I take another gulp of water and reach for my phone. It's Friday. Antoine is either just waking up or just getting into trouble.

He answers on the second ring.

"Yoooo, Shai! What it do?" he says, loud as hell. Club-volume voice. No music behind him though, so he must be home.

"Nothing. Cooling down from a workout," I say, stretching my calves on the counter's baseboard. "What's up? You sound wide awake."

"I'm getting into something tonight. Thinking of hopping over to Monaco. The Ares Grand Prix afterparty is jumping all weekend. You pulling up?"

"Monaco?" I laugh. "Bro, you just woke up. How the hell you already thinking about a different continent?"

"Because I'm Antoine," he says like it's an explanation. "And because you never do anything fun anymore. You work, you code, you tinker, you read, you lurk in that penthouse like Batman. I'm tired of it. I need my best friend back."

"I didn't go anywhere," I say, even though I know damn well he's not wrong.

"Shai... your ass hasn't touched a casino table, a yacht deck, or a nightclub since when— a year go? You didn't even come out with for my birthday this year."

I don't answer.

"That's what I thought," he says. "We hitting Monaco. Get dressed."

"Toine..."

"Nope. No excuses. Put on some of that low-key billionaire swag you do. And don't start with the 'I'm busy' speech. You're rich, not dying."

I sigh. "I've got a meeting Monday. We need to finalize the Q4 projections."

"And we will. After we touch a little international soil and remember we're human beings and not robots who live inside spreadsheets."

"I don't live inside spreadsheets. That's your job."

"Exactly. And I'm telling you—it sucks. You need air."

He's pushing. Hard. And the sad part? He's not wrong. I've been grinding so long I forgot what outside feels like. I pay for a jet I barely use. I own property in three countries and haven't stepped foot in two of them in years. My idea of fun is buying a new monitor.

"Alright," I say finally. "Fine. Monaco."

"That's my dog!" he says, damn near blowing out my eardrum. "I'll call Wayne. Jet wheels up in two hours."

"Make it three. I need a shower."

"Bet. See you soon, bro."

He hangs up before I can object.

I head to the closet. Color-coded. Lined like a boutique. Rosa keeps it immaculate—she's the only person I trust in my space. I grab a pair of A. Testoni Black Labels, the ones with the dark–mid brown shift and the metal buckle. Not too flashy, not sloppy. I pull down a soft espresso-colored cashmere V-neck and tailored slacks. Clean. Understated. Masculine without trying to be.

I hit the shower, let the hot water melt the rest of the stretching out of my spine, then stand under the air-dry vent to dry off. I rub a little curl cream in my hair, brush the sides, line the edges with my trimmer.

Then I pull out the bottle.

Initio Parfums — Side Effect.

Warm rum, tobacco, vanilla, spice. It doesn't scream money. It whispers confidence. The kind of scent that makes people remember you even when they try not to.

I hit two sprays. Enough to shift a room, not drown it.

As I'm slipping my watch on, there's a knock. Right on time.

Antoine.

I open the door, and he steps in wearing a designer fit that probably cost someone's mortgage. Rings on both hands, chain sitting heavy, hair freshly cut.

"Shai! Look at you!" he says, adjusting my collar like a proud uncle. "Damn. You clean tonight."

"My stylist organized my closet. I just picked what was reachable."

"You look like money with discipline," he says. "Love it."

I grab my phone, wallet, passport just in case, then follow him out.

We step into the hallway—and there she is.

614, my neighbor.

But now she's not in sweats and slippers. No, she's giving a whole different vibe. Fitted jeans hugging the right places, soft shawl over a simple top, stilettos clicking across the marble. Hair down now, loose waves brushing her shoulders. Makeup light, like she didn't try too hard but still nailed it.

She's... different like this. Not better, just—polished.

I shift out of her path automatically.

Antoine, naturally, damn near breaks his neck.

"Excuse me, ma'am," he says, chest puffed, voice dropped two octaves. "My name is Antoine. Welcome to the building. If you need help with anything, I'm your guy."

She gives him a polite smile—the kind women give men they don't want but don't want to be rude to.

"Thank you," she says. Then she looks directly at me. "Oh, 616... the wine opener worked perfectly. Thanks again."

"Anytime," I say, nodding once.

Antoine's soul leaves his body.

We all get into the elevator. Antoine is performing, leaning on the rail, acting like he's starring in a fragrance commercial. She's on her phone. I'm wishing the elevator was faster.

"Yo," Antoine says too loudly, "I can't wait to hit Monaco! Strip is gonna be wild!"

She doesn't react, though the corner of her mouth betrays mild amusement.

"Toine," I warn, "I'm trying to relax this weekend. You told them separate rooms, right?"

"Of course!" he lies.

"Separate rooms, Antoine."

"Shai, I got you," he says, holding up three fingers like a fake Boy Scout.

The doors open. She steps out first and walks straight toward a waiting Mercedes GLC Coupe. Clean. Tasteful. No color-wrap nonsense.

Antoine watches her like a man watching his future wife walk away.

"Bro..." he whisper-yells. "She is BAD. Lord have mercy. I'm about to get my life right. I'm talking church every Sunday. Meditation. Celibacy. Therapy. All that."

"You don't even know her," I say, stepping into the back of the Maybach. "She could be a serial killer."

"Worth it," he says, climbing in after me.

"Good evening, Shai," Rich says from the front. "To the airport?"

"Yes, Rich. Thank you."

We pull off. City lights roll by. Antoine pops open the champagne like he's the one paying the fuel bill.

"Well, I don't see you doing better," he says.

"I don't need to do better," I reply. "I'm not looking for anything."

"You never are."

"Because emotions break the heart, Toine. And I don't do broken."

He nods. He knows not to push.

I look out the window.

A quick, sharp thought of how perfectly manicured her hands were slips through my mind.

CHAPTER FIVE

614 - Elia

Ladies' night. Thank God.

Between moving into a half-empty penthouse, dodging Tony's on-again, off-again dramatics, and trying not to spiral into a full existential crisis... I deserve a drink. Or three.

I do one last mirror check.

Hair laid.

Outfit immaculate.

Lip gloss glossing.

Cheekbones doing the Lord's work.

Cell phone? Keys? Purse? Perfume?

Good.

One more sip of wine before I go.

Do not judge me — I know everybody pre-games.

I lock up and head down the hall, and of course... the universe plays games. I run right into 616 and her friend. Why is it that men insist on trying me with recycled pickup lines? Sir, please. I have lived enough life to recognize Dollar Store game.

We exchange a few words — her friend tries way too hard, 616 keeps it neutral — and then we're sharing an elevator like a sitcom pilot. Pretty sure he was staring at my butt. I knew I should've stood in the back.

As soon as the doors open, I slide out and head to my car — my 2026 Mercedes AMG CLE-Coupe. She purrs like a dream. I tap my screen, queue up my girl Jazmine Sullivan, and glide onto Sunset like I'm in a music video nobody asked for but everybody would watch.

When I pull up to Lola's in West Hollywood, the hostess takes me to the back corner where my girls are already halfway through their first round.

"Ladies?" I say, leaning in for hugs.

"Hey Miss, how you doing?" Melissa asks, squeezing me tight. She smells rich. Like escrow and closing costs. Melissa is the real estate plug for every A-lister in L.A. — confident, direct, and allergic to broke behavior.

"I'm fine," I say, sliding into my seat. "Listen. I want a clean night. No pity. No crying. No bringing up Tony. Just drinks, laughs, and foolishness. Understood?"

They nod in unison, which means absolutely nothing. Melissa immediately clears her throat like she's preparing to testify.

"Ok, I'm just gonna say this," she begins. "One of my wealthiest bachelor clients had a showing today. I can check if he's open to a date. I hate seeing you go through this mess."

"Thank you, but no thank you," I say as my drink arrives. "I'm writing off men until I get myself together. I'm not leaving one circus to audition for another."

Melissa shrugs, unfazed. "Suit yourself. But he did say he doesn't date because he doesn't trust women, and he hasn't been intimate in a long time. Girl... you better strike while that man still remembers what to do."

Austin bursts out laughing. Austin is a basketball wife married to one of the Lakers' black-card starters. Everything she says sounds expensive and slightly chaotic.

"That man needs somebody to warm him up," Austin adds. "A late-night booty rub at minimum."

"That's why I have a secret drawer," I respond without shame. "Most men are a waste of time anyway. I can do bad all by myself."

"And that right there is why you need a man," Austin says. "Nothing like a man's touch."

"Pass," I say. "I'm not interested right now."

"You writing off men?" Austin asks slowly. "Like... permanently? You not becoming one of them lesbians, right?"

I choke on my drink.

"What? Girl, no! I'm just saying I'm not dealing with anybody right now."

Natalee jumps in. Natalee is our certified hood-to-Hollywood success story — an NFL wife with a ride-or-die spirit and zero filter.

"Well, don't knock it till you try it," she says. "A woman knows what spots to hit. Trust."

Melissa rolls her eyes. "Nat, please. Everybody knows you was in the streets before the league found you."

"Eating ain't cheating!" Natalee shouts, quoting Sommore from Queens of Comedy, and the whole table falls out laughing.

Lord, these women.

"Speaking of lesbians," I say, taking a large sip, "my new neighbor is one. I guess. One of those masculine females. I went over earlier to borrow a wine opener, and when she opened the door... I wasn't expecting that. These are multimillion-dollar penthouses. I was just surprised."

Melissa gives me a look. "You better be careful before she shows up trying to open more than your wine."

Austin yells out, "I need something big, stiff, and real!" The entire lounge turns to stare before she waves them off like she's accepting an award.

Natalee leans in. "Well, is she cute at least?"

I pause.

Why am I pausing?

"She's... attractive. Handsome? I don't know the word. But pretty, yes."

Natalee claps her hands. "Well, if you don't want her, I might."

"Well we gone be fighting, cuz I ain't dyking!" Melissa says, another reference to Sommore's scene in The Queens of Comedy.

The table explodes again.

I shake my head. "Y'all are insane. And yes - definitely your type, Nat. But she was polite enough... eventually."

The night goes on — gossip, trends, cheating scandals, my next role, Austin's husband's nonsense. I love these women. They exhaust me, but they lift me too.

When I finally pull off into the night, SZA humming through the speakers, I think back to the hallway. To 616. To the way she looked past her friend's foolishness. Cool. Unbothered. Centered.

Not saying we'll be friends.

But I'll keep it cordial.

She does have style.

And she smelled... good.

I sit with that thought a little longer than I planned.

Warm. Clean. A little spicy. Masculine without trying.

I turn the music up and laugh at myself.

My phone vibrates.

Unknown Caller.

"Hello?"

"Enjoying the new penthouse?" Anthony's voice is calm. Familiar.

A pause.

"614 has beautiful light at night."

My breath catches. My hands go cold around the wheel.

I end the call.

Still trying to figure out why I can't get the smell of Initio out of my nose.

CHAPTER SIX

616 - Shai

Why do I do this to myself all the time?

When I meet a woman, all I really want to do is relax and chill, grab a bite, watch a movie, and see where the night goes. That is it. No drama, no Instagram stories, no "what are we" conversations. I am not looking for a relationship. I do not need anyone to take care of my home; that is why I have Rosa.

I know some of them see dollar signs when they look at me, and I am honestly thankful I am not a man, because God only knows the problems I would have then. Still, I am not stupid. If you are coming into my home, there are rules.

Waiver signed before entry.

They are willingly entering my home, knowing exactly who I am.

They are at least twenty-five and have shown valid identification.

They are willing and consenting to whatever may occur, even though that is rare. I just enjoy the company sometimes.

They also agree to be recorded during their stay so they cannot say things changed behind closed doors.

It sounds extreme until you have lived through the alternative.

Three years ago, this girl I barely knew came over after a party. We watched a movie, ate wings, and she passed out drunk on the couch. That was it. Next day, she was on the phone with her friend—loud—talking about how she "spent the night with that Intel-Ligent money" and might have to "make it worth her while." I heard every word from the kitchen. That was the night the cameras went up and the waivers got drafted.

Now, if I ever end up in court, I am ready.

"No, your honor, nothing changed. Exhibit A — four hours of us sitting here watching TV, having drinks, and me escorting her to the door. Signed. Sealed. Delivered."

I laugh to myself. I am just waiting to tear somebody up like that. You will not get me.

This is the protocol I keep trying to drill into Toine's thick skull. You need to protect yourself. A lot of women are out here shopping for a meal ticket. Antoine had three pregnancy scares this year alone. Three. He better clean it up before he has to marry one of these women, because his mother will not have her grand-baby raised out of wedlock. Oh no. She cracks me up, but she is serious.

Now I am getting to my point.

I have been dealing with this chick Nicole for about a month, but it is nothing to me. She digs me, and I think she is cool, but I am not into relationships, and I have told her that on numerous occasions. Repeatedly. In English and Spanish. Now, every time she comes over, she starts sipping a little and talking about how I need someone to come home to. How she knows how to take care of me. How we "move the same." Blah, blah, blah.

Tonight, she took it up a notch. Started asking what it would look like to move in. Asking where "her side" of the closet would be. Talking about how we would look at company events and charity galas once she "cleaned me up." That was when I mentally checked out. Cleaned who up... have you seen me?

I do not have time for the shenanigans, so tonight she politely got escorted out the door. Not just out of my door — I walked her downstairs and out of the building, then told Ray, our night doorman, to notify security if she comes back.

Nicole stood on the curb with mascara streaks on her cheeks, arms crossed, shivering in that thin little jacket, staring at me like I had ruined her life.

"You are really just going to throw this away?" she asked, voice shaking. "After everything I have done for you?"

"We had wings and Netflix, Nicole. This is not a divorce hearing," I said, keeping my tone calm. "I told you from day one — we are friends who hang out. That is it."

She looked like she wanted to slap me, cry, and beg all at the same time. Instead, she turned away and started pacing on the sidewalk, phone already in her hand. That was when I knew it was time to go.

Ray watches all of this, shaking his head.

"Oh, you got you another crazy one?" he says, laughing. "You sure know how to pick them."

"I know. I think I need to accept that I am meant to be alone. People do not understand friendship when they have other motives," I say, turning toward the elevator.

I almost step on 614's toes. I did not even realize she was behind me.

"Oh, excuse me. I did not see you there," I say, sliding past her.

"No, it is ok. I was going to let Ray know there is a woman outside crying hysterically. I did not know if she was about to go postal, but I think I have my answer," she says, smirking.

Her timing is immaculate.

"Hey, some women cannot deal with rejection," I say, trying not to sound too cocky as I head into the elevator.

"Hold it, I am coming up. I need to check something really quick," 614 says.

"Of course I will. Not," I laugh, letting the elevator door close — but I do not press a floor, so it stays on the lobby when she pushes the button.

The doors open again, and when she sees me standing there, she lets loose.

"You know you're an ass?" she says. "Why am I always being cordial, nice, speaking when I see you, and all I get is a nod? You need to get it together. Not everyone is out to bother you or hurt you. I am just trying to be polite."

She has some fire in her. I will give her that.

"Well, I do appreciate your honesty, and you are right. I am an ass. I apologize. I will work on correcting my destructive assholish behavior," I say, being sarcastic.

I lean back against the wall and giggle to myself. As soon as the doors open on our floor, she darts out and storms down the hall, heels clicking like a soundtrack.

"Hey!" I call after her. "Wait a sec."

She opens her door but stands in the doorway, facing forward.

"What?" she says, not looking at me.

"I apologize. I do. I don't trust people I do not know, and you're right — you have been nothing but kind to me. I am just not one for change. It takes time for me to come around, but I do eventually. I am a nice, laid-back person. I promise," I say, trying to sound as sincere as possible.

"Look, we're neighbors. That is it. We do not have to talk or communicate. I do not know you. You do not know me. We can leave it there. I will return your wine opener," she says.

She walks inside and slams the door in my face.

I turn around and walk to my place, taken aback by how she talked to me. She does not owe me anything, and I do not owe her anything, but I admit I have been rude. The other day, I saw her struggling to get her trash out the door. I did not help. I just stared until she figured it out. It was funny. You can tell she never had to do things like that for herself. Probably always had a man around. Or a team.

I guess I could give her a break. She seems cool enough. Maybe.

Just as I get into my PJs and pour myself a glass of wine, there is a knock at my door. It is probably her; no one else can get into the building without calling first, and she said she would bring back my wine opener.

I open the door, and there she is, holding the wine opener out for me to take. She has changed: powder-pink boy shorts, a pink spaghetti-strap tank, and pink-and-white Puma slippers. Fresh face, no makeup now. Softer.

"So what are you about to do?" I ask as I grab the wine opener.

"Nothing much," she says, still irritated, but calmer.

"Ok. Let me make this up to you. How about you put some clothes on and come back over? We will have dinner and chill. Sit and be friendly for once. How does that sound?" I say, testing the waters.

"I am ordering out," she says, flat.

"Ok, well, come get some of Rosa's cooking. She always makes extra in case Antoine comes over. I'm sure I have one movie in here you have not seen. And the best part is I have wine. Lots of it. And the good stuff," I say, looking into her eyes, trying to get a smile. "I am not taking no for an answer. And I will not make you sign my consent form. That is a big step for visitors. I mean, I can trust you, right?"

"Yes, you can trust me. But why do I have to put clothes on if we are sitting in the house?" she asks, confused.

"Well, I did not know if your man or significant other would be mad if you went to your neighbor's place like that. You do have on boy shorts, and I think I saw some cheek. I am just saying — that is not exactly first-meet-and-greet attire," I say, laughing.

"Well, we are both women, right? You do know that I am straight, right? And you are standing here in a tank and PJs. Are you going to get dressed too?" she asks.

"Yes, I do understand, and no, I am not," I reply without hesitation.

"And I do not have a boyfriend. I have a husband, but we are going through a divorce. Now, can I trust that we can be chill and cool without you trying to hit on me?" she asks, laughing lightly.

"No. Trust me. You do not need to worry. I respect all women, and if that is not how you go, I am the last person who will try to convert you. Too many emotions come with doing things like that," I say. "You are safe here. I just want to be friendly and have some company," I add, looking her straight in the eyes.

We hold eye contact for a beat too long. She looks away first.

"Well, in that case, you can trust me too," she says as she walks inside.

I cannot lie — boy shorts always do something to me. I am going to try my hardest not to look. Do not look, do not look, do not look...

Damn it. I looked.

I feel a little guilty, but it was worth it, I think to myself as I smirk and close the door.

I head into the wine room and grab a bottle of my best white to go with the linguine pasta dinner Rosa left simmering. I open it, refill my glass, and pour hers. I take a second to reset — this is neighborly, nothing more — then hand her a glass and lead her to the movie room. She looks pleased to see I have one of her films in the library.

Our shoulders brush as we walk side by side. I pretend not to notice.

I have every movie saved and stored on a multi-petabyte server, but I still enjoy the old-school DVD library. I am a hoarder and will always buy physical media. I probably still have some VHS tapes around here for my old VCR.

"Did you like it?" she asks as she browses the shelves.

"Did I like what?" I ask, watching her.

"My movie. Unspoken Bonds," she says, eyes on the cases.

"I thought it was ok. A little slow at first, but once it picked up, it was good. I did not know you played in that," I say, lying. I had picked it up recently just in case she ever asked.

"You are funny," she says. "I mean, with all the streaming services, why do you still pick DVDs? We can find everything online. You ever heard of Netflix?" she laughs.

"It is like streaming music versus vinyl. I would rather have the vinyl. It is raw. Plus, I always enjoyed going to Blockbuster and picking out a movie. One day, I want to give my kids that experience. Have a popcorn stand and everything — you know, candy, popcorn, turn it into a real Blockbuster night," I reply.

"That's cute. I like that," she says, sliding Unspoken Bonds back in place and pulling out The Conjuring: Last Rites instead. "Ok, now this? This one still scares me."

"You are a horror person?" I ask, taking the case.

"Horror and thrillers. I like what keeps me on my toes," she says.

"I like anything that makes people sit a little closer," I say.

She rolls her eyes, but she is smiling.

I lead us back to the living room. She takes a seat on the couch while I load the movie. She tucks her legs under her, close but not too close. Our knees are almost touching when I sit down.

"You know this one still gets me every time, even though I know where all the jumps are," I say.

"Seriously. Me too. I still flinch at the same parts," she says.

"I am going to grab the salads. Would you like more wine?" I ask, then catch myself. "Never mind. I will just bring the bottle."

Our hands brush when I pass it to her. She pulls back fast. I pretend I did not notice that either.

"Yeah, do that," she laughs. "Hey, 616... are you ever going to tell me your name? Not like I do not know already, but I would rather hear it from you."

"I have grown to like 616, 614," I say, walking out of the room.

"Would you like me to call you Elia?" I ask as I set up her place setting.

"No, it's fine," she says, smirking as she sips.

"Fine with me, 614 is a little easier to get right." I say, placing her salad and breadsticks down and taking my seat beside her.

"So, it has been about four months since you moved in," I say, keeping my tone easy. "How are you adjusting to the building?"

She lets out a small breath. "It is... different. Quiet. I like that. Still getting used to doing everything on my own, but... it feels peaceful here. Safer, somehow."

"People or place?" I ask.

"Both," she says softly. "Even you... a little bit."

I nod once, like it is no big deal. It is.

We say grace — which surprises her, I can tell — and I start the movie. After we finish our salads, I run back to the kitchen and make our dinner plates. I set them neatly in front of her and top off her wine.

"You are a great host, and this dinner is to die for," she says after her first bite.

"Yeah, Rosa has been with me since the beginning of starting my company. I didn't want too many people in and out of my home, so I sent her to culinary school. She loves to cook, so it worked out," I reply.

She glances toward the hallway where the equipment is set up, then back at me. "Intel-Ligent... I saw that on a billboard the other day. Do you work there or something you just contract with?"

"It is my company," I say, wiping my mouth.

"Like... you own stock, or..."

"I built it, brick by brick. I'm the CEO."

She blinks. "You are the CEO of Intel-Ligent? You?"

"Yes, me," I say, smirking. "Why is that so shocking?"

"I don't know. I pictured a forty-five year-old white guy in a Patagonia vest," she laughs. "Not... you."

"Sorry to disappoint."

"That is not disappointment," she says quickly. "Just... unexpected. So the guy... what is his name..."

"Antoine Joseph," I say.

"Yes. I have seen him somewhere as well," she says, leaning in.

"Yes, he is my COO. He is the face of the company, though. You met him last weekend in the hallway," I say, remembering how she played him.

"Oh yeah. That guy," she laughs. "That's funny. So that is why you have all this Intel-Ligent equipment and tech stuff in here."

"Pretty much. Antoine says I need to leave the technical work to the people we pay to do it, but I like tinkering. You have to keep up with the times. Technology changes daily. I have to stay ahead of the competition," I say, taking a bite.

"Well, that is good. I was wondering how you made it to the top of the food chain. I am surprised Pete did not tell me this," she says.

"Well, I have a rule. If you do not know who I am, I prefer to keep it that way. Most people are not reading tech and software journals or magazines, so they would not know me. I am not a limelight person. I leave that to Toine," I say.

She sets her fork down, studies me for a moment, smiles, and nods. "Well, CEO, can you rewind the movie now that I just missed five minutes?"

I nod. "Sure I can."

After I rewind the movie, I gather the plates and place settings. As I start the dishwasher and wipe the counters, she comes into the kitchen.

"More wine, please," she says, waving an empty bottle.

"Yeah, go in the wine closet and grab another. Pick whatever you want," I say.

She comes back with a modest bottle of Robert Mondavi. Refreshing. I half-expected her to grab the $2,000 bottle of Domaine de la Romanée-Conti 2008 I have been saving for a special occasion.

"Good choice," I say as I open it. "Did you pause the movie so I do not get yelled at again for making you miss something?"

"Of course. Now come on. Dinner was great, thank you, but I would like you to sit and enjoy some of it," she says, tugging my arm.

I can tell the wine is starting to hit. Hers and mine.

I join her in the living room and refill our glasses. I grab my Ralph Lauren throw and lay it across her. Our fingers graze again. She thanks me and settles in, wine in hand, eyes locked on the screen. As the movie plays, there are moments our shoulders almost touch. Every time it happens, one of us shifts — just a little — like we both agreed to keep this in the safe zone.

She looks comfortable. That is what I like to see. When someone can relax in my space as if they have been here before, it says a lot.

Maybe she is cool. A little bit.

"Would you like more wine?" I ask as the movie ends and I turn off the TV.

"No, thank you," she says. "I have taken up enough of your time for the night. I should get home."

"Ok," I reply, carrying our glasses into the kitchen.

When I walk back in, Elia is folding the throw blanket and placing it neatly on the sofa.

Damn it. I look again.

In my defense, she is bending over, and it is right there. An excellent view, if I might add. But I will respect her. She is straight, and I know that. She is cool. I am no dog. Not with her.

"I had a great time tonight. It felt good to let go for a few hours and relax. Thanks again," she says as I open the door. "Next time at my place. I will make dinner, and you pick the movie. Deal?"

"Deal," I say, standing in the doorway, making sure she gets into her apartment safely.

"See you later, 616," she says as she opens her door.

"See you soon, 614," I reply as she walks in.

Damn it. I did it again, I think to myself as I close my door.

***

614 — Elia

Well, who would have known she could be so nice? I had a good time with her, even though I am sure she checked me out a few times. Maybe that is why she wanted me to make sure I was dressed. I mean, they think just like men, right? I should have known.

But I was fine. I'm not going to trip over that, I decide as I undress and slide under the covers. It has been a long time since I felt that relaxed in someone else's space without worrying about what they wanted from me.

As I start to doze off, the craziest thought pops into my head:

Could I be with another woman?

Not just drunk-kiss-in-the-club-with-your-friend-for-attention stuff. Really be with a woman.

No. That is crazy talk. Do not let this girl get into your head like that.

I roll over and stare at the ceiling, annoyed at myself. I can already hear my mother's voice, talking about abomination and hellfire. Then Nat's voice cuts right through it:

"Do not knock it till you try it, girl."

Geez, what is going on? I think as a strange stir hits my gut and a hot flash rolls through me. Curiosity and guilt, arm-wrestling.

"Lord, please do not start with me right now," I mumble, even though I am not sure which side I am asking Him to handle.

This cannot be happening to me right now, I think, finally slipping into sleep.

CHAPTER SEVEN

614 - Elia

I am halfway down the hallway before I realize I am crying.

Not the cute, one-tear-down-the-cheek movie cry. The stupid, hot, embarrassing kind that sneaks up on you when you've held it together too long. My eyes burn, my nose is clogged, and my vision is blurry enough that I almost walk right past my own door.

Perfect. Exactly how every actress wants to come home—puffy-eyed and snotty, like a raccoon that lost a fight with its own trash can.

I fumble with my keys, drop them, and they skid across the hardwood in this echoey little sound that feels way too loud at two in the morning. I lean my forehead against the door, just breathing, trying to get it together.

You're fine, Elia. You're fine. You did the interview. You smiled. You laughed. You dodged the questions. You didn't say his name. Gold star.

I bend down to grab the keys, and that's when the door across the hall opens.

"Rough night?"

Her voice is soft, but it still makes me jump. I look up, and there she is—616, Shai—standing in her doorway in gray sweats and a black tee, barefoot, curls loose. She looks like she just got out of bed, but somehow still fully awake. Of course.

"Jesus, do you move without sound?" I ask, trying to wipe my face without looking like I'm wiping my face.

"Perk of being a ninja," she says lightly. Her eyes flick over me once, nothing too obvious, but she sees everything. "You good?"

I open my mouth to say yes. What comes out is a weird, broken noise that sounds more like a laugh and a sob had a baby.

So that answers that.

Her expression shifts, just a fraction. The playful edge drops.

"Come here," she says. Not a question. She steps out into the hallway, pulls my keys gently from my hand, and unlocks my door like she's done it a thousand times. "You can fall apart inside. These hallways have eyes and ears."

I hesitate, just a second—because that's my default setting: hesitate, calculate, perform, protect. But I am exhausted. Bone tired. Soul tired. I follow her in.

She flicks on the lamp in the corner instead of the overhead, like she's been here long enough to know the layout. Warm light, shadows, soft edges. My place suddenly looks smaller with her in it. Or maybe I just finally feel how small I am in it.

"Sit," she says, nodding toward the couch.

I drop my bag on the floor and sit, pulling my knees up like I'm trying to fold into myself. She disappears into the kitchen without asking for permission like she owns stock in my cabinets.

"You want tea? Water? Vodka?" she calls.

"Tea," I say, my voice thin. "Please and thank you. Vodka probably turn this into a way worse situation."

She chuckles under her breath, metal clinks, cupboard doors open. The normal sounds of someone moving in a kitchen. It grounds me. I stare at the wall and feel the tears start again, slower this time, like my body finally realized it has an opening and it's going to take it.

Work was fine. Hair and makeup, interview, pretend to be unbothered while strangers dissect your life like a crime scene. The problem wasn't work. The problem was the last question.

"So, Elia, any contact with Anthony these days?"

Like they were asking if I'd seen an old high school friend at the grocery store.

I swallow hard and wipe my face again. By the time she comes back, the tears are just sitting there, heavy. She sets a mug on the coffee table and hands me a tissue without saying anything about it, which I appreciate more than I should.

"Chamomile, honey, and a little lemon," she says. "I would've added whiskey, but you look like you might break in half if I breathe too loud."

"Thanks," I say, voice scratchy. I take the tissue first, blow my nose, then reach for the mug. My hands are shaking just enough to make the tea ripple.

She doesn't sit right next to me. She takes the chair at an angle, close but not crowding, one ankle resting on her knee, elbows on her thighs. Watching me without staring. Waiting.

"It was a long day," I say finally.

"I can tell," she says. "What happened?"

"It's nothing," I start, automatic. "I'm just tired."

She tilts her head, eyes narrowing the slightest bit, not buying it. "You're an actress. You know when someone's lying because you do it for a living. So do I. Want to try again?"

I let out a humorless laugh. "Wow. Drag me, why don't you."

"I'm not dragging you," she says calmly. "I'm offering you a rare chance to not perform. You can take it or not. I'll still drink my tea and enjoy my splash of whiskey."

It's the way she says it—casual, no pressure—that makes something in my chest crack. I stare down at the steam rising from the mug, the way it curls and disappears.

"They asked about him," I say quietly.

She doesn't say anything, so I keep going.

"Anthony."

The name feels like a pebble in my mouth. Small, but sharp. All these stupid highlight reels flash through my mind: the wedding, the red carpets, the interviews where we sat side by side and lied on command.

"They always get there eventually," I say. "They clock the ring finger, the change in my mood, the timelines. They act like they're just doing their job, like they're so sorry to bring it up, but their eyes light up like Christmas. Trauma makes good TV."

Her jaw tightens. I notice it because I'm used to reading faces, and hers is usually relaxed. Controlled. Right now it isn't.

"What did you say?" she asks.

"I gave the approved answer," I say bitterly. "We're no longer together, I wish him the best, I'm focused on my work, blah blah blah. I smiled. I laughed. I made them feel comfortable asking me about the worst year of my life."

The last part comes out sharper than I expect. My eyes sting again. I sip the tea to give myself something to do, something to hold.

"Did he cheat?" she asks, voice even. No tabloid curiosity. Just a data point.

"No," I say. "That would've been easier. At least then I'd have something simple to point to. What he did was quieter. Slower."

I stop there. Long enough that she doesn't interrupt. Long enough that I almost don't continue.

I take a breath.

"It was... the way he made me feel crazy about my own needs," I say. "Like I was overreacting. Like I was ungrateful. Like I should be lucky someone like him even wanted to be with me in the first place."

I laugh, but it comes out wrong.

"Imagine that," I say. "Me. Being told I should be grateful a man wants me. In this face. In this body. With my career."

She doesn't laugh. Her eyes go soft instead. That somehow makes it worse.

"And then when it all came out," I continue, words rushing now that the dam is broken, "it wasn't just my heart. It was my brand. My image. Every headline. Every comment. Team Anthony, Team Elia, who did what, who deserves what. I couldn't even be sad in private. I had to grief-manage."

"Grief-manage," she repeats quietly.

"Yeah," I say. "There was a schedule for when I could cry. Fifteen minutes in the shower. Twenty in the car. Ten between hair and makeup. The rest of the time? Smile. Hit your mark. Be unbothered. Be goals."

My throat closes up. I push the words through anyway.

"And the worst part is—" I stop, swallow hard. "The worst part is that sometimes I still miss him. Not the version that hurt me. The version I thought he was. The man I married in my head. And I hate myself for that. I hate that someone who broke me like that still takes up space in here." I tap my temple. "And in here." I rest my hand lightly on my chest.

The silence that follows isn't heavy. It's... full. She lets it breathe. No cheap comfort, no "you're better off," none of that Instagram therapist nonsense.

"I don't think that makes you weak," she says finally.

"Yeah, well, it feels pathetic," I say.

"Feeling something doesn't make it true," she says. "Grief is messy. Loyalty doesn't shut off when someone disappoints you. You loved him. That doesn't vanish because he didn't know what to do with it."

I stare at her. "How are you so sure?"

Her mouth twists, a wry almost-smile that doesn't reach her eyes.

"Because I live in rooms full of men who don't know what to do with me," she says.

There it is—the pivot. Up until now, Shai has been... smooth. Untouchable. The cool neighbor with the Maybach and the smart mouth. Right now, she looks like something else. Someone else.

"What do you mean?" I ask.

She leans back in the chair, runs a hand over her face, and exhales slowly.

"You ever sit at a table and know everyone there is waiting for you to slip?" she asks. "Not because you're bad at what you do. Just because they're annoyed someone like you made it in."

"All the time," I say. "Welcome to Hollywood."

She nods. "Now imagine that, but the table is mostly old white men who have been in power longer than you've been alive. They're used to seeing people who look like them and think like them. You walk in—Black, queer, younger, with more money on paper than half of them—and suddenly every move you make is a test."

The way she says it—flat, matter-of-fact—hits harder than any dramatic monologue would've.

"I thought money fixed that," I say quietly.

"It doesn't," she says. "It just changes the zip code of the disrespect."

I huff out a small, bitter laugh. "Say that."

She smiles without humor. "I sit on boards, I sign checks, I green-light projects, and still, at least once a quarter, some man looks at me like I broke into his office and started playing CEO. They call it 'concern' or 'due diligence.' What it really is, is 'We're going to poke holes in everything you do until we find a reason to say we were right about you not belonging here.'"

My stomach twists. Not because I've lived that exact experience, but because I know that look. I've seen it in directors, producers, journalists. The quiet calculation. The mental tally.

"So what do you do?" I ask.

"I over-prepare," she says simply. "I outwork them. I show up earlier. I leave later. I learn the room. I read the board packets two, three times. I anticipate every question, every angle. And even when I'm right, I make sure they think it was their idea."

"That sounds exhausting," I say.

"It is," she says. "It's also survival. I have investors, employees, kids in after-school programs whose grants depend on the profit from the companies I run. I can't afford to be the stereotype they're waiting on. So I live with this constant hum in my head that says, 'Don't give them a reason to take it all away.'"

There's a tightness in my chest again, but it's different this time. Less about me, more about... recognition. She looks powerful on the surface, and she is. But underneath, she's running the same program I am: don't mess up, don't be too emotional, don't be too loud, don't be too much, don't be too real.

"That sounds like imposter syndrome," I say.

"Oh, I have that too," she says dryly. "But this is different. Imposter syndrome is when you doubt yourself even though you're qualified. This is... knowing you're qualified to sit at the head of a table you built and still knowing people are waiting for any excuse to pretend you're not."

We sit with that for a second.

"So let me get this straight," I say. "You're Shiloh Mercer, CEO of Intel-Ligent, rich enough to lose a million dollars and call it a rounding error, and you still feel like that?"

"Every time I sit at certain tables," she says. "Not all. Some rooms are mine. Some rooms, I built. But the ones I had to fight my way into? Yeah. I walk in already knowing at least one person thinks I'm a diversity hire with a good tailor. It's not until they realize who I am that their posture changes."

I shake my head. "That's insane."

"It's America," she says. "Insane is the baseline."

I crack a smile despite myself. She sees it, and her shoulders drop a little, like she's relieved she didn't break me further.

"Why are you telling me this?" I ask. I don't say, You don't owe me that. But it's there.

"Because you think you're weak for missing a man who hurt you," she says. "Meanwhile, you've spent years proving yourself in an industry that would throw you away the second you stopped making them money. You think you're pathetic for having feelings. I think you're human for having them and still showing up anyway."

The words land in me like a stone in a lake, heavy and deep. Ripples spread.

"Nobody talks to me like that," I say quietly.

"Like what?" she asks.

"Like I'm not... a product," I say. "Like I'm allowed to be messy. Like I'm not just a brand they're trying to keep from cracking."

"Maybe that's the problem," she says.

I sip my tea. It's cooler now, easier to drink. I hadn't realized how tightly I was holding myself until I feel my shoulders actually drop.

"Do you ever get tired of carrying it?" I ask. "All of it? The company, the expectations, the... whatever it is they put on you."

"All the time," she says. "But I'd be more tired if I let them win."

"That sounds heroic," I say.

"It's not," she says. "It's petty. I worked too hard to sit where I sit. I'm not giving them the satisfaction of watching me fall apart. They already assume I will."

"You sound like my mother," I mutter.

"Is that an insult?" she asks.

"Depends on the day," I say. "Tonight? No. Tonight it's a compliment."

She smiles, small but genuine this time.

We sit there in the quiet for a moment. The kind of quiet that doesn't feel empty. My living room is still the same—same couch, same bookshelf, same candle I never light—but somehow it feels... softer. Less like a set. More like a place a person lives.

"I'm sorry about Anthony," she says after a while. "Not for the headlines. For the way he made you doubt yourself. That part pisses me off."

"Why?" I ask.

"Because you're... you," she says, like that explains it. "You deserve someone who understands that being with you is a privilege, not a favor."

My throat tightens. I look away, blinking fast.

"You don't even know me," I say.

She shakes her head. "That's not true."

"Oh really?" I ask, trying to deflect. "Enlighten me, neighbor. What do you know?"

She ticks off on her fingers. "You hate early mornings but you'll get up for work because you respect the crew. You're polite to service staff, you tip well. You read real books, not just scripts. You talk to your mother even though she drives you crazy. You pretend you don't like scary movies, but you do. You bake when you're stressed but you order pizza when you're sad."

I stare at her. "How do you—"

"I pay attention," she says simply. "Patterns. You're very consistent."

I throw a pillow at her. She catches it, laughing softly.

"Creep," I say.

"Observer," she corrects. "Point is, I know enough to be sure Anthony didn't deserve what he had. And you missing him doesn't change that. It just means you loved honestly. That's not something to be ashamed of."

I exhale slowly. My chest feels... less tight. The ache is still there, but it's not swallowing me whole anymore.

"Thank you," I say. "For... all of that."

"Anytime," she says.

I glance at the clock on the wall. It's almost three.

"I'm sorry for dragging you into my emotional meltdown," I say. "You probably have some billionaire thing to do in the morning."

"I have a meeting at nine," she says. "With three men who think I shouldn't be running my own company."

"Fun," I say.

"Oh, it'll be a blast," she says dryly. "I'll go in, smile, let them circle, then remind them nicely that their bonuses depend on my 'unqualified' decisions."

I snort. "I kind of want to watch."

"You're not invited," she says. "But I'll give you a recap."

We fall into another quiet. I drain the last of my tea and set the mug down.

"I should let you sleep," she says, standing. "You've got work tomorrow too. And an entire city waiting to read your face for clues."

"Yay," I say flatly.

She walks to the door, then pauses with her hand on the knob.

"Elia?" she says.

"Yeah?"

She looks back at me, eyes steady. "You're not weak. You're not pathetic. You're human. And anyone who made you feel otherwise... was wrong. Period."

The words go straight through me. No fluff, no sugar. Just clean truth.

I nod, because if I try to speak right now, I might cry again.

She seems to understand. She opens the door, steps into the hallway, then leans back in for one last thing.

"And for what it's worth," she adds, "if anyone ever asks you again about him on camera, you're allowed to say, 'That's not a topic I'm willing to discuss today.' You don't owe them your pain just because they're rolling."

"That would start a PR avalanche," I say.

"Maybe," she says. "Or maybe it would start a boundary."

She gives me a small smile, then steps out fully.

"Goodnight, 614," she says.

"Goodnight, 616," I reply.

She closes the door behind her, and for the first time in a long time, the silence in my apartment doesn't feel like it's swallowing me. It just feels... quiet.

I pick up my mug, take it to the sink, then catch my reflection in the microwave door. Eyes swollen, nose red, makeup smeared.

I should hate this version of myself. But I don't. Not tonight.

Tonight, I look like someone who survived something and is still here.

I turn off the light, crawl into bed, and pull the covers up to my chin. My phone buzzes once on the nightstand—a calendar reminder, an email notification, something work-related. I flip it over so the screen is facedown.

For once, I don't feel guilty choosing sleep over performance.

As I drift off, one thought loops in my mind, soft and steady:

Maybe I am not as breakable as they want me to believe.

CHAPTER EIGHT

614 - Elia

I am preparing for a two-week trip to the East Coast to go over a movie role I have coming up and make a few appearances on some shows. In this industry, you have to keep your face known, or you will be forgotten quickly. I am heading out tomorrow morning, still wondering who scheduled morning interviews. I am almost sure Anthony will come up, and I am not ready to discuss that with the public. I made it completely clear to my publicist: I want a clean trip.

I hate being up early, but I have to make sure all my bills are caught up and my affairs are in order before I head out. I call down to the front desk to let them know I am on my way and to have my car waiting. Pete is the sweetest old man. I need to make sure I give him an excellent gift when he retires.

I grab a light jacket and head out the door to run errands. As I close my door, I see my neighbor is heading out.

"Where have you been, stranger?" I ask. I have not seen her around in a few weeks, not since we hung out that last Saturday.

"Hey, you. I was out of town for a speaking engagement. You know me, always willing to influence our youth," Shai says, smiling. "What have you been up to?"

"Nothing much. I have some work to do for a new project coming out, so I am flying to New York tomorrow for two weeks," I say as we head to the elevator.

"Well, congratulations. So you will be gone for two weeks?" she asks, looking a little bummed. "Just when I was starting to like you."

"Oh really? So now you do not like me anymore because I am going away for a few days?" I say, acting unbothered.

"No, for real. I was looking forward to our next movie night, but it's cool. I will get through," she says, smiling.

"Well, as soon as I get back, I will set a reminder to let you know so we can get together. Cool?" I ask, knowing she is full of it.

"Yeah, sounds like a plan," she says as we step off the elevator. "Well, take my number in case you get bored or need someone to talk to," she adds, handing me her card.

"Ok, yeah, I will keep that in mind. Hey, Pete," I say as I walk past the front desk.

"Hello, young lady," Pete says, like he is genuinely happy to see me. "Be careful out there. It is supposed to rain today."

"It never rains in Southern California, Pete." I say with a smile as I head to my car. As I get in, I notice 616's chauffeured Maybach pull up.

"Well, that would be a nice car to take me to the airport tomorrow," I say as she steps out.

"All you have to do is ask," she says with a smile and gets into the back seat of her car and the driver shuts the door.

I smile and shake my head. She is too much, I think as I drive off to meet with my agent.

My day is not as long as I thought it would be. I am home by one in the afternoon and ready to relax on my couch with a good book. It is dreary outside, that gray L.A. drizzle that makes you want to stay wrapped up in a blanket and mind your business. When I get in, I put a pot of tea on and head to my room to get more comfortable. I throw on a pair of sweats and a tee, my usual in-house uniform. I tie my hair up and remove my makeup. I hate makeup; it destroys the skin, so I make sure I put my moisturizer on and let it soak in.

As I sit in the kitchen waiting for the teapot to whistle, I decide to text 616 to see if I can really use her car for the airport. I hate waiting for cars, and they kind of weird me out.

"So is that a yes or no?" I text. Her response is immediate.

"Are you asking?" she replies just as my pot whistles.

My heart does that little skip it has no business doing. I roll my eyes at myself, pour my tea, and curl up on the couch with my blanket before I answer.

"How did you know it was me?" I ask.

"This is my personal line and not many people have this number. So for a random number to pop up, I can only assume it was you", she texts back.

"Oh ok. Well yes, I am asking. May I please get a ride to the airport tomorrow?"

"Sure. Just let me know the time, and I will have the car downstairs waiting."

I feel a little weird asking, but I have to admit she's cool with me and I'm comfortable with her since our dinner and her coming to my rescue in the hallway. My thumbs hover over the screen longer than they should before I finally type.

"Ok. 5 a.m. Thanks a bunch."

"Anytime", she responds almost immediately. *"Enjoy your day, 614. Maybe I will see you later."*

I stare at the three dots blinking like they might say something else. When they disappear, I answer.

"Maybe you will", I reply.

Then it hits me. I am flirting with this person, and I do not want to sound crazy, but I think they're flirting back. Actually, I know she is flirting back. But I know I can't go down this road. If something like this ever got out, it would destroy everything I worked so hard for.

It's just senseless flirting. No harm in that, as long as we keep it innocent and nothing more, Elia. It is keeping my mind off the usual crap I am dealing with. It is just something to do.

I pick my book up and begin to read. I have been hooked on Freida McFadden lately—this one, The Housemaid, has been on my nightstand for a week, can't wait to see the movie. I can lose hours in her twists, but my exhaustion must have caught up with me, because before I know it... I am out cold.

It feels like as soon as I start reading, I am awakened by a knock at the door. Startled, I hop up, spill tea on my sweats, and knock over my plant. Great.

"Who is it?" I ask, trying to pull myself together and blot tea off my thigh at the same time.

"Your neighbor."

I open the door a crack and see her standing there.

"Hey, come on in," I say. "I must have fallen asleep reading, and your erratic knocking made me spill my tea all over me. Thanks."

"Anytime," she says, smiling.

"So what is up? Can I offer you something to drink?" I ask.

"No, I am fine, thank you. I just wanted to stop by and see you before you left," she says, glancing around my place. "Nice place. Looks very... cozy."

"Thank you," I say, grabbing a bottle of water. Her eyes slide over my bookshelf, the half-folded throw, my little stack of scripts on the coffee table. I feel oddly exposed, like she is reading more than the room. "What time is it?" I ask, not realizing how late it is.

"It is about 7:30," she says, checking her Cartier.

"Oh my God, I slept forever. I must have been tired," I say, taking a sip of water. "Well, I will be up all night."

"Yeah, well, that sucks. Are you all ready for tomorrow?" she asks, and I nod.

"Good. The car will be downstairs at 4:45 sharp, ok?"

"Wait, I said 5," I say.

"Well, I did not want you waiting. It will be there when you come down. Ok?"

"Yeah, no, that is fine. Thank you again," I say, flashing an innocent smile.

"As I said, no problem. Well, I guess I will leave you to it," she says, heading toward the door.

"Leave me to what?" I ask, even though she clearly heard me say I will be up all night.

"Whatever it is you big stars do when preparing for something: sleep, eat, do not eat, purge, wax, makeup, weaves... I am sure there is something," she says, laughing.

"Ha-ha, but that is all getting done tomorrow, so no, I do not have anything to do but probably call and check in with my mother. Oh, how I love to hear her antics," I say.

"Well, good luck with that," she says, opening the door. "Text me if you need me."

"Sure. Thanks for stopping by," I say, a little irritated that she did not offer to hang out. My chest drops a little as soon as she turns.

"Anytime," she says and leaves.

Just like that, I feel a little bothered. Why? I do not know. Maybe I expected her to want to chill or hang out, start a conversation, something. Whatever. I am not going to stress over this. She is just a friendly neighbor. That is all, I tell myself as I walk over to my wine rack and grab a bottle of red.

Maybe I will have a salad.

Nah. I could go for pizza.

I grab my phone and call Johnny's Pizzeria and order a small pie and a Caesar salad. What a good mix, I think as I make my way to the couch with a freshly poured glass of wine. The apartment feels extra quiet, the kind of quiet that makes you aware of every little sound—the fridge hum, the rain tapping the window, my own thoughts.

As I get comfortable and start channel surfing, my phone vibrates. It is a text from 616.

"All you have to do is ask", it says.

I stare at the screen. My face heats up. Ask what?

She is a smart ass. It seems like she can read my mind. Then I laugh to myself at the thought—she is a techie; she probably has cameras or something in here.

"What am I asking for this time?" I reply.

"To come over so you will not be lonely", she says. *"I am very keen at reading people, and I could tell by your body language you wanted me to stay. So why did you not ask?"*

I pinch the bridge of my nose. Are you serious right now?

"Are you freaking kidding me?" I text, a little pissed she read me that well. I am still trying to figure this girl out, but she bothers me and intrigues me all at the same time. My stomach does this annoying flip I do not approve of.

"No. Why would I do that?" she replies.

"If I wanted to hang out, I would have asked you to hang out", I say back, trying not to sound needy. I reread the message three times before hitting send, still hearing my own lie.

"So you want to come over?" she asks.

"No. I just ordered some pizza, and I am probably going to sit and watch one of these stupid reality shows", I type.

"Ok... so you want to come over", she replies, obviously ignoring my plans.

"Yes", I send back before I have a chance to think. My thumb betrays me.

"Ok good. But this time I am going to need you to actually throw some clothes on. No pink boy shorts and T-shirts from Baby Gap, ok?" lol

"OMG you really know how to get under my skin, do you not?" I write, smiling. That was kind of funny. Whatever. I have to bite back a grin.

"I am having a little get-together. Antoine is bringing some people over to chill and hang out. Do not worry—everyone signs non-disclosure agreements when they enter, so you do not have to worry about that. Cell phones and recording devices are confiscated upon entry. Ok?"

"A bit thorough", I text. *"Do I get frisked upon entry also?"*

"All you have to do is ask", she replies.

I roll my eyes so hard I could sprain them.

"Ughhhh whatever. Maybe I will stop over. What time?"

"Good. I will see you when you get here. Let us say 9."

"Fine", I reply. *"Do you mind if I bring a friend?"*

"Is it a female, and is she cute?" she asks.

"Yes and yes", I reply, not letting it bother me. I tell myself it does not.

"Well then, of course you can", she responds.

Smart ass, I text back.

I call Nat to see what her plans are for tonight. She is the only one who really gets this, and I want her there to assess the situation.

"Hey, girl," she answers.

"Hey, what are you doing tonight?"

"Nothing. I was going to sit in the house and watch some reruns. What you got going on?" she asks.

"Well, my neighbor invited me over. She is having a get-together, and I did not want to roll alone. You want to come?"

"Girl, I will be there in an hour," she says, just as I am buzzed to pick up my delivery.

After I eat my salad and take two bites of pizza, I start to get dressed. Natalee gets there around 8:45, and we have a glass of wine as I catch her up on what is going on. Her face says more than her words do.

"Elia, it seems like she's cool and you might be a little razzle-dazzled," Nat says.

"I mean... I am not gay. Shai is cool, and she is cute, but I am not like that," I say.

"But she does something to you, does she not?"

I pause. I hate that she is right. There is a tightness in my chest that only shows up when 616 is involved, and I do not know what to do with that.

"I cannot lie. Yes. She is smart, funny, and an asshole, but I feel like I am drawn to her."

"I know what you mean. Look, relax and take it one day at a time. Do not force yourself to be so closed-minded about living life. You only live once. Now let us get over there so I can see what the hype is about."

"Thank you, Nat. And please do not tell the other girls. That would be the last thing I need—at least until I figure all this out."

"Girl, you know I got you," Natalee says as we hug.

It is about 9:10 when we finally head out the door. In the hallway, I hear music, and a few women are getting off the elevator. Figuring they are going to Shai's place, I wait for them to knock first.

We walk in last, and I notice everyone is being checked and their cell phones are going into little cubby lockers. This is too funny. She really does cover all bases. The lights are dim, warm and golden, music sliding between R&B and Afrobeats, the kind of vibe that makes people loosen their shoulders and forget they have jobs in the morning.

"You are late," she says to me, naturally the time-obsessed one.

"Perfection takes time," I say, expecting to hand over my phone and sign something. "This is my good friend Natalee. Natalee, this is..."

"My name is Shai, pronounced like 'shy,' but spelled S-H-A-I, just in case you ever wanted to write my name or something. Anyway, it is a pleasure to meet you, Natalee," 616 says, shaking Natalee's hand.

"You two are good. I have a nice bottle of white on ice for you in the kitchen. I will catch up with you in a few," she says before heading over to the women who just walked in. "Natalee, please make yourself at home."

I can feel the eyes on my back as I walk to the kitchen. No search. No cell phone confiscation. They must be mad. I giggle to myself.

We get into the kitchen, and I grab the bottle from the ice bucket. I pour us a glass of wine into the two glasses placed next to it.

"Elia, she is adorable. And rich," Natalee says. "And if you cannot tell she has a thing for you, then you are blind. Tell me why your wine is in the kitchen set up all nice and neat while everyone else is getting their drinks from the bar. You are special."

"I know, Nat, but I do not want to jump the gun. I do not know," I say, not wanting to talk about it. "Let us head into the party."

We walk back to where everyone else is and sit off to the side of the bar. It is a nice setup—about twenty-five to thirty people. Everyone is either dancing, laughing, or posted up in little pockets of conversation. I notice 616 keeps glancing in my direction. Every time our eyes catch, she looks away like she was not checking, and I pretend I did not see her.

I smile and continue talking to Nat, until someone walks up behind me.

"Fancy meeting you here," a familiar voice says.

"Hello, Antoine," I say without turning around.

"Good evening, Elia," he says. "What brings you here?"

"My friendly neighbor invited me," I say, glancing over at her. Yes, she is watching, trying to look engrossed in another conversation but clearly bothered. There is a tightness in her jaw she thinks she is hiding. "Natalee, this is Antoine, Shai's best friend."

"Nice to meet you, Natalee," Antoine says. "What is better than one beautiful lady? Two," he adds, amused with himself. "Well, I must say I am glad you could make it," he says, smiling just as another woman walks up and grabs him.

"Hey, I want to finish this conversation later," he says as she pulls him away.

I nod, hoping he forgets.

"Who is that, Elia?" Natalee asks.

"That is Antoine. Shai's right-hand man and COO of her company, Intel-Ligent," I say.

"Girl, he is cute too. And Shai is the CEO of Intel-Ligent? You struck gold," Natalee says.

"It is not all about the money, Nat. I have my own money. I am good."

"Yeah, Elia, I know—but you do not have that kind of money. She is a bazillionaire," Natalee says, pouring more wine.

"There is no such thing as a bazillionaire, Natalee. And stop thinking money is the root of happiness. It is not," I say, aggravated.

"I know it is not, Elia, but it sure helps the tree grow," Natalee says.

"Whatever, Nat. You are lucky you are my girl," I say with a smile, just as Shai walks over.

"How are you ladies this evening?" she asks.

"We are fine. Enjoying your event. Thank you for the wine."

"You are quite welcome. You know where the wine closet is if you need more. I can set more on ice if you like," she says politely. This is for Nat's benefit.

"How polite of you," I say, playing along. "But we are fine. We are at the bar, so we will have drinks here. No need for special treatment," I say, staring right into her eyes.

"As you wish," she says, smiling.

"Stop it, please," I say, shaking my head.

"What? I am just ensuring that my guests' needs are met," she says.

"Well, thank you. Are you drinking?" I ask.

"Yeah, I am sipping on a smoked old-fashioned," she says, back to her usual self.

"Good. Sip some more. And I will have a Whiskey smash, please. I have had enough wine," I say, and she calls the bartender over.

"Nat, you want one?" she asks, and Natalee nods.

"So Antoine came over?" she asks as the bartender hands us our drinks. "He is very entertaining," she adds, obviously fishing.

"Yeah, Natalee would love to be entertained. Wouldn't you, Nat?" I say jokingly.

"Girl, if I was not married," Natalee laughs.

"Yeah, most women do," Shai says. "He seems to like you, Elia."

"Well, I am not interested in him," I say, staring straight at her. The words hang between us heavier than they should for such a simple statement. For a second, the room noise dulls, and it is just us and that truth sitting between us.

"Well, ladies, I have to make my rounds," she says, breaking our eye contact. "I will check in with you later."

She smiles at me, nods at Natalee, and walks away. I watch her as she moves through the crowd—smooth, laid back. She smells good as always, that same warm scent I now recognize, wearing black slacks, a black V-neck tee, and black loafers, of course with red bottoms.

The night goes on, and after three more Whiskey smashes, Natalee is on the dance floor shutting it down. I am half-tempted to get out there, but I am not going to make a fool of myself just yet. It is too fresh, I think, and smile.

It is around midnight when 616 walks back over, the smoke drifting off her freshly made Old Fashioned still lingering in the air.

"You ok over here?" she asks. I can tell she is a little tipsy, but not sloppy—just looser around the edges.

"Yeah, I am fine. I am probably about to leave. I have an early day if you do not recall."

"No, I do. Five a.m., right?" she asks.

"Yes. Four forty-five," I correct.

"Right," she says, smiling. "Well, I hope you enjoyed yourself. I wish we had a little more time to talk, but I understand."

"All you have to do is ask," I say, looking up at her, knowing she is too stubborn to do it.

"Good one. Use my words against me," she laughs to herself.

I watch her thinking. Maybe she is used to women doing whatever she wants. Maybe she is not used to asking for anything when everything is handed to her. Maybe this is new for both of us.

I call over to Nat to let her know I am leaving.

"You are more than welcome to stay, Nat. I live right across the hall," I say as I gather myself.

"Yeah, girl, I do not have anything to do. I am going to hang out, if that is ok with Shai," Natalee says.

"No, that is fine. I will see to it that Natalee makes it to your place when she is ready," 616 says.

I look at 616 as I get up to leave, waiting for her to say something. Stay. Sit. Five more minutes. Anything.

As I open the door, I feel her come up behind me. Her hand hovers near the small of my back for half a second, close enough that I can feel the heat, but she pulls it back before she actually touches me.

"I think I should see to it that you make it to your door safely," she says, following me out.

"Thank you. I think I can handle it from here," I say as I open my door. I pause in the doorway for half a beat, giving her one last chance. "Please see to it that my friend makes it here safely. Goodnight, 616," I say, closing the door behind me and wondering why she did not ask.

I climb into bed and fall asleep with one thing on my mind: 616 and her stubbornness.

CHAPTER NINE

614 - Elia

I'm just waking up at 4:00 when there is a knock on the door. I open it to see Shai carrying her in like she weighs nothing. Natalee doesn't even stir. I grab a cold water bottle from the fridge and two Aleve from the bathroom cabinet, put them on the table, grab a pillow, grab a throw blanket, and get her settled on the couch.

"Thank you for looking after her," I say as 616 stands there watching me.

"Oh, no problem. She had a good time. Especially when the kamikaze shots came out. You left just when it got good." She smirks.

"Yeah well, you can have another one when I don't have to be up at the ass crack of dawn," I say, heading to my bedroom with her right behind me.

She sits in my room while I hop in the shower. I'm quick—ten minutes, tops. I throw on a fitted red and white Balenciaga track suit and matching Nike max pros, something comfortable for the plane. When I step out, towel drying my hair, she's watching me like she's trying to memorize every move.

"I wish you'd tell your friend I'm not interested." I pause. "Are you ok?" I ask after noticing how quiet she got.

"Sweatpants, hair tied, chilling with no makeup on... that's when you're the prettiest. Hope you don't take it wrong," she says softly.

Thank God my back is to her because I blush so hard I almost burn.

"Well, thank you," I say as I turn around.

"I'm sorry if that was out of line. I know you're straight. I shouldn't have said—" she starts, stumbling.

"Geez, I would think you'd have better game than that," I say, and she smiles.

"I meant it. But I respect your boundaries," she says, a little embarrassed.

"It's not that deep. Trust me. And since you're already up, grab my bags, please. Thank you." I say as I head out.

I leave Natalee a quick note: left early, sweats in my closet, I'll give her a call once I land and I'm situated. Then we head to the elevator in silence. Downstairs, the chauffeur opens the door, loads the bags, and Shai slides in from the other side.

"So you decided to ride?" I ask her.

"Yeah, why not? Car rides put me to sleep," she says as she opens the chilled drawer and pulls out two mini vodka shooters. She throws one back and hands me one.

I shrug. "Why not?"

I take it—with water, because I am a lightweight—and by the last sip I'm already warm.

"It's ok. You can sleep on the plane," she says.

"Yeah... I don't sleep on planes. Too many people, too much going on, luckily I'm in first class so I can get some work done." I admit.

"You can sleep on this plane," she says with that little arrogant smile that tells me she knows exactly what she's doing.

"Good morning, Rich. Take your time. I want to enjoy the view," Shai says.

"We all love the scenic route, but I have a plane to catch. I don—"

She cuts me off.

"Relax. Have a drink. Enjoy the ride."

And for some reason, I do.

It's 5 AM but the streets still have life—Uber drivers, club leftovers, the usual LA nightlife residue. The music is low, mellow, and the liquor is settling. We talk about nothing and everything. She pulls over twice to give a couple of homeless people cash.

"I hand out money, sometimes," she says, looking out the window. "I know most of it goes to liquor or drugs. But I hope... maybe it buys them a meal. Or a room. Something."

Her eyes are soft, tired. A quiet kind of sad.

"You can't save the world, Shai. You'll go crazy trying," I say, taking her hand. Warm. Steady, Vulnerable.

"I'll go crazy if I don't."

She looks at me, and I melt.

I don't care that she's a woman.

I like whatever this is.

So I kiss her.

Her lips are soft. Slow. Intentional. She kisses like she feels everything. The butterflies instantly flutter in my stomach, and I pull away because it hits me too fast.

She looks confused. Hurt.

"Did I do something?"

"No... I didn't expect myself to..." I trail off.

She pulls me into her lap, straddling her, and kisses me deep. Neck, lips, jaw, slow and warm and purposeful. I moan without meaning to, because God, she knows what she's doing. Her fingers brush my nipple through my bra and I almost lose it.

I'm seconds from ripping clothes off when she stops.

"Umm... we're here," she says.

I'm pissed - and embarrassed for being upset.

I look out the window.

"...This is not LAX."

"Yeah... I decided you should take my jet. You need real rest."

The door opens.

"Damn, we couldn't get five more minutes?" I mumble, blushing.

“We’ve got five hours,” she says, taking my hand.

The jet isn’t just a jet, matte black exterior, custom interior, soft-lit, modern, with the kind of quiet that only comes when someone paid for true privacy.

Inside: a lounge, an office suite, a full bedroom, rainfall shower, and a breakfast dining alcove.

“You can have this room,” she says, pointing to a private suite with a queen bed and floor-to-ceiling LED dimmable panels.

She kisses my forehead and leaves to change.

I swap into a pair of shorts and a tee, fully aware I’m teasing her. When the plane levels, I head to the breakfast area. A flight attendant greets me with a menu and a smile.

“I’ll have the egg-white omelet, wheat toast, turkey bacon, and a mimosa.”

Shai arrives, hair still damp, wearing soft black joggers and a black tee.

“You ordering?” I ask.

“No. I have already put in my request.”

She tops her orange juice off with champagne creating a mimosa.

“So... drinking problem?” I ask.

“The only problem I have is when the drinks run out,” she says, sipping. “Kidding. I work hard. I play when I want.”

“Understandable.”

We eat. The food is stupid good.

“You should be tired,” I say.

“I am. But I can go a few more hours. I'll sleep on the way back.”

The mimosa hits just right. I follow her to the lounge, lay against her, and we put on a movie. Her fingers trace my waist, slow, teasing. I get hot immediately.

I pull back without meaning to. Shai pauses, searching my face.

I don’t make her wait. I cup her face and kiss her slowly.

She kisses back, deeper this time.

She wraps her arms around my waist and I melt into it. I bite her lip and slide to her neck, kissing slowly, dragging my tongue, feeling her shiver.

We're breathing heavy, kissing like we can't get close enough.

Then she picks me up — literally lifts me — and carries me to her bedroom, still kissing me.

She lays me down gently.

I want her. Badly.

She kneels at the end of the bed and lifts my feet. She kisses my toes, then the arch of my foot. A slow, confident trail — the kind that knows exactly how to unravel a person.

She kisses the back of my knees, down the back of my thighs.

I am dripping wet already.

At my inner thigh she teases me with her tongue over my shorts.

I grab her curls, moaning.

She pulls my shirt off.

Takes one nipple in her mouth while her hand plays with the other.

It's soft, sensual — and then I whisper:

"Harder."

She sucks harder. I feel it winding up too fast, too deep.

I'm about to cum. I don't want to yet.

She lifts her head and kisses me slow, then pulls my shorts off.

Mmm. Yes. I'm ready.

She kisses down my sides, across my hips.

When she licks my hipbone I almost lose it.

And then—

Her tongue slides over me. Slow. Warm. Wet.

I grab her head.

Her tongue moves everywhere — teasing, circling, tasting.

There's heat pooling in my stomach, rising fast, sharp, hot.

She starts sucking my clit and I grind into her mouth.

I can't hold it.

I grip the sheets, her hair—

And I explode.

My body convulses.

I'm trembling, cumming hard, breath shaking.

She kisses up my body and kisses me slow while I'm still cumming through the aftershocks.

She turns me over. I'm on my knees, legs jelly.

Her fingers slide across my swollen clit, then into me—slow. Deep.

My moan breaks in my throat.

I push back, taking her in as far as I can.

She fucks me deeper. Faster.

"You like that?" she murmurs.

"Yes—" I moan.

"Tell me."

"Yes... yes, I like it when you fuck me!"

She hits the spot, hard. Her hand reaches around and pinches my nipple—

And I explode again.

Cum running down my leg.

My body collapsing onto the bed.

Orgasms rolling through me, one after another, uncontrollable.

I claw her back with each one, moaning into her neck.

Finally, I come down. Breathing. Weak. Melted.

"So this is what it's like?" I whisper.

"What—being with a girl?"

"Yes."

"No. This is what it's like being with me."

"Did you have to break me down like that the first time?"

"That was just a teaser."

"Just a— excuse me?" I laugh, clit throbbing.

"So you never had a multiple before?"

"Honestly? No. Never."

"Well then... that's a first for both of us. I joined the mile-high club, and you had a multiple." She laughs.

"That's two for me," I say as I kiss her, tasting myself. God. Her lips alone could start something again.

"Get some rest," I tell her, rolling over.

She slides behind me and wraps her arms around me.

Damn. Really? This good?

I tingle at the thought.

Well... you only live once.

I drift off.

—

I wake up as the plane is taxiing.

I get up quietly, shower, dress, gather my bags.

My phone is blowing up; I'll call my manager later.

I walk back and kiss Shai softly. She stirs.

I kiss her again and leave.

Her captain says "Once the tarmac is clear and we have finished refueling we will ensure to get Ms. Mercer back to the West Coast. Have a safe trip Ma'am." He says shaking my hand as I exited.

Loyalty. I love it.

When I step off the jet, a black SUV is already waiting on the tarmac. The driver steps out immediately — tall, sharp suit, posture straight like he trained for this.

"Ma'am, good morning. My name is Raul," he says, opening the door for me. "I'll be your driver during your stay in New York. Ms. Mercer has instructed me to take exceptional care of you. Anything you need, day or night, you call me directly." He hands me a sleek black card with his number embossed in silver.

"Your accommodations and all incidentals are already handled."

I blink at him, because I sure didn't arrange any of this.

He loads my luggage and pulls off smoothly.

And then, as we turn the corner into Manhattan traffic, the SUV glides under a private awning — dark stone, warm lighting, a small discreet entrance with no signage except a tiny gold plaque.

Aman New York.

My jaw damn near hits my lap.

This isn't a hotel you accidentally end up at.

This is the kind you get invited to — quietly.

Raul parks, steps out, and opens my door.

"Welcome, ma'am."

The staff already has my room key. No check-in line. No questions. No clipboard. Just a soft, "Right this way," and an elevator that feels like a whisper.

My suite door opens into marble, warm wood, black stone, soft lighting — the kind of expensive that doesn't need to brag.

And yeah... I don't need to ask how this happened.

Penthouse suite, skyline view, marble everything — and immediately call Stacy. Three hours later I'm styled, beat, pressed, and walking into my workday like nothing happened.

But everything happened.

CHAPTER TEN

616 - Shai

I woke up the second she left. The whole damn room still smelled like her skin and that light vanilla lotion she pretends isn't intentional. The pilot pinged me the second she stepped off the jet, waiting on my word, and I told El Capitan to prep for departure.

But instead of getting up, I laid back down like an idiot, staring at the ceiling, replaying everything.

Thinking about her.

Thinking about how she purposely wore those boy shorts because she knows good and damn well it does something to me.

Thinking about how bad this could end if I let myself slide into anything emotional.

I don't do love.

Not the soft kind.

Not the "look me in the eyes and see my soul" kind.

Shake it off, Shai. You don't do love... but the way she looked at me before she left... I felt that somewhere I don't even admit exists.

Funny how one night can make your rules look flimsy as hell.

"Rise and shine, Toine!" I say when he finally answers.

"What are you doing up so early?" he asks, voice sounding like gravel and regret.

"Money never sleeps, fool. Pick me up at the private terminal. I'm landing in twenty."

"What time is it?"

"Damn near 3:30 PM."

"See you in twenty." He says hanging up.

I gather my things, sign off with the crew, hand out their envelopes. They enjoy working for me, and I take care of them. No shortcuts.

Toine's waiting outside. I get in, debating if I should tell him anything.

"So what's up? Where you coming from?" he asks, pulling onto the road.

"I had to fly to NY for something."

I pause. He's my best friend — my only real confidant besides Rosa. I could tell him the truth... or something close.

"So what happened after I dipped out this morning?"

"Same ole'," he says. "Took a few chicks back to the crib and made some videos. Didn't take it down until around nine. You disappeared after dropping ole' girl across the hall. I'm saying... you smashed?"

"Nah, I just took her across the hall and helped her get settled. Something light."

"Yes, she was a mess by the time she left this morning," he laughs. "I had her doing mad shots. She held her own, though."

"Yeah, she's cool as hell."

My stomach growls.

"I'm starving. Swing by the steak shop."

"Bet."

He stops at a light, looks at me like he's waiting on his moment.

"So... are you gonna put me in with Elia?"

"Nah. I can't do that. Elia ain't feelin' you like that."

"How you know? She told you that?"

"Yeah. She told me she wasn't interested."

I can't help laughing.

"Oh, so you just gon' laugh at my pain? That's jacked, Shai!"

"I'm laughing with you, not at you. You can't get everybody, Toine. Save some for us little people."

"What you mean by that?" he shoots back.

Here we go.

"I took her to NY this morning and... let's just say I rode sky on the mile high," I say, giggling.

"Damn, Shai. For real? You messing with me, right? You just gon' crush me like that?"

"Between me and you, right?"

"Yeah, of course. Fuck it — bros before hoes."

He says it like he means it... but I see the way his eyes flicker. Toine never hides his emotions well.

We grab our food, and he drops me off at the penthouse.

Rosa definitely had her hands full cleaning up after last night's madness. When I open the door, the place is spotless — lemon, eucalyptus, touch-less lights rising automatically as I enter. My OLED wall-panel displays a soft ambient skyline loop.

"Rrrrosssaaa, my favorite woman in the whole world," I say, hugging her, purposely rolling R's in an exaggerated manner.

"Shai... good afternoon. You leave this house like a tornado passed through," she fusses.

"I know, Rosa. I'm sorry. I appreciate you."

She gives me a long look.

"You look different today. What you been up to?"

Sharp as always.

"Nothing. Just tired."

"You need settle down and stop running wild following Antoine," she mutters. "I am not going to be around forever to clean up mess, Shai."

"Yes, ma'am."

I am the closest thing to family Rosa has left in the area. After her son died in that motorcycle accident, I covered the funeral, moved her into a safe place, gave her more benefits, stock options in the company, more stability. She still shows up every day because grieving women never sit still.

"What's for dinner?"

"Your favorite. Steak, Asparagus, Mashed Potatoes..."

"Don't know what I'd do without you."

I shower. Steam helps, but not enough.

Every time I close my eyes, I see Elia.

The passion in her kiss.

The surprise in her moan.

The way she shook under me.

The way she didn't want to let go.

This is how people get in trouble, Shai.

Feelings are a luxury you don't allow yourself.

I grab my phone.

A text from her:

"Good afternoon, sleepy head. Did you make it home ok?"

Lord.

My chest tightens in a way I don't appreciate.

"Yes, I'm home. About to get some work done. How's your day going?"

Her reply is instant — too instant for someone "not thinking about me."

"It's going. I'm tired. Still got a lot of work. Thank you for the treats. You're sweet when you want to be."

"Don't mention it. Just wanted you taken care of. Raul will look after you."

"He seems nice. I'll call you when I'm done for the day."

"Ok. Have fun."

I bury myself in work — projections, dev updates, hub messages from the engineering teams on our encrypted workspace exchange. I don't stop until one in the morning.

My eyes burn. My body feels like it's moving five seconds behind my brain. I push away from the desk and collapse onto the couch, letting my head sink back into the cushions.

I'm trying not to think about her.

Failing.

My phone lights up.

Elia.

My damn pulse stutters.

I debate letting it ring once, just so I don't look too eager, but I swipe immediately.

"Hello?" I say, low.

She sounds soft, worn, sweet in a way that hits me somewhere I don't like acknowledging.

"Hey... sorry. I know it's late."

"It's fine," I say. "I wasn't asleep yet."

"You should be," she murmurs. "You had a long day."

"So did you."

There's a breath on her end. Not a sigh—something closer to hesitation.

"I just... wanted to hear your voice before I crashed," she says quietly.

That's it.

That's all it takes for my chest to tighten.

"You good?" I ask.

"I'm okay. Just tired. It was a lot today."

"Yeah," I say. "Same here."

Silence drifts in, but it's not empty. It feels like standing too close to a warm door you're not supposed to open.

She laughs softly. "I know you're probably exhausted. I don't want to keep you up."

"You're not," I lie. "I'm good."

"Shai..."

"Yeah?"

"Thank you. For today. All of it."

I swallow. "Anytime."

Another small pause—comfortable, almost tender.

"I'll let you get some rest," she whispers. "We can talk more tomorrow if you're free."

"I'll make time," I say before I can stop myself.

She breathes out like she heard more than I said. "Goodnight, Shai."

"...Night, Elia."

I don't move for a long time after the call ends. I don't like how much I wanted to hear her voice. I don't like how natural it felt.

This is how trouble starts.

And I'm already in it.

CHAPTER ELEVEN

614 - Parallel Days - 616

614 - Elia

New York hits different when you're tired.

I wake up before the sun touches the blackout shades — somewhere around six, maybe a little after. The Aman suite is too quiet, too still, the kind of silence that makes you remember every detail you're trying not to think about. My body feels sore in that slow, echoing way... partially from yesterday's travel, partially from a morning I absolutely cannot afford to replay right now.

I roll onto my back and stare at the ceiling for a second.

No calls. No cameras. No handlers.

Just... breathing.

It's the first moment I've had to myself since this trip started.

I grab my phone from the nightstand.

No missed calls from Shai — which makes sense. It's barely past six here, which means it's after three in the morning in LA. She wouldn't be awake yet. We texted and had a quick call before crashing, but we kept it light. No labels, no deep dive. Safe. Controlled. Necessary.

A text from Raul: *"Car is confirmed for 10 AM"*.

A text from Stacy from last night: *"Big day tomorrow. Reset the narrative. Get rest"*.

I laugh a little at that. Rest. Right.

I stretch my legs and instantly regret it — that familiar pull shoots up my thighs. Not painful. Just... undeniable. A reminder. I rub a hand over my face and shut that down quickly.

“That stays in yesterday,” I tell myself as I swing my legs over the edge of the bed.

I take my time in the shower — steam, hot water, a few extra minutes just letting the tension slide off my shoulders. By the time I’m done, the haze in my head has lifted enough to feel functional.

It’s barely 7:15.

I make myself a cup of coffee from the in-room bar and stand at the window while the city wakes up forty floors below. Break vans. Delivery trucks. People with somewhere urgent to be. Everyone moving fast while I’m trying to slow myself down.

This is my first full day here.

Long hours. Cameras. Interviews. Smile on command.

And I need to look like I slept eight hours and haven’t had a single emotional thought.

At 7:58, my suite phone buzzes.

“Morning, Ms. Girard. Your team is on their way up.”

Showtime.

Glam floods in at eight sharp — garment bags, rolling racks, makeup kits, curling irons, fabric tape, sensible chaos. The room fills instantly with energy and chatter, and I let myself be moved, lifted, tilted, powdered, pinned. It's routine. Muscle memory. Something I can disappear into.

By 9:15am, we’re almost there.

Hair set.

Makeup seamless.

Wardrobe narrowed down to two options.

Stacy steps in like she owns the place — adjusting a sleeve, fixing a curl, checking the jewelry, scanning me for any cracks.

“Car in forty-five,” she says. “Remember — lifestyle tone. Bright, clean, upbeat. Focus on the project and the charity. No heavy personal angles unless you open that door.”

I nod, grounding myself in the version of me they came here for.

Even if my pulse is still somewhere back on that jet.

"Got it," I say, sipping my tea. I glance at my phone again. Nothing new. A part of me I don't want to acknowledge relaxes at the fact that Shai hasn't texted anything weird. No "round two?" No slick comments.

Good. Boundaries. Adulting. Whatever.

Raul has the door open before I reach the curb. New York air hits hard—exhaust, coffee, that cold metallic smell of skyscrapers.

"Good morning, Ms. Girard," he says. "We're right on schedule."

"Thank you, Raul. How are you?" I ask.

"I am well," he says, giving me a small smile in the rearview once we pull off. "The city is busy today. Stay ready."

Story of my life.

The studio is fifteen minutes away and once we arrive, Stacy runs through talking points while a PA mic's me. The host pops into the green room for a quick hello. We exchange the usual pleasantries: "Love your work," "Thanks for having me," "Huge fan," "You look amazing." It's all choreography.

By the time I walk onto the set, I'm in full mode. Smile. Wave. Cross leg. Sit at an angle. Chin down, eyes up. I could do this in my sleep.

The first half is easy.

We talk about the movie—my character, the director, how "excited" I am to be stretching myself artistically. We talk about my charity work, the youth program I partner with, the importance of representation on screen. The audience claps right on cue.

And then... she pivots.

"So, Elia," the host says, her voice dropping into that soft, fake-sincere register they use for sensitive topics. "You've been very open in the past about your personal life. Fans really connected with your marriage journey, and a lot of them still comment, asking... how is your heart these days?"

There it is.

Not Anthony's name. Not directly. Just his ghost, sitting in the chair between us.

My spine goes rigid for half a second. I hear Shai's voice in my head from that night on the couch: You're allowed to say, 'That's not a topic I'm willing to discuss today.' You don't owe them your pain just because they're rolling.

The words sit on my tongue. Heavy. Possible.

I taste them. I almost say them.

Instead, I smile.

"My heart is... healing," I say. "I think anyone who's loved deeply and gone through a transition knows it doesn't happen overnight. But I'm grateful. I'm learning a lot about myself, about what I want, and I'm really focused on pouring that into the work and the people who pour into me."

It's not a bad answer. It's honest. Kind of. But I feel the little twist in my stomach anyway. The tiny betrayal.

I had a chance to draw a boundary. I chose the brand.

The audience claps like I won something.

We cut to commercial. The host squeezes my hand like we just shared a moment. "You're so strong," she whispers. "Thank you for sharing."

I want to say, You're welcome, but my throat is tight.

Instead, I nod. "Of course."

The day doesn't slow down after that.

Raul shuttles me from studio to studio, each lobby a variation of the same: glass, plants, security desk, people pretending not to stare. I do an evening radio spot, a pre-taped late-night bit, and a quick table read with the director and cast.

By 8 o'clock, my cheeks hurt from smiling. My publicist is thrilled. My team's group chat is blowing up with links and clips, everyone sending flame emojis and "QUEEN!!!" like I'm not one glitch away from losing it.

In the SUV between stops, I finally let my head fall back.

"You ok, Ms. Girard?" Raul asks, catching my reflection in the mirror.

"Yeah," I say. "Just a long day."

He nods once. "You carry it well."

I huff a little laugh. "Comes with the job."

My phone is in my hand before I realize it. My thumb scrolls to the last text from Shai.

Don't mention it. Just wanted you taken care of. Raul will look after you.

You'd think that would annoy me—somebody swooping in and arranging my life without asking. But it doesn't. Not today.

Today it feels... nice.

I start to type something—You were right, these people are exhausting—then erase it. I type Miss you and delete that so fast my thumb cramps.

By the time we get back to the hotel, I've talked myself into exhaustion.

Stacy peels off in the lobby. "You were amazing today," she says. "Trends are already up. Rest. Tomorrow we hit the morning shows again."

I smile, hug, all that. Once I'm in the elevator, the mask drops. My shoulders sag. My jaw unclenches.

The suite is dim when I walk in. Turn-down service. Soft music. A little plate of macarons on the table with a card.

Compliments of the Chef. Welcome to New York.

I flop on the bed fully dressed and stare at the ceiling.

It takes a good ten minutes before I admit what's actually buzzing under my skin.

I don't want to talk to my co-star. Or my director. Or Stacy.

I want to hear her voice.

I grab my phone, roll onto my side, and hit call before I can talk myself out of it.

***

616 - Shai

There's a special kind of hell reserved for days when you're both tired and in charge.

By the time I finish brewing my coffee Antoine has already forwarded three "urgent" board messages and a flagged thread from Legal, as he sat on the stool in the kitchen.

"That was fast," I say as he walks into my office with Antoine trailing behind me.

"That's capitalism," he shrugs. "You really thought you were going to sneak in a quick New York run and not pay for it?"

He's not wrong.

I throw on a blazer so the old men on the board call feel less threatened, and step into my home office, walls lit low, my encrypted screens already pulling up the hub.

"Let's get it over with," I mutter.

Antoine laughs. "They've been circling all morning. Be nice."

"Nice is for people who sleep and they can wait until my coffee has marinated a little bit." I say with a smirk sitting down behind my desk in my home office.

I log into our secure conference grid, and as soon as my camera connects, three of the executives straighten like I just walked into the office boardroom.

Eight faces populate the wall screen. Six older white men, one white woman in her fifties who tries too hard to be "one of the guys," and a younger Asian guy from one of the newer funds who watches everything like it's a case study.

"Afternoon, everyone," I say. "Let's make it quick. I've had a long morning."

That gets a chuckle, but not the warm kind. The polite, corporate kind.

We go through the numbers—projections, burn rate on the new AI safety initiative, a few acquisitions on the table. I know this stuff cold. I live it. I built half of it.

Still, the questions come.

"Are we confident this is the best allocation of capital at this time?"

"Has Risk signed off on the expansion runways?"

"Would it be prudent to bring in an outside operator if we're scaling at this speed?"

They never ask, "Do you know what you're doing?"
They just wrap it in enough jargon to pretend that's not what they mean.

"I'm confident in this allocation," I say, voice cool. "Yes, Risk has signed off. And no, we don't need to bring in 'an outside operator' to run the company I built from a laptop in my dorm room. Any other concerns?"

One of them clears his throat.

"It's just that... with so many initiatives running in parallel, we want to ensure nothing is slipping through the cracks. We've all seen founders who tried to do too much."

There it is.

I smile, slow and sharp.

"And you've all seen founders who were never allowed to do enough," I say. "I'm not one of them. You're free to review the materials again. I'm happy to walk through any line item you don't understand. But we're moving forward as planned."

Silence. A muscle jumps in one guy's jaw. The younger one looks... impressed, maybe. Or entertained.

Antoine leans against the far wall off camera, arms crossed, fighting a smirk. He loves when I do this dance. I don't.

"Very well," the chair finally says. "We'll trust your judgment."

You don't have a choice, I think. Out loud I say, "Thank you. I'll have my assistant send a follow-up summary."

We disconnect. The screen goes black. My shoulders drop half an inch.

"You handled that," Toine says.

"I always do," I reply. I rub the bridge of my nose. The familiar hum in my head is loud today. The one that says, Don't slip. Don't give them a reason.

Toine studies me for a second.

"You good?" he asks.

"I'm fine," I lie. "Just tired."

"Yeah, but this ain't just tired. You've been... off. Since you got back from New York."

"Drop it, Toine."

He raises his hands. "Say less. I'm just saying—if this girl got you out here glowing and groggy, at least let me hate properly."

I throw a pen at him. He dodges, laughing, and leaves me alone with my screens.

The rest of the day is a blur of messages and code review threads. I hop into 3 product stand-ups, kill a deal that doesn't smell right, green-light a beta that does. On paper, it's a productive day.

In reality, I am distracted as hell.

Every quiet moment, she pops up.

The way she fell asleep on my chest.

The way she whispered "harder" like she surprised herself.

The way she looked at me when she said she trusted me.

Trust is not a word people throw at me lightly. They trust my decisions, my money, my name on a deal. They do not usually trust me with their feelings.

I check my phone more than I want to admit. Nothing from her beyond the earlier exchange.

"Good afternoon, sleepy head. Did you make it home ok?"

"Yes, I'm home. About to get some work done. How's your day going?"

"It's going. I'm tired..."

I reread it twice between calls.

"She's just being nice," I tell myself. "You are not thirteen. Relax."

By midnight, my eyes are burning from screen time. I kick my shoes off and collapse on the couch. Rosa has already gone home. The place is quiet in that expensive way—insulation and tech making the city feel a world away.

I flick on Fall of the House of Usher. Might as well watch rich people fall apart worse than I am.

Somewhere around episode two, my phone buzzes in my hand.

Elia.

My heart does that annoying jump.

"You sleeping?" she asks when I pick up.

Her voice is soft, edges blurred by exhaustion and New York.

"No," I say. "Just finished work. Why are you still up? It's after one in the morning, you should be sleeping after the long day you had."

"I know," she sighs. "I'm just getting in. I wanted to call you before I went to sleep."

There it is again—that hit, low in my chest. The one I don't want to examine too closely.

"I appreciate that," I say, keeping my tone light. "But you don't have to feel obligated. We cool either way."

"Shai... about this morning," she says quietly.

I sit up a little. "Ok."

"It happened because I wanted it," she says. "I'm glad it happened.

I swallow and jump in before she can keep going — before she says something I don't know how to hold.

"You don't owe me anything," I tell her. "If you never want it to happen again, it won't. You're still my friend. I'm not going to push you into something you're not used to."

There's a quiet beat on her end. Not hurt. Not offended. Just... thinking.

"Shai," she says softly. "I know you're not trying to pressure me."

"Yeah. I understand," I say. "I know you're not... this way. And I won't create anything messy for you. I respect your world. Just know I'll never hurt you."

There's a pause. I hear her breathing.

"I know that, Shai," she says. "I trust you."

I lean my head back against the couch.

"And I trust you," I say. The words come out easier than they should.

She exhales on the other end, a little laugh wrapped in a sigh.

"Look... forget the mushy stuff," she says. "How was your day?"

"Long," I say. "Board circus. Old men worried I'm going to tank their boats while I'm the one keeping them afloat. You?"

"Also long," she says. "Interviews. Everybody wants to ask how my heart is without actually caring about the answer."

"Did you give them what they wanted?" I ask.

"Unfortunately," she says. "I stayed on script. I thought about what you said... that I don't owe them my pain. But when the lights came on, the brand answered before I could."

I'm quiet for a second.

"That doesn't make you weak," I say. "That makes you a professional. You survived the day. That's enough."

"Maybe," she says. "Still felt like I let myself down a little."

"Welcome to leadership," I say. "We stay disappointing ourselves in ways nobody else even notices."

She laughs, tired but real.

"Sounds like we both had a rough one," she says.

"Yeah," I admit. "We did."

Silence settles between us. Not awkward. Just... full.

All I hear on her end is that insulated hush—no street noise, no chaos, just the kind of silence you only get in a suite forty floors above the city. Her voice sounds closer than it should. On mine, it's just the low murmur of the show I forgot to pause.

"You watching TV?" she asks.

"Yeah. Fall of the House of Usher," I say. "Rich people with problems. Makes me feel better about mine."

"Text me which episode," she says. "Maybe I'll put it on so we can be fake watching together."

Something in my chest loosens.

"Deal," I say.

Her breathing evens out little by little. I lie back on the couch, phone pressed to my ear, eyes half-closed.

We don't say goodnight. We just... fade.

Somewhere in that quiet, we both fall asleep, two overworked idiots in different time zones breathing into the same line, pretending this is casual.

And I hate how much I want it to happen again.

That's what scares me the most.

CHAPTER TWELVE

614

The next two weeks flew. I was so busy doing PR in New York that it felt good to be heading home. As Raul drove me toward the terminal, all I could think about was 616. We had talked almost every night since I left. Her past, my past, Antoine, my mother, the business, friends—nothing felt off-limits anymore. I had gotten to know her in a way I did not expect, and I could not wait to feel her arms around me again.

She lived a lonely life, a quiet kind of depression wrapped in genius. If it were not for Antoine, she would have no one.

"Thank you, Raul," I said as he opened my door. I reached into my purse for a tip, but he gently raised a hand.

"No, Ma'am. Shai already took excellent care of us. We do not accept tips when she is the one who booked."

Of course she did.

When I stepped aboard the jet, I froze.

Two dozen long-stemmed white and yellow roses.

Three bottles of wine.

Soft jazz playing low.

A folded note on the table.

Sit back and relax. Enjoy your ride. I wish I could have been there this time, but you have waited this long; a few more hours will not hurt. Jess will take good care of you.

P.S. There's a bottle of SirDavis in my room under the stand if the wine is not enough.

– 616

Am I really living this life?

The sight hit me harder than I expected. I stood there for a moment, gripping the note, feeling something warm and terrifying rise in my chest. Anthony still wanted me. He begged for us. He called and texted and refused to sign anything. Yet here I was—being seen, tended to, understood by someone who had known me for a matter of weeks. Someone who read my moods without me opening my mouth. Someone who cared in a way that felt dangerous. A woman. A woman who was making it very hard to pretend I did not feel what I felt.

I took my bags into the back room and stretched out on the bed. I meant to rest for a second—but it turned into an hour… then two.

I woke to someone crawling behind me, a familiar kiss brushing the back of my neck.

"Hey, you," I whispered, eyes still closed.

"Hey," she murmured as she pulled me close. Her scent—Le Labo's Another 13, clean and addictive—wrapped around me. "How are you feeling?"

"I am better now."

She kissed my shoulder. "Come on. Let me get you home. I will take your things to the car."

"No… just let me lay here for a minute," I complained, half-asleep, half-gone.

"Let me get you comfortable at home," she said, scooping me right off the bed like it was nothing.

We got into the car. Rich grabbed the luggage without a sound. The moment we pulled off, I turned toward the window and melted into the memory of our last ride in the Maybach—her hands on me, her mouth on me, the way she made me feel like my body belonged to her.

I glanced over at her.

Quiet luxury from head to toe.

A soft Loro Piana cashmere hoodie in deep red.

Matching ribbed joggers from The Row.
Minimalist Tom Ford sneakers.
A smooth leather Celine cap.
No logos.
Just wealth.

She kept switching between her iPhone and her encrypted work device—the matte-black one her execs used. Her thumbs flew as she sent rapid-fire instructions to engineering, product, and operations. One minute she was my quiet, teasing lover. The next she was all business—firing off orders, troubleshooting something in real time, her voice low and focused in that way that always reminded me she ran an empire.

I can admit it now. I was turned out. Completely.

When we pulled into the garage, she told me to wait so no one saw me slipping out of her car. Once it was clear, I followed her upstairs, giving her space the way she needed. It stung a little, but I understood. Her entire life depended on no scandals.

The moment the door closed behind us, I headed for the shower. I needed water, silence, and a minute to breathe.

The shower felt like heaven. A reset. A cleansing of the two longest weeks of my life.

When I stepped out—body towel, hair towel, robe tied loosely—I padded into the kitchen and found a freshly poured glass of wine waiting for me. She was on the couch watching college football, a glass of her own in hand, typing into her phone with that CEO intensity.

"Thank you for the wine," I said as I settled next to her.

"Anytime," she said, still watching her phone.

"What is wrong?"

"Nothing. A few servers failed over. The team is handling it. They're pushing diagnostics now." Her phone vibrated again. "It does not look critical. I would go in if it was, but my team is solid. They know the playbook."

Real CEO talk. Calm. Controlled. Lethal.

"Well, I was going to get something to eat. Are you hungry?"

"No. Do not worry about that. Rosa is making dinner. It should be done soon. No need to put anything on."

Her smirk made my stomach flip.

"Acting like you don't want it," I muttered, walking toward the counter for the bottle.

Before I could reach it, her hands wrapped around my waist. She turned me around and lifted me onto the counter. Her lips brushed mine—soft, intentional, hungry.

"I never said I did not want it."

My towels hit the floor.

The entire kitchen changed temperature.

She took her time this round—hovering just long enough for my breath to hitch, kissing just slow enough that my body leaned into her without thinking. It was the build-up that got me. The restraint. The way she made me wait for her mouth, her hands, her rhythm.

She devoured me.

Not rushed.

Not messy.

Skilled.

Focused.

Calculated.

The release hit me so hard my brain blanked. My legs trembled. My toes cramped. I knocked an entire fruit bowl off the counter. I could barely breathe when she finally came up for air, checking her phone like she did not just ruin my life on a granite countertop.

She carried me to the bedroom when I could not walk. My legs were useless. I tried to protest, but she slid between my legs again, and my protest died in a moan.

What happened next?

Physics should study it.

NASA should take notes.

Hours later, I woke alone but wrapped in the comforter she tucked around me. The imprint of her body was still warm.

For a moment, I touched the places she had kissed—my neck, my waist, the inside of my thigh—and the guilt hit me like a weight. Anthony was calling. Begging. My husband. My history. And here I was, shaking from the way another person—another woman—had touched me. This was not casual anymore. This was not harmless. This was not just something to "pass the time." It was becoming something I could feel in my bones.

My phone had blown up with missed calls from the girls. I scrambled to shower again, threw clothes on, and headed to Lola's for our monthly meet-up.

"Hey ladies," I said as I sat. Their eyes scanned me immediately.

"You are glowing," Melissa said, narrowing her eyes. "How was your trip?"

"My trip was fine," I said, sipping my drink.

The conversation swung to Anthony—how he called Melissa about selling the house, how he refused to sign the divorce papers, how he missed me. I ignored two calls from him right there at the table.

Then my phone rang again.

My heart jumped.

"Hey you," I answered, trying to ignore Melissa staring into my soul.

"How did you sleep?" she asked.

"I slept great... thank you. Where did you disappear to?"

"I went to the office with Antoine. We had to finalize the root-cause analysis from last night's incident."

"Sounds... interesting," I said, trying not to smile. "Text me when you get in."

"Enjoy your girls' night."

When I hung up, the interrogation began.

I lied.

Badly.

"Someone I met in New York," I said.

Natalee gave me a look of pure girl, you are terrible at lying.

It started to feel suffocating—the lies, the half-truths, the way my heart jumped every time my phone lit up. I excused myself to the restroom just to breathe. I leaned over the sink, stared at my reflection, and tried to fix my face so I didn't look like a woman who had just been ruined on a private jet. I argued with myself quietly—You're married. You know better. You know this is risky. But every time I blinked, I saw her face over mine. Felt her breath on my neck.

I splashed water on my cheeks and walked back out like nothing was wrong.

The rest of the night blurred—drinks, gossip, marriage talk I did not want, and reminders that I was still technically someone's wife.

On the drive home, I tried to convince myself not to overthink any of this.

She was just fun.

Just a distraction.

Just something new.

But the truth sat in my chest like a secret I was scared to say out loud:

I wanted her.

And every time I thought of her... my whole body reacted.

CHAPTER THIRTEEN

616

It is about 11 p.m. when I leave Mikey's place and head home. I enjoy hanging with him because he is so mysterious, but a genius. He enjoys showing me the latest gadget he bought or just talking to me about software programs. He taught me a lot, and for him to be thirty-five, he knows his stuff. He is one of the few people I can sit in silence with for three hours and not feel like I am wasting time.

He lives alone in a loft-style studio apartment with about eight computers set up, and all he does is work. Four ultra-wide monitors mounted on the wall, two custom rigs running virtual machines and penetration tests nonstop, another box dedicated to packet sniffing, and one tower that he swears is "only for things the government should never find out about."

Mikey writes in languages half my engineers only read about in college. He builds his own tools when he cannot find one that does what he wants.

He is the same idiot who once hacked Intel-Ligent into the ground as a prank just to prove how bad our old security vendor was. I fired the vendor and hired him the next day.

He has a little cocaine habit, but it does not hinder his performance, so I let it slide—for the moment.

He says it keeps him up; he hates sleep. I get it. But I swear, if it ever starts dragging him under, I will pull him out by force and put him through an intervention he will never forget. I will protect him... but I will protect the company too. And if it comes down to choosing, I will protect the brand at all cost, even if it kills me to do it.

I get in the house about 11:30 p.m. and realize it is Friday and I have not heard from Antoine. I wonder what he got into tonight. I change into some shorts and sit at my computer to check emails, send out some, and do a little work. The usual—incident reports, board pings, two journalists trying to get cute with "anonymous source" stories. Delete, archive, delegate.

It is about 12:00 a.m. when there is a knock at the door. Of course, it could only be 614, so I disable the surveillance and immediately open the door to see her standing there in some boy shorts, a wife-beater with no bra, might I add, and some pumps, holding a bottle of wine.

"Damn, where have you been all my life?" I ask as I watch her walk in. She sure knows how to get it going. I just want to attack her, but I am cool, so I keep my composure. Control first. Always control.

"I am going to grab some glasses. Have a seat," she says and walks into the kitchen. She has apparently been drinking and is feeling a little freaky, but I do not mind at all.

I turn the fireplace on—electric, of course—and put on a Quiet Storm mix, by my favorite playlist creator Jaz Mone'. Just as she comes back in with the wine. It feels like she is moving in slow motion. I take that moment to admire the curvature and the walk. Not many women can get that walk in stilettos, when it looks so... effortless. She hands me my glass and sits down right next to me. Smelling delicious, looking delicious, I can almost guarantee she tastes delicious, but I am going to be good. I watch, taking it all in.

"So you like?" she says, straightening her leg out so I can see her shoes. "I got them in New York. I just wanted to break them in before I wore them."

"Very nice," I say, eyeing up her thighs.

"Here, let me stand up so you can get a better view," she says, standing up.

"Oh yeah, they fit good. Real good," I say, not once looking down. "I may need to get me some of them," I add as she laughs.

She stands right in front of me, and I sit up on the couch. I take my hands and gently glide up her legs to her waist and pull her down on me. I kiss her lips, softly and slowly, as she puts her arms around my neck, spilling a little wine down my shoulders. She pushes me back on the couch and starts to lick and kiss my neck and shoulders, getting the wine that spilled. I throw my head back, enjoying her tongue and lips. She begins to ride me, back and forth, as she lets out a soft moan and I am awakened to the sound of my phone ringing in the distance.

Damn... really?

"Hello," I answer, trying not to sound asleep.

"I am sorry. Did I wake you?" 614 responds.

"No. Not at all," I answer, smiling about the dream I did not want to wake up from.

"Well, you sound like you were asleep."

"I must have dozed off at my desk for a minute. What time is it?" I ask.

"It is about 1:30."

"So how was your night?" I ask, trying to shake the dream.

"Ughhh... you know... normal girl talk. Very... ummm... eventful," she replies.

"I am sure," I say, laughing to myself.

"Why is it freezing in here? Maybe I do not know how to work this thing, but it says 70. It feels like 50."

"Well, I do not mind keeping you warm if you want," I say, smiling. "I was just about to take it down anyway."

We both know what that means now. No need to say it out loud.

"How easy is it for you to do this to me?" she asks after a few seconds.

"Do what?"

"Just break down my defenses. It is like I cannot say no. I am not saying that I want to, but... I do not know, it is just a little overwhelming," she says.

"Ok, well, you do not have to come. I—"

"No, I am not saying that. I am just saying this is all so new to me. I have never really been this drawn... you know what, never mind. Open the door," she says, hanging up the phone.

We really do not hang up anymore. We just relocate the conversation.

I walk over to the door and open it. Elia is dressed in an oversized sweatshirt and some sweatpants. So much for dreams coming true, I say to myself. Do not get me wrong, she is still hot, and I have a great imagination, so I am fine.

"That cold?" I ask.

"You have no idea," she says, taking off her sweatshirt and grabbing a throw blanket.

"Can I get you anything?" I ask.

"No, I am fine. I had enough to drink for tonight. I just want to relax until I fall asleep."

"Ok," I say, crawling up behind her.

We lay on the couch and put on that new Diddy documentary on Netflix—*The Reckoning*. I have seen enough of these exposés to know how they go, but something about the slow unraveling of power and secrets always pulls me in. It is the kind of background noise I fall asleep to—a little truth, a little conspiracy, a little reminder the world is darker than people pretend.

Shows used to feel simple. Now everything is layered, heavy, always pushing an angle. Even documentaries feel like they are trying to teach you a lesson you did not ask for.

"Diddy knew damn well... chickens always come home to roost." I shake my head as I cue episode three again. Some people really believe they're untouchable—that consequences are something meant for other people.

I used to think I was different. Careful. Smarter. As long as I wasn't the one making promises, I told myself I wasn't the one breaking them.

I can already see myself in some future documentary, sitting under bad lighting, pulling a Bill Clinton—*I did not have sexual relations with that woman.*

Funny how that logic works.

Chickens don't care whose yard they wander back into.

I pull her close to me as she nestles in my arms; she closes her eyes and falls asleep.

I watch her sleep for some time. I watch as the blood courses through the vein in her neck with every pulse. How her eyes tend to flutter from time to time. Her lips part slightly as she drifts deeper in. She looks like she drools, I think to myself, smiling. I kiss her neck softly not to wake her, close my eyes, and hope and pray I can continue the dream I was having earlier.

It is about eight in the morning when Rosa comes in and awakens us. I thought she was off on Saturdays. Goes to show how much I pay attention to the little things. I tell Elia she can go lay down in the bedroom as I get up to go see what Rosa is doing.

"Rosa, what are you doing here today? I told you to take the weekend off. Go shopping, catch a movie, catch a cold, but take some time, Rosa," I say to her.

"Today is five-year anniversary, Shai. I need work. I went to cemetery and laid flowers... You want breakfast?" she asks as I see tears in her eyes.

"Sure, Rosa, make that breakfast for three," I say, giving her a hug.

"Shai, no mushy stuff," she says, waving her hands, smiling, just as Elia enters the kitchen.

"I am going to head across the hall and fix myself. Ok?" she says, fixing her ponytail.

"All right. Rosa is making breakfast," I say to her, walking her to the door.

"Yeah, give me like ten minutes. Good morning, Rosa."

"Good morning," Rosa says not turning around.

"Ok." I close the door and head to the bathroom, knowing I have to fix my breath situation.

I wash my face and brush my teeth before heading over to the computer to check my emails. I have no calls, so that is a good thing, and my emails are just necessary updates. Server status green, legal thread long, board thread longer. Nothing on fire yet.

There is this pharmaceutical project Antoine got me to invest in, and I have my worries. This is Antoine's baby, but I like to know what is going on. The Premmission series: a neuromodulation protocol aimed at disrupting trauma pathways and editing how the brain stores certain memories. If it works, it changes the way PTSD, addiction, and some forms of depression are treated. If anything goes wrong, it looks like we tried to play God with people's minds.

This is the idea that is going to skyrocket Intel-Ligent, according to Antoine. I am giving him leeway on this, but I am watching. Big swings make big headlines. The wrong kind.

"Are you hungry?" I ask as 614 walks through the door.

"Yes," she says, taking her seat as Rosa brings over food.

"Good, Rosa makes an excellent breakfast," I say, pulling up my first news article on my iPad.

Rosa finishes setting the food out, and I invite her to join us. I do not mind eating with Rosa. Most snotty people do not eat with "The Help," but I think that is downright ridiculous, especially if it is just me. Now, if I were having dinner guests or something like that, then that is different of course, and Rosa is more than "The Help" to me.

She has seen me broke, pissed, drunk, and bleeding. That is family, she is family, not staff.

I continue reading my daily news. The next war; you know, the usual depressing information, as 614 and Rosa talk recipes or whatever they are discussing.

"So what is on your agenda?" I ask 614 as Rosa gets up to take the plates.

"Sit around here and bother you all day," she says, smiling.

"How about something a little more relaxing," I say to her.

"What could be more relaxing than laying on the couch in my PJs watching re-runs and drinking wine?" she asks.

"Well, today is a tough day for Rosa. I want to do something for her and you, since it is not cool for us to be all out in public. I figure you two could go have a spa day and do a little shopping. It would mean a lot to her and to me," I say.

"It is not that we cannot go out in public..." she says, as I stare back at her, please do not feed me crap. "We can go out in public, just in a very secluded place. That is all."

"Sure..." I say, drinking some orange juice.

"Well, I do not have a problem at all taking Rosa out. Besides, what girl would not want to shop at the expense of someone else?" she says as she straddles me.

"I knew you were a gold digger," I say, laughing.

"You know some women would take that offensive, but I have my own money. My pockets may not be as deep as yours, but I do ok," she says, kissing my neck.

"I know, that is why I appreciate you," I say as we start to kiss. It always starts to get so heavy and passionate. I mean, the sexual attraction is definitely mutual.

"What are you going to do while I am out tearing up the strip?" she asks playfully.

"Probably hit up Antoine and go play some ball or something. I could use a good workout," I say, rubbing her and still trying to get some.

"Basketball sounds good," she says, closing her eyes. "No, we cannot start this right now," she says, moaning as I kiss her neck.

"Why not?" I ask, still kissing her.

"Because Rosa is wandering around and I am still sore from yesterday," she whispers, still moaning to my kisses.

"Are you wet right now?" I ask her as I rub her nipples.

"Nope," she says, obviously lying. I can feel the heat radiating through my PJs.

"Ok, well let me just touch it," I say, sliding my hands down her sweats. She is dripping wet. I massage her clit with my fingers, knowing this is not going to take long, it is already swollen. I hear her moan softly as she starts to move her hips.

"No, we cannot... ahhhhh!" she lets out a moan just as I slide inside of her. She bites down on her lip as she takes in two and starts riding them slowly. I hold onto her hip with my free hand, feeling the way her hips rock back and forth. I think, as her hips start moving faster, with her face in my neck, one hand in my hair, and the other hand gripping my upper back, I feel her walls tightening.

"I am coming," she whispers in my ear. I feel her riding become tighter as she is trying to hold on. "Oh... wait, do not move," she says softly as she pulls me tighter, trying not to moan loudly as she comes, biting down on my neck to muffle her scream. I get my hair pulled, bit, and scratched all at the same damn time. Damn, she gets me going.

"You have to stop doing that," she says, gently pulling my hand out and laying her head on my shoulder.

"What? Giving you orgasms? Ok," I say, kissing her forehead.

"Yes. A girl can get used to that. Next thing you know, I am walking around here crying, make-up running down my face, looking crazy while you have me banned from the building!" she says, laughing.

"Ha-ha. Oh, you have jokes. She did not get half of what you are getting. She was here, let us just say, for my enjoyment," I say.

"And what do you mean for your enjoyment?" she asks with that look women give when you say something wrong.

"I mean... you know, she serviced my wants. I was not even on her like that," I say, knowing that I started something.

"Mmmm-hmmmm," she says, nodding. "So... are you full of enjoyment with me?"

"Of course I am. What kind of question is that? I enjoy doing you, that is where my pleasure comes in. You do not need to worry about anything right now. I know you are not into the entire girl-on-girl thing. It is fine, baby. Trust me," I say, kissing her forehead, trying to reassure her that it is not a big deal. "I enjoy you."

If I say it enough, maybe she will stop trying to label this and just feel it.

"It is fine," she says, obviously a little bothered. "Tell Rosa to be ready around one. I am going to shower and get ready." She gives me a peck and walks out the door just as Rosa emerges from the back room with her iPod on and duster in hand.

"You are going out today. So put the duster down and walk away," I say. "Elia wants you to be ready by one."

"No, Shai. I am fine. I promise," she says in her broken English.

"I will not take no for an answer. Have a seat and drink a mimosa. You are going out for a spa day," I say, guiding her to the spare bedroom. "Turn on Telemundo and relax!"

I head to the kitchen to make her a mimosa when my phone rings.

"Toine, what is good?" I ask.

"Nothing. What you up to?"

"I was just about to hit you up. You want to go ball a little bit?" I ask him, walking Rosa's drink into her.

"Yeah, that sounds good. Been a minute since I hit a basketball court up anyway. What time?"

"Around one or so. I will meet you up there."

"Ok, cool. By the way, we are ready to start on the first test for the first Premmission series. This will determine if it will be approved by the FDA or be bounced back. We are hitting the budget pretty close, Shai."

"What do you mean hitting the budget pretty close? Especially since I am sure I am not the only investor in this?" I ask him.

"I know. I have gone over the charts myself, and everything seems to be checking out..."

"I want a full report on my desk Monday morning, Toine," I say, maintaining my cool. "Clinical burn rate, cash runway, risk register, everything. No slideshows. I want the raw numbers and the audit trail."

"Shai, I understand, but I am telling you, if this pops—when this pops—the way it is supposed to, we will be multi-billionaires. I feel it, Shai," he says, trying to reassure me.

"Toine, I have ten million dollars floating around out there. Something better pop, and I better not see one glitch in the paperwork, or I will shut this project down. Understood?"

"I got you, Shai. When did you become such a boss?" he asks jokingly.

"When I got ten million on the line," I say. "See you in a few hours."

"All right," he says, hanging up.

This is not a game right now. Antoine puts his money up for any get richer quicker scheme. This dude is already a multi-millionaire, but I guess that is not enough. I am sure it is going to pick up, but I do not want anyone slacking on responsibilities thinking I am cool.

I worked hard to get where I am, and I will be damned if I fall into some bullshit. Not going to happen. I sit down at my computer and hit Mikey on the secure chat.

SHAI: You up?

MK: Always. What is on fire?

SHAI: This Premmission thing... talk to me.

MK: Technically, it is sound. Concept is wild but not stupid. Memory reconsolidation, targeted neuromodulation, very bleeding-edge. But something around the data flow feels off. Too many hands touching the numbers. That makes me itch.

SHAI: Wish you would have voiced these concerns earlier.

MK: You already know I am always watching, Shai. I wanted to see who tried to get clever before I called it out.

"Antoine believes in this thing, and I am not going to lie, I believe in it, but I think I may have jumped the gun on this a little bit," I type.

MK: Trust no one, Shai. Not even me. Lock your access. Watch the wire transfers. Follow the paper, not the pitch. There is not much you can do now. Ride it out and watch it closely. I am on it. Do not worry about it.

"Enough said," I reply.

And just like that, my ghost signs off.

I never told Antoine that I kept Mikey on to run and watch the backside of my company. As far as Antoine knows, Mikey is just our securities manager. He runs things from his home, making sure we are not being hacked or jeopardized. He has no idea that Mikey is my go-to guy, and I like it like that.

When there are hundreds of millions on the line, trust no one, and even though I would trust Antoine with my life, there is no harm in having someone else monitoring all activities. I have multiple accountants watching each other. That is the way of the game. Love is just an emotion, and trust will get you killed. That is the rule. Feelings are a luxury. Risk is not.

It is about 12:30 when I finish making phone calls, checking emails... you know, the usual routine. I take a shower to get ready to play some ball. Yes, I know I am going to just get sweaty all over again, but it is cool, I will just shower again.

As I step out of the shower, I notice 614 standing in the doorway, leaning up against the frame. Damn this chick is bad. She always has heels on, and damn it, that is the biggest turn-on for me. She is dressed in a simple orange blouse with the one shoulder off, a pair of nice fitting capris, and of course open-toed orange and tan heels.

Usually, I would be embarrassed and pissed at the same time for someone sneaking up on me like this. They would immediately be kicked the hell out and deleted. I step out of the shower with calmness unlike me in this situation and stand in front of the body dryer as she stands there watching with her arms across her chest. Looking like she has something to say, but does not. Just stands there. So I just stand there and watch her. As much as I want to fuck her right here and now, I do not. Self-control is a bitch.

"What is wrong?" I ask her, breaking the silence as I start to lotion.

"Nothing... just wondering what I got myself into," she says, not moving.

I watch her as she looks me up and down, checking out my tattoos and my physique. She has never seen me naked before, so this is a first, but hey... there's a first time for everything, right? I put my polo briefs on, spray down with body spray, and put my wife-beater on before replying.

"What do you mean by that?" I ask, walking up on her.

"Nothing... I have to go. Rosa is waiting," she says, walking out of the room.

"Well, wait, let me give you a card," I say, looking for my wallet.

“Do not worry about it. This one is on me,” she says as she and Rosa walk out the door.

I stand there speechless for a minute, trying to figure out what happened. Well, whatever. They will be gone for a few hours. I will deal with it then, I guess. She is already doing math in her head—where this goes, what it costs her, what it makes her look like. I cannot blame her. I designed my whole life around avoiding that math.

I throw on a white V-neck T-shirt, some basketball shorts, some J’s, and a hoodie and walk out the door. I hop in my Bentley and ride to meet up with Toine, all the while thoughts of 614 running wild. Why does this chick have this hold on me? Usually, I can can a chick real quick, but... I do not know. Whatever, I think to myself as I pull up.

No better way to relieve stress than on the court. Ready up.

We play for like three hours before we call it quits. We decide to recoup by having lunch at one of our favorite spots by the courts. This is not going to do anything but put me to sleep. We both order lemonade, chicken, and waffles.

“So I met this chick. Her name is Chantae,” he says as the plates arrive.

“Really... and you actually know her name. I am proud of you, boss,” I say back, laughing.

“Yeah, she is cool too. She has me taking walks and talking. You know, an intelligent chick,” he says, taking a bite.

“That is what is up, Toine. It is good to finally see someone has your attention for more than a night. How long has this been going on?” I ask him.

“About a month. I did not want to rush into telling you because I know you think I am playing when I say things like this. So I just wanted to make sure that it was the real deal. You know.”

“Yeah, I feel you. So what do you think?” I ask him.

"Nothing right now. I am just taking it one day at a time," he says, laughing.

"Well, that is cool. I cannot wait to meet her."

"Yeah, I actually wanted to set something up to hang out or something. You know, chill with some drinks," he says.

"Cool with me. I am sure we can arrange that."

"So what you got going on tonight?" he asks me as we finish up our lunch.

"I do not even know yet. Elia felt some kind of way this morning over some bird giving me head. I do not know what to think of it. You got this check?" I say, laughing.

"Ha-ha, you are funny, boss man. Yeah, I got it. So you still with ole girl?"

"Yeah man, I mean I do not know where we are going, even if we are, but we are chilling," I say.

"Well, you are obviously going somewhere if she is catching feelings. Damn, Shai, what you do to her?" he says, laughing.

"I put it down. What can I say?"

"Well, you sure bagged a good one. Damn, I wanted to marry her."

"I am so sure," I say as we get up.

"I will definitely see you on Monday. I need that full report and presentation, Toine."

"Are we in boss mode or friend mode?" he responds.

"I am always a boss. I am in bossy friend mode," I say as I get in my car.

"Later. Maybe I will see you tonight," he says as he speeds off. He sure does not need a Ferrari driving like that.

CHAPTER FOURTEEN

616

I get in about seven, and I see that 614 and Rosa are back already. There are a few bags and Rosa's shoes in the doorway. Well, what is going on here, I think to myself as I hit the living room and see the two of them on the couch watching something on what I will assume is Netflix.

Great.

"Five minutes, Shai. Almost over," Rosa says.

"Hey," I say as I walk over to 614 and kiss her forehead.

"Hey, baby," she says, not even taking her eyes off the TV. "I mean..."

"It is fine, relax," I say with a smile. The word hits different now, but I let it pass. No need to spook her when she is finally letting herself slip.

I go into the kitchen and grab a bottle of water. Damn, is this what it is like with women in the house? Netflix, bags, being ignored, and my 120-inch being taken over.

It is Saturday, and I have some games to watch, but I dare not roll in there. I go into my bedroom instead and turn the game on in there, shaking my head, when Elia walks in.

"So how was the game?" she asks.

"We got our asses kicked most of the time. I am going to be sore later, but I had fun," I say, getting out some clean underclothes so I can take a shower.

"Here, I will run you a bath," she says, going into the bathroom.

"Thank you. So tell me, how was spa day and shopping?" I ask, stripping down to my briefs.

"We had such a good time. Rosa told me about Mexico, and it is funny because I have never been there, but it sounds wonderful. Then we had lunch, she told me about her son, working for you, about how you need to settle down and stop dealing with trash... yeah, a very eventful day."

"Great..." I reply as I take my briefs off and get in the tub. I lay my head back and close my eyes, enjoying the hot water. "I must be getting old. Toine and I used to ball like that, and I never felt like this."

"You are not getting old. Just out of shape," she says, and I feel her slide in between my legs, resting her back against my chest.

"Oh, you scared me. I thought you were Rosa for a second," I say jokingly.

"Ha-ha, let me find out you and Rosa have a thing going on," she says, laughing, running her nails softly up and down my leg.

"Would you not like to know?" I laugh back.

"This feels so good. I love baths," she says.

"I know. I just do not know the last time I took one," I say. "Did you pee in the water?"

"Are you seriously asking me if I went pee in the water?" she says, laughing. "No, did you pee in the water?"

"I did not know you were getting in," I say, laughing as she turns around to get out. "Nah, I am kidding for real. I did not pee. I knew you were going to get in. For real. I do not marinate in my own urine. That is nasty."

"So why would you say that and put that idea in my head?" she asks, not knowing whether to get out or stay in.

"I was just joking. I swear. Bad joke?" I say, still laughing, lying in the same spot.

"Terrible joke," she says, turning back around and getting back in her original position.

"Ok, I guess I will scratch that one off my list of funny things to say."

"Yeah, please do. Horrible," she says, shaking her head.

"Can I ask you something, 616?" She asked after a few minutes of silence.

"Of course."

"Are you satisfied? I mean... with me?" she asks, lying there.

"Yes. Why would I not be?"

"Because I do not touch you or go down on you. What do you get out of it?"

"I get off by you coming. The way you feel when I touch you inside, wet and warm. The way you moan in my ear like I am giving you the greatest pleasure. The way you hold me tight and claw my back as you cum. The way you bite my lip when I hit your spot. Feeling you tighten around me when you are about to explode. That is what gets me. I do not need you to touch me or give me head. I am fine," I say, kissing her neck.

"I just want you to know that I want you just as much as you want me, if not more. The things you do to me... I have never felt. You caress my body. You cater to me in the bedroom. I am not just another hole to be poked until you get off. It is always right, every time. You fuck me when I want it and make love to me when I need it. I just do not want you to think this is a one-way street," she says, still gliding her nails down my legs.

"Trust me, I do not. I want you all the time, anywhere and everywhere, dressed up or in sweats. It took everything I had in me not to grab you up this afternoon when you were standing in the doorway. I want you. I just do not want you to come over and give me head from time to time because you are bored."

"I just have a lot going on. You know, with the divorce and you..."

"Elia, do not worry about me. I am here for you, but you must take care of yourself first, and whatever I can do to help you, just tell me. You never have to fight things alone. If this stopped tomorrow—because I would want one more night—then I would still be your friend and take care of you. If you are not doing me dirty in ending it, I respect you for the woman you are. That is why you have made it farther than any other woman has or ever will," I say to her.

The words come out easier than they should. I do not do love, but this... is dangerously close to something that looks like it.

I watch as a tear falls from her left eye. I know this must be hard for her. Going through a divorce, dealing with me, re-establishing her career with new management, ex-husband calling, new place, new life. She told me how things changed so quickly for her. She had shared everything with Anthony, and to break away from him, she had to cut away from it all.

I grab her close, and we sit in silence until our fingers wrinkle and the water turns cold.

"You ok?" I ask as we step out of the bath.

"I am fine. Thank you," she says as she starts the shower. "I am going to take a quick shower. You coming?"

We hop in the shower, and I wash her, and she washes me. I allow her to get close to me, even though I have never been this close to anyone. I know this is weird for her, so I just give her the time she needs to become comfortable. I watch her, lathered, nipples hard, seeming to enjoy every minute. I enjoy every minute. Water, steam, her back under my hands—this is more dangerous than any deal I have ever signed.

We get out of the shower and stand in front of the air dryer together. I cannot stress enough that I have never had these intimate moments with anyone, but with her, it is... different.

I throw some briefs and a wife-beater on, grab the lotion from under the sink, and walk her over to the bed. Even though I know she had a spa day today, I take my time and lotion her. Laying her on her stomach, I work her shoulders, down her back, thighs, and legs, smiling as she giggles when I get to her feet. I roll her over and do the same as she lies there. I kiss her as I come up, and we just take this moment to connect. Her eyes closed, my eyes closed, we sit lip-to-lip, softly touching, lost in the moment until my phone goes off.

Of course.

"Do not answer," she whispers, knowing that I have to.

"Hello," I say, never breaking eye contact.

"Yeah, I am on my way over," Toine says.

"Now is not a good time, Toine."

"Why, what are you doing?" he asks me.

"Spending some time right now."

"That is cool, but Tae is leaving tomorrow for a week, so I wanted to bring her by to hang out for a little bit."

"All right, man, what time?" Knowing how important this is to him, I do not want to let him down.

"It is, what, 9:30? I will be there by 10."

"All right," I say, and we hang up.

"Hey, baby, Antoine is about to come over so I can meet this chick he is feeling before she leaves. He just wants to hang out for a bit, have a drink or two. So you want to hang out or head home?"

"Ummm... I mean, do I have to worry about anything?" she asks.

"No. I will provide my normal security measures. You are safe with me. You trust me, right?"

"Yeah, I trust you, but it is not you I am worried about."

"Look, just throw on something. I am going to get dressed and get the bar set," I say, getting up.

I throw on a black V-neck T-shirt, a grey cardigan, some black linen slacks, and some grey and black Christian loafers to blend it. I watch her take over my bathroom, fixing her hair, neatly putting her clothes on, and spraying some shimmer gloss stuff. I am supposed to be getting the bar set, but I take my time just so I can watch her process.

Wearing all black, she matches her makeup precisely with neatly lined dark eyeliner and mascara. I watch as she slides her last foot into the six-inch black Christians she obviously bought earlier today.

"What a coincidence. Are you trying to match me?" I ask, coming up behind her as she puts her jewelry on.

"No... it is just what I happened to have at the moment," she says as we stand in front of the mirror together.

"I must say... I make you look good," I say with a smile.

"Ha-ha, yeah right. You definitely have that backward," she says just as my bell buzzes.

"The sad part is, you really seem convinced that statement is true," I say, laughing as I kiss her neck and head to the door.

"Yeah, whatever, we will see," she yells at me.

"Hey, baby, stay in the room until I perform the check. I will get you when I am done."

"Ok, babe," she yells from the bathroom.

I enable the security so that it can match and track the faces entering and get my lockers set up for personal items. Antoine is probably going to have a problem with this, but I can respect someone's privacy. With the Internet, you cannot trust anybody. I turn the fireplace on, set some '90s jams on, and set the vodka and wine on the bar just as he knocks at the door.

"What is going on?" I say as I open the door.

"Nothing, bro, what is up?" he says as we clap it up. "This is Tae," he says as she walks in.

"Pleasure," I say as I extend my hand.

"I have really heard so much about you," she says as she also extends her hand.

"Hey, Toine, I have to take security measures. No disrespect though."

"Nah, it is cool. Your girl here?"

"Yes, my friend is here, so you know I have to follow protocol," I say, correcting him.

"I understand completely," he says as I have her follow the procedures, sign the confidentiality agreement, and hand over her cell phone and recordable devices. Same rules for everyone. I am not losing my company over somebody's Instagram story.

"So, Tae is it? What can I get you to drink?" I ask, heading over to the bar, taking a moment to feel her out before I bring out Elia.

"I will have a vodka and cranberry. Thank you," she says, standing around the bar.

"You can have a seat in the seating room," I say, handing her drink. Toine makes his standard drink, Hennessy and Coke, and leads her into the sitting room.

I make Elia a whiskey smash and make my way to the bedroom to get her.

"Hey, baby, you ready?" I say, walking into the bedroom to see that she changed her hairstyle.

"Yeah, coming out now," she says as she walks out of the bathroom looking to die for. I am honestly hoping this is lust and not love. I do not do love, but she... makes my eyes smile every time I see her.

"Thank you for the drink," she says as she grabs the glass and starts to walk into the room.

"Wait... let me see you," I say, grabbing her arm and pausing her mid-stride.

"Let you see what?" she says, turning to look at me.

"All of that." I stare at her for a second before I grab her hand and lead her into the sitting room to sit around the fire.

"Hi, I am Elia," she says, approaching Tae.

"Hello, Chantae," Tae says as they exchange a little handshake.

I watch Toine as Elia enters. He is focused, but trying not to be. I mean, he really cannot trip because Tae is just as pretty and mannered, but you know dudes, it is always the one they cannot get that is the one they want. I cannot even say "a dude," that is just human nature.

"Antoine," Elia says as she takes her seat.

"Elia," he says, drinking his drink. I shake my head at the two of them.

"So now that the introductions were made, what is going on?" I ask, trying to get this night moving.

We continue to make small talk for some time over drinks. It is not long before the liquor is on the table and we are just making drinks at will. Elia and Antoine finally come around, laughing and making jokes. Tae eventually loosens up and relaxes. It is no longer a proper meet and greet. Before you know it, we are all sloshed. The heels come off, and everyone is just comfortable.

It turns out to be a good night.

"Toine, you cannot beat me," I say. For some unknown reason, he has it in his head that he can beat me on the pool table.

"Ok, well let us go to the game room and fix this issue," he says, trying to stand.

"Game on," I say, grabbing my drink.

"Here they go. Tae, you want another drink?" Elia asks as she prepares hers.

"Yes, thank you. Well, we want to play too," Tae replies.

"Not a problem. Baby, can you shoot pool?" I ask 614. "We can play partners."

"Sure, why not," 614 responds, which lets me know that she cannot.

"Tae and Elia know damn well they cannot play," Antoine says as he grabs the Hennessey bottle and leads the way.

"How do you have all these rooms?" Elia asks as she enters the "Man Cave."

"I purchased two flats and had the walls knocked down. I wanted a house in an apartment," I say, shrugging it off. She has never ventured into this side of the apartment. There is really not much more to show. I have one bedroom, a formal dining area, and a massive gaming center. This is usually where we watch football on game day. Six flat screens, pool table, arcade games, PlayStations, Xboxes, Wiis, ping pong, chess, darts; you want it, I got it. I can be a big kid at times.

"And when do you have the time to play all this?" Elia asks, amused by my inner kid.

"We used to play heavy when I first got it, but business took over. As we expanded, we became too busy to have game nights. Call of Duty, 2k, and Madden 24-hour marathons. Now it is really only used for football season or when Toine and I have our competitive moments," I say as I input the code in the security system and we all watch the room come to life.

"Oh no, you do not have the original Pac-Man," Tae says excitedly, running over to the machine.

"Yeah, and Toine has the high score. I gave up trying to beat it," I say, laughing.

"House rules," I say as Toine racks them up.

The night pretty much goes on as expected. The liquor flows, and I realize 614 is not as bad at pool as I would have expected. We win three out of five games, and Tae actually beats us all in beer pong. We have an excellent night. With Elia on my arm, I feel complete. Whole again. Even though I cannot take her out in public, I guess I will just have to respect that. For now, this is what "together" looks like—closed doors, NDAs, and my name on every liability.

We are all so wasted by 3:30 in the morning that Toine and Tae just crash in one of the spare rooms, and Elia and I stumble into my bedroom and fall out on the bed.

I wake up about nine o'clock fully dressed, and Elia naturally wanders into the bathroom. I slide out of the bed and head to the bathroom once Elia walks out to wash my face and brush my teeth. Once I finish, I go into the kitchen area where I see Tae and Elia making breakfast.

"Ummm, where is Rosa?" I ask, nervous.

"She is somewhere around here," Elia responds, dancing around the kitchen as they listen to Xscape's Traces of My Lipstick. Truly classic album.

"Well, what are y'all doing in my kitchen?" I say, taking a seat at the table.

"Making breakfast," Elia says as she hands me some orange juice and gently kisses my lips.

"Nobody cooks in my kitchen but Rosa. I do not trust y'all like that, honestly," I say, grabbing a banana and peeling it.

"Well, you do not have to eat," Elia says, singing into a spoon.

"Whatever. Where is Toine?" I ask.

"He is still asleep," Tae says as she puts some biscuits in the oven. "How do you turn this thing on?" she asks, staring at the stove range.

"It is touch. Here, let me," Elia says, reaching over and turning the stove on. "Who says I do not know my way around a kitchen?" she says, smirking.

"A blind man can feel his way around a kitchen. That does not necessarily mean that he can cook," I say, heading into my office.

I sit down at my computer and begin to check emails. Of course, business as usual. Mergers and buyouts, marketing analysis, the normal. I notice an email from an anonymous address, the subject line reading,

You Want To Read This. It is routed through the secure relay Mikey set up for anything that cannot go through standard corporate mail.

Thinking it is spam, I leave it alone until Mikey can do an analysis on it. Just then, Mikey pops up in our secure chat.

MK: Ready for your vacation?

SHAI: Not really, but I guess I have to.

MK: Well, have fun and do not forget about the little people. :)

SHAI: I will try not to. Hey, MK, I got an email from an anonymous sender. Subject line says, "You Want To Read This." Check it out and do some research. Let me know what you find, but not until I return from my vacation. I just want to enjoy it.

MK: Ok, will do. Thanks for the bonus, by the way. One day I am going on a permanent vacation, and if you keep handing me bonuses, it will be sooner rather than later.

SHAI: Yeah, I will be putting a stop on the check.

MK: Too late.

He signs off.

I close out my screens and head into the kitchen to see Rosa coming to the rescue, grabbing plates and setting the table, arranging my meal the way I like it. I really appreciate her.

"Shai, they burn the kitchen down. No more cooking in my kitchen," she says, laughing.

"I was wondering when you were going to come in here and get this mess in order," I say, taking my seat.

"When you go on vacation, Shai?" she asks as she lays my fork, spoon, and knife neatly in front of me.

"I am leaving tomorrow," I say, patiently waiting to taste this breakfast 614 made.

"What vacation?" 614 asks, stopping what she is doing to look at me.

"Well, I was going to tell you over breakfast, but I booked us a one-week stay at an exclusive resort. Private beach, no cameras, nobody, just us," I say, grabbing a piece of bacon.

"Really?" she asks, smiling.

"Yes, we leave tomorrow morning. So, I guess once you are done burning my breakfast, you can go pick some stuff up," I say, grabbing my iPad to check the news.

"Very funny," she says, smiling, laying my plate out and kissing my lips.

"Something sure does smell burnt," Antoine says as he walks into the kitchen.

"Welcome to breakfast in hell," I say as he takes his seat across from me.

"As hungry as I am, I would eat anything right about now," he says, grabbing some orange juice.

"Well... you are about to get your wish," I say, taking my first bite.

We all sit and eat breakfast, talking and laughing about last night. I am seeing a different side of Toine. He seems to really like Tae. For once, he is not chasing chaos—he is actually trying to build something.

Between Tae, Premmission, and this anonymous email, I can feel the ground shifting. Vacation or not, a storm is coming.

CHAPTER FIFTEEN

614

After breakfast, I head over to my place. I have been spending so much time with 616 that I have neglected my own duties. Now I have this surprise trip I have to be ready for tomorrow. Great.

I am excited. I have this week off before I have to buckle down and get to work, so a vacation sounds excellent. I know that I have to call my mother. I have been ignoring her calls for days.

"Hello," she says as she answers the phone.

"Hello, Mother," I reply.

"Oh, here is my daughter that would leave her elderly mother to fend for herself," she throws back at me.

"Mom, you are far from elderly, and if you were incapable of self-support, I have some nice nursing homes all lined up for you," I say with a laugh.

"Of course you do," she says.

"What are you doing, Mother?" I say as I walk into my closet to decide what I need to pick up when I go out.

"Oh, nothing much, cleaning and such. I have been trying to tell you I am heading to Vegas for a trip. Play some penny slots," she says.

"Oh yeah, well that is great, Ma. Glad to see you getting out," I tell her.

"Yeah, Gladys, Ruth, and the girls put together a little trip."

"Well, that is good, Mom, but is it not a sin to gamble?" I ask, waiting for a response.

"It is not gambling if it is just for fun," she snarls back, knowing I have a point.

"Ok, whatever you tell yourself," I reply. "Listen, I am going to be out of town for work for about a week, doing press and meetings. So if I do not answer right away, do not panic. I will call you when I can."

"Mmmm-hmmm... Have you talked to Anthony?" she asks.

"No, Mother, not recently, but I will speak to him soon enough. Ok?"

"Well, alright. I just want to see you two work this thing out."

"Sure, Mother," I say as I get a call through on the phone. "Hey, Mom, I have to call you back. Have fun tonight and remember to take your cell phone and medication. Call me if you need anything."

"Ok, baby. Love you," she says as she hangs up.

"Hello," I answer, switching to the incoming call.

"Hey, girl," Natalee says on the other end.

"Hey. What is going on?" I ask as I throw some clothes on my bed.

"Nothing much. I have not heard from you in a few days, so I decided to check in on you."

"I am fine. Shai and I are going on a vacation tomorrow for a week," I say, trying to hide my excitement.

"From the looks of it, she really likes you," she says.

"Yeah, I guess, but you know I am not trying to get back involved like that. I just got out of a commitment, and I am not trying to get back into it."

"I understand, but you cannot fight that bug," she says, laughing into the phone.

"I am not trying to fight it, I am trying to stomp it out before it has a chance to lay eggs," I say, laughing back.

"Well, have fun on your trip and call me. Let me know how it goes."

"Ok, girl. I will," I say as we hang up.

The second the line goes dead, the guilt creeps back in—my mother praying for reconciliation, my best friend low-key cheering on my situationship with a person she will not even let herself fully name out loud. Divorce, God, Shai, career—it all feels like four different storms circling the same house.

I take the rest of the day to get myself together. Make the necessary calls and arrangements before I leave to go on this vacation. I set up an outgoing message for my emails and the business line stating I will be out of the office for the specified dates and to contact my agent for relevant information.

I take a quick shower and throw something on to run errands and get things needed for my trip. I decide to call 616 and see if she needs anything while I am out.

"Hey, baby," I say as soon as she answers the phone.

"Hey, beautiful," she replies.

"I am about to head out and do some shopping, and I wanted to know if you needed anything while I was out?"

"No, but if you see something I may like, just pick it up," she says with a chuckle.

"Ummm… ok. What are you doing?"

"Nothing much, relaxing. Going over some paperwork."

"Ok, well I will be back in a few. Can I take the Maybach?" I ask, really feeling like being spoiled.

"Hahaha, that is funny," she replies as if I said something funny.

"What, Shai? I am serious."

"You do know my license plates are very identifiable," she throws back.

"Ok, and why should I care?" I say.

"Because if that gets out, Elia, you are going through a divorce, and you are riding around in the Maybach of what the world loves to call a well-known lesbian. Let us be honest, you may get a pass if it were Ellen's, but nobody is going to let that go. You will get back and walk into a media frenzy. You have to pick your battles, babe, and this is not one. You know you can have anything, but I do not want you to go through that. Not now. How about I order a car service?" she replies, and even though she has a point, it is not the point I wanted to hear.

"No, it is fine. I understand. I will talk to you when I get back," I reply and hang up.

I just want to yell. Maybe I do not care what people think right now at this point. I know she has my best interest at heart, but why can I not go out with the person I want to go out with. This sucks, but all in due time, I guess.

I put the thought to the back of my mind and call down to the front desk for them to get my car. I grab my keys, my purse, and my phone and head out the door. Why can it not just be easy, I think to myself. Why does loving who makes me feel safe have to feel like a career risk and a spiritual crime at the same time?

I make several stops at various stores on Rodeo Drive. I want to make sure I look excellent for my baby during this vacation. I make a stop at the Gucci store to see what gift I can find for her. I want to get her something special, but that is hard to do because I do not know what she has already.

So I just decide to grab her some Gucci accessories: a wallet, scarf, sunglasses, and a pair of sandals that came out today. I am pretty sure she does not have them. I will swing by Louis Vuitton and see if I see anything there.

As I am walking out of the Gucci store, someone bumps into me, causing me to drop my purse, bags, and my phone. Without saying excuse me, the person continues to jog on like it never happened. As I bend down to pick up my things, a familiar voice speaks to me.

"I don't like you walking around unprotected. Things happen." Anthony says as he bends down to help me pick up my items.

"Anthony, what do you want?" I ask, gathering my bag when he notices the Gucci items.

"So who is he, Elia? I mean, I do not see you wearing any of these items," he says, staring at me.

"A friend of mine's birthday is in a few days. I was just getting some things," I say, grabbing my purse.

"Well, I would hope that you would not be dumb enough to cheat on me. That could make the divorce harder than it has to be," he says with a smirk.

"Anthony, are you done?" I ask, trying to move past him.

"No, Elia, I am not done, and neither are you," he says as he pulls me close and smiles just as the paparazzi snap a picture. "Now we would not want to piss off your fans. I will walk you to your car, and this will be a great photo op for you, especially with the new movie coming out," he says as he grabs my arm and escorts me to the car.

My shoulders tense the second he touches me.

In awe and afraid of this situation, I walk to the car, smiling for the camera when inside I am absolutely infuriated. We get to my car, and I throw the bags in the trunk. Noticing all my shopping, he immediately asks if I am going somewhere.

"I am minding my business, Anthony. Is that ok with you?" I ask sarcastically.

"Elia, you will lose this war. You're standing on a career I built. Don't make me remind you of that. By the time I'm finished with you, your name will not be worth a stand-in on a sitcom," he says, still smiling like we are having a great conversation.

"I am sorry you feel that way, Anthony, and if this is your way of getting me back, it is going to take a little more than a threat," I say as I slide past him and get into the car, thankful that the camera guys are lingering around because I know his temper. That just pissed him off.

Just as I get ready to close my door, the gentleman that bumped into me earlier comes running up to my car.

"Ma'am, I apologize about earlier. I was about to get a ticket. I figured this was your phone I saw laying by the store," he says as he bypasses Anthony and hands me the phone.

"It is no problem, thank you," I say, just really wanting to get out of here. He takes one look at Anthony, turns around, and walks away, probably sensing the hostility in the air.

"You have a good day, Elia," Anthony says as he walks away. "I will see you soon, baby," he says and strolls gracefully into the crowd of shoppers.

Ugh, that just really ruined my mood. I just want to get home to Shai. I decide to call her to see if she has eaten.

"Hey," she answers. "You done spending?"

"Yes, in fact, I am. I just had the worst episode ever," I reply. "I just want to get home to you. Did you eat?"

"No, but Rosa has steak in the oven. You know I am not one to eat out and stuff. I like home-cooked," she says. "Come on back. I will have the wine waiting."

"Ok, be there in a bit," I say, and we hang up.

I ride home in silence, just thinking about what happened. I have been riding a fairy tale the past few months with Shai, and I have neglected to pay attention to my real issues. I have to handle this with Anthony.

I know Shai is going to be upset when she sees the pictures, and I can bet that Anthony set that up. What an ass. I can see the headlines now.

"Anthony and Elia: Rekindling the Flame?"

Why will he not just leave me alone? Once I get back, I am finishing the divorce, but for now, I am going to appreciate lying in the sand with Shai.

I decide to make one more surprise stop at a secret store for adult items, so to speak. I want to spice the mood up and have some fun. I grab a few things and head out the private exit. This is going to be fun, I think to myself, ready to give her all of me and prepared to learn whatever I need to.

I pull up to the building and step out of the car as they grab my bags and assist me with getting them to my apartment. Once I get in, I call Natalee and tell her about Anthony and his shenanigans. We talk for a few before I let her know I have to go tell Shai before it is splattered all over the web.

I grab some clothes so I can take a shower and get comfortable before dinner and head over.

"Hey," I say, jumping into her arms as she opens the door.

"I missed your face," she says as she kisses me.

"Oh my God, so let me tell you about my day," I say as I grab my glass and head into the bedroom. I proceed to tell her about Anthony, the incident with the paparazzi, the threats, and the promises. She sits there taking it all in, listening very carefully.

"Are you ok?" she asks as I finish. "I mean, do you want me to get you security from here on out? Do you want me to handle this?"

"No, it is fine, it is just threats. He is just going through something right now. It is fine, baby, I promise. I just want to go enjoy you and our vacation. I will get the divorce finalized as soon as we get back," I say as I start to strip to hop in the shower.

"Are you sure, Elia? I can and will protect you," she asks again.

"Yes, love, I'm sure. He is all bark, no bite," I say, trying to reassure her and me at the same time. I can honestly say he has never hit me, but he had no problem grabbing me up from time to time. I do not want to worry her, so that is something I will keep to myself for now. If I say it out loud, if I name it as abuse, then I have to explain why I stayed. Easier to smooth it over and pretend I am stronger than I feel.

"Ok, well take a shower. Dinner will be ready shortly," she says as she kisses me on the back of my neck and heads out of the room.

"Oh, and you do not want to join me?" I ask, naked and exposed, wanting to feel her close to me.

"Nope, I am holding off until we get to where we are going," she says, dropping her head and quickly exiting the room.

"Suckerrrrr!" I yell, closing the shower door. I am going to make the next few hours very interesting. Let us see how long she can go. Letting the water overtake me, I close my eyes and I just let it all go. I am where I want to be.

***

616 - Shai

Once Elia is in the shower, I head to my office and hit Mikey up on the line. Realizing I do not know what I am dealing with regarding Elia and her previous situation, I decide to do some recon.

"MK, I need some recon. Elia Girard and her husband. Who is this guy? Who is she? What is the story? I know we did a brief search earlier, but I want an in-depth view. I want to know what I am dealing with with this guy. I will hit you on the secure line tomorrow before I leave for the details," I send.

"Damn, you are really making me work. LOL. I am on it," he replies.

"Great, check is in the mail."

"That is what I like to hear," he says, signing off.

I go into the kitchen to see Rosa setting up the dining area. I advise her that I want to have dinner on the balcony tonight and to set some candles up and make it really nice. It is a beautiful night, and we are up high enough, so we do not have to worry about getting caught.

I grab a bottle of wine and head to the balcony to wait. It is a special night. It has been almost 8 months since Elia and I started this affair thing. I am surprised that it lasted this long honestly, but scared at the same time. Six months is where things usually burn out or blow up.

The fact that we are still here means this is either something real... or a bigger mistake than I planned for.

"Awwww, this is so beautiful," 614 states as I get up to pull her chair out.

"I'm happy that you love it," I say as I walk back to take my seat.

"You know a girl can get used to this kind of treatment," she says as Rosa comes out with our salad plates.

"Well, do not," I say with a laugh.

We talk about small things for the first portion of dinner. I point out a few constellations in the sky, and I show her where she could see Venus. She listens and observes me like I am the only person in the world, hanging on my every word as I do hers.

She is my friend, and that is what I love the most. The sex is easy. This—sharing the sky, laughing over nothing, letting silence sit between us—that is the part that scares me.

"I have something for you," she says, getting up as we finish dinner.

She comes back in with boxes neatly wrapped and places them in front of me. I can see the excitement on her face knowing that she accomplished a great feat. No one has really ever taken the time to think about me. Why is she doing this? Does she want me to love her knowing that we can never be?

I open the first gift, which is a Gucci wallet and a scarf. I love them because scarves go well with my attire, and I needed a new wallet, even though I am a creature of habit and I hate change. I will use this now. I will get used to it. I also receive a pair of metal navigator Gucci sunglasses. Not many sunglasses fit my face, but these are hot and they work well.

"Baby, I did not want you to get me all this stuff. I was thinking some J's or something," I say, smiling, obviously happy. She then grabs another box and hands it to me.

"This is for our trip," she says, smiling as I open up the shoe box and see a pair of Gucci sandals. I like Gucci. "I do not want you wearing J's the whole time we are on vacation. So I like these better."

"I do too. Thank you, baby. I must admit you have outdone yourself today. Something so simple can mean so much," I say, trying my sandals on.

"What do you get someone that has everything?" she asks. "So I figured I would start again. I have absolutely no idea what you have and do not have. I need to do an inventory of your closet."

"Anytime. I too have something for you," I say, reaching into my cargo pocket.

"Babe, you did not have to. You have done..." she starts to say before I cut her off.

"No, I wanted to," I say as I hand her the box. I watch as her eyes open and water at the five-carat diamond earrings. "Diamonds are a girl's best friend, right."

"Yes, of course, but I cannot accept this gift, Shai. I mean, they are beautiful," she says, putting them on.

"Hahaha, oh, you can't," I say, laughing, sipping my wine, watching her look in the mirror admiring them. I got her the earrings as a diversion. The real gift I will give while on vacation. This is like getting jewelry from the Piercing Pagoda compared to what I have for her. I cannot wait. If these earrings make her react like this, the real gift might actually break her.

"Oh, you are the best," she says as she comes over and kisses me. "What can I do for you?" she asks as she starts to kiss my neck.

"Nothing. You have done enough," I say, trying to fight the urge. "We have a long day tomorrow. We should get to bed," I say, lifting her up as I get up.

"Fine," 614 says as she grabs her wine. "It is only 9:30. What the hell?"

"Early bird gets the worm," I say, dimming the lights and heading into the bedroom. I really just want to lie in bed and cuddle.

I climb into the bed and grab the remote. As I turn the TV on, I watch her. She knows I want her, and she is determined to get me tonight, but it is not going to happen.

I watch as she takes her tee off, exposing her hard nipples. Then she takes her Victoria's Secret sweatpants off, clearly in view to show me her thong. I watch as she starts to lotion, which she does every night to keep her skin moisturized. Man, that lotion smells excellent, I think to myself as she slides under the cover.

"Baby, I am cold," she says as she nestles into me, pressing her nipples against my arm.

"Well, if you had some clothes on..." I say as I put my arm around her, pulling her close.

"Take yours off so we can have some body heat."

"Negative," I say. She is trying hard, boy. Damn. I want to, but I cannot. Must fight the temptation. One night. I can give us one night of just sleep. I owe her at least that much discipline.

We close our eyes and drift off to sleep with Girlfriends playing in the background. I did not give in. I am proud of myself. I can say no to her, and as hard as it was to do, I had to prove to myself that I could. I fall asleep with her on my mind, in my arms, and in my heart.

I awake a few hours later to check in with Mikey.

"Clear," he says as he picks up the secure line.

"Hey, what is going on?" I ask.

"Nothing much. From what I see, she is clean, as to be expected, but Anthony is in with some pretty shady people. I mean this guy has mob connects, but the main thing that caught my attention is he is in heavy with a corporate financing group. I mean, bank statements show multiple transactions between him and an offshore account for millions. I do not even think she knows this guy's worth or debt, if that makes any sense.

I am going to have to dig a little deeper to find out the trace, but to sum it up: this dude is dirty and always has been from what I see. He used her as a puppet, sort of like a mask to hide his shadiness, but with her out of the picture, it will all come to light, especially with the divorce. Once someone starts to dig, what they may find will rock him to the core. I can ensure he will do anything he needs to do to keep it from coming out."

"Hmmm... damn it. So where are we?" I ask, taking it all in.

"All we can do is sit back and watch for now. You have kept it clean so far, but trust no one, Shai. This is not the type of guy to lose, especially to another female, no offense. I will see what else I can find about this mystery account maybe to give us some leverage just in case. Nothing wrong with having an ace in the hole, but until then, stay smart."

"Ok, did you have a chance to look into that email?" I ask.

"No, but it will be done. I will have a full report on everything by the time you get back."

"Cool," I say, hanging up the phone, taking it all in. I mean, what does he have to do with me. He does not know anything. I do not even know this dude, so whatever. I am ok; I am better than good. I am great, I think to myself just as Elia enters the room.

Lying to myself has always been my favorite coping mechanism.

"Let us get ready to go, baby," I say, grabbing her hand, leaving my desk, work, and the worry behind me.

CHAPTER SIXTEEN

NECKER Island

616 - Shai

Once the jet landed on Terrance B. Lettsome Airport in the Virgin Islands, we transferred straight to a yacht for the thirty-minute sail to Necker Island. Yes, that Necker Island. Richard Branson's playground.

Because I had booked an exclusive hire for the week, we had the full run of the island. Aside from staff, it was just her and me.

It sounded lonely on paper.

It did not feel lonely at all.

"Ugh, babe, I am not feeling too well," I said, gripping the rail. My stomach rolled.

"Awww. Come here. Let me get you some water," she said, already sliding an arm around my waist. "You are just a little seasick, baby. Come lay down."

She led me below deck to one of the cabins and eased me onto the bed.

"Never been on a boat before?" she asked, brushing hair from my face.

"I am fine with land and air," I muttered, breathing through nausea. "Water... not so much."

"We will be there in a few, babes. Just lay here until then, okay?" She tucked herself against me. "Let me find out you are a little baby."

"Nope. I am a warrior. Believe that," I said, wishing my stomach would cooperate.

When we finally docked at Necker, it was worth every second of that ride.

Crisp, clear water.

Manicured, ridiculous landscaping.

Open pavilions, warm wood, white stone, soft fabrics—the kind of quiet wealth money cannot fake.

The staff lined up to greet us, smiling, already briefed. This was going to be a good week.

We were shown to our quarters for the stay: an open suite with ocean views on three sides, outdoor shower, private path straight to the sand.

First things first: I needed a shower and a reset.

By early evening, I had my equilibrium back, and we eased into the night with what I thought would be a simple patio dinner: some music, lobster, wine.

Necker does not do "simple." Course after course appeared—tastings, pairings, amuse-bouches I could not pronounce. We nibbled, we sipped, we settled.

"You look beautiful tonight," I added, letting my gaze linger.

"Thank you. All for you," she said, smiling.

"I would hope so. You know, I have never done this with anyone," I said. "I have not met anyone who made me want to smile this much. I appreciate you."

"I may not have had a hardest life," she said, "but I know what it is like to be unhappy. I know what it is like to cry and feel lonely in a room full of people. To have it all until you realize you have nothing. I get you, Shai. You do not fool me with that mask you hide behind. You are still missing the one thing that will complete you."

"Antoine loves me," I said, laughing it off.

"Yeah, along with every other fine girl he gets a whiff of," she shot back.

"You have a point." I pushed my plate away and stood. "Come on, two left feet. Give me something to laugh at."

"You dance? I have to see this," she said, taking my hand.

I pulled her close. The song was something I had never heard, but in that moment it became my favorite track on Earth.

"I could dance with you forever," she murmured. I felt her eyelashes brush my cheek.

I closed my eyes too.

Cool breeze on my back.

Warm body in my arms.

For the first time in a long time, I held someone like I was afraid to let go.

"Come with me," she whispered, tugging my hand.

She led me into the bedroom—open walls, candles, the ocean laid out like a painting you could walk into. From the bed you could step straight onto the sand.

"Stay right here." She guided me onto the edge of the bed. "Do not move."

I watched her disappear into the bathroom. I assumed lingerie. Maybe a little show. I finished my wine and tossed back two shots of vodka just to be safe.

I was going to give it to her tonight.

That was the plan.

Until I saw her step back into the room.

Black knee-high leather boots.

Black catsuit, unzipped just enough.

And in her hands: cuffs, a feathered tickler, a small flogger, and chains.

Time out.

My hand went straight for the vodka. I poured another double.

You did this, Shai.

She walked to the bedside table, laid everything out with quiet intention, then turned toward me.

"Sooooo... you need a drink or...?" I cleared my throat.

"No. Just come sit on the bed," she said, taking my arm.

"Have you ever done this before?" I asked.

"Nope," she said, pushing me gently back. "But I did read Fifty Shades of Grey."

Great.

Relax. Safe words exist. You cannot always be in control, Shai. Breathe.

She turned on a '90s slow-jam playlist, and Az Yet's "Last Night" floated into the room as she climbed on top of me and kissed me—slow, soft, intentional. Her lips were warm and patient.

Then she stopped.

Something slid against my forehead. A moment later she tied a blindfold over my eyes. My heart rate doubled. I do not like being unable to see. I did not stop her.

My sense of touch sharpened. I reached for her hips, but she moved my hands away.

I felt her unbutton my linen shirt, one button at a time. Kisses along my neck and collarbone. Nails tracing my tattoos like she was reading Braille.

Her tongue followed the ink.

Warm. Steady. Confident.

I felt my body start to unclench.

A metallic clink.

Cold cuff around my wrist.

Then the other.

Arms above my head.

A tug to test the strength.

"Is that too tight?" she whispered.

I shook my head.

"No."

***

614 - Elia

I had been told one thing: have fun with it.

So I did.

With her blindfolded and secured, I took my time. I kissed her lips, her jaw, down the center of her chest and stomach until I reached the tie of her linen pants. I loosened the knot, slid them off, revealing her black Polo briefs.

I stepped back, watching her.

Even blindfolded, her head tracked my movements.

"Is there a safe word?" she asked.

I let a beat pass. Took a sip of wine. Enjoyed the silence.

"Do you want one?" I asked, picking up the feather.

"I do not know. Am I going to need one?"

I did not answer.

Instead, I flipped open her pocketknife and carefully sliced through her sports bra. Her breasts rose with her breath.

I straddled her, ran the feather around each nipple until they hardened. Her hips moved on their own, rubbing against my clit through the suit.

I bent down, took one nipple into my mouth, teasing the other with my fingers. Her body jerked.

I switched sides.

She whimpered this time.

She was close.

I was not ready for her to finish.

I slid down and pulled off her briefs in one motion.

I kissed the inside of her thigh, then lower, letting my tongue glide over her bottom lip once, twice.

When her hips tilted, I wrapped my lips around her clit.

Her whole body exhaled.

I took my time—small circles, slow rhythm, building her up. When she climbed high enough, I pushed a little harder, alternating licks and suction.

She grabbed the chain between the cuffs, knuckles white.

I did not stop until the wave passed.

Somewhere in that, I broke too—quietly, legs clenched—but I did not show it.

When she went limp, I slid off the bed, secured her ankles with the padded cuffs clipped to the footboard, snug but not cruel.

I removed her blindfold.

Her eyes widened.

"Is this you?" they asked silently.

I smiled.

I unzipped the catsuit slowly. Her gaze followed every inch.
Boots next.
Then wine—held in my mouth as I kissed her, letting her taste everything at once.

Then I pulled out the eight-inch strap.

Her eyes widened again.

I strapped it to her, guiding her hands so she understood the mechanics. The small vibrator pressed snug against her clit. I clicked it on low.

She shivered.

I turned, straddled her in reverse, and sank down onto the toy.

The vibrator hummed against her, syncing with my movements. I adjusted my pace to hit my spot every time.

"Baby, I am about to cum," she managed.

I dialed the vibration down.
I wanted her to wait.

Breathing louder, bodies slick, heat everywhere—when I was close, I turned the vibration to max.

She bucked hard.

That pushed me over too.

We came together.

When the tremors faded, I lay on her chest, listening to her heartbeat slow.

The red marks on her wrists caught my eye. I slid off, released the cuffs, then kissed her.

"Really?" she finally said. "You could not have warned me?"

"Warned you about what? Did you enjoy it?"

"I did. So are we going to talk about that whip?" she called from the bathroom.

"No. It was just a scare tactic. I guess it worked?"

"Whatever. Come on, let us take a shower. I owe you one," she said, scooping me up.

***

616

I woke alone to a cool breeze across my face.

It was only 8:30 a.m.

I checked the room, the bathroom, then paused at the open wall.

She was walking up from the shoreline, towel over her shoulder, book in hand. She almost fell out of the hammock twice before getting settled.

I smiled and went to wash up.

"You want breakfast?" she called as I rinsed my face.

"That would be nice," I said.

She came up behind me, arms around my waist, head between my shoulder blades. My eyes closed on instinct.

What is happening to me?

Our hearts synced.

Then mine sped up.

I kissed her forehead, breaking the spell.

"What is for breakfast?"

"They have it all laid out. Choose whatever you want," she said, taking my hand.

The rooftop spread was ridiculous.

"This is beautiful," I said. "Truly unforgettable."

We sat. I pulled my chair so I could see both her and the ocean.

"So, we have been talking for some time," she said. "How do you feel about this whole situation?"

"That is how we are starting our day?" I smiled.

"Why do you avoid serious questions?"

"I am not avoiding. I am just..."

Nothing slick came.

"I am just shy."

She burst out laughing.

"That is the biggest crock of bull I have ever heard."

"What do you want to know? We are on a private island—clear skies, blue water—and you want to know how I feel. This should say it." I reached for her hand. "I would not have wanted to experience this with anyone else."

She flushed.

The wind lifted her hair.

Sun hit her cheek.

Jawline, neck, pulse—everything soft and steady.

She was one foot away.

I missed her.

"When was the last time you vacationed like this?" she asked.

"Toine and I used to take quick trips. Weekends. Nothing this long. I had a company to run, and I like to be in everything or at least know everything."

"So you are miserable right now with no phone, no iPad, no laptop," she teased. "I will let you check them later. Maybe while I am in the tub or napping."

"Oh, that is my permission?" I smirked. "I am not the one who breaks promises. We agreed: no electronics. Who do you need to call?"

"My mom and Natalee. Just to let them know I made it safely," she admitted.

"Babe, that is not work. The rule is no work. Everyone I talk to is tied to work, so I am blacking it out for the next five days, seventeen hours, thirty-five minutes and... seventeen, sixteen seconds."

"You are so anal retentive. And that is the exact time, is it not?"

"It is. I set a timer."

"The countdown to you being rid of me?"

"No. The countdown until the fantasy ends and we go back to being prisoners in our own homes."

"Why torture yourself?"

"It is not torture. I just like to keep track of things."

"Give it to me." She reached for my wrist.

"Elia—"

"We are going to live in the moment," she said, unclasping my watch. "Promise me we will have now and worry about everything else later."

"Do not lose that watch. It is one of my favorites."

"Promise me or this thing is going swimming with the fishes," she said, dangling it.

"Okay, okay. I promise."

"Good." She dropped into my lap. "Now let us go sightseeing."

After a slow kiss and long hug, we changed and met the concierge. They walked us through activities and helped plan the week.

I wanted to explore—animals, birds, the island.

The tour took two hours, ending at a ridge-top picnic area overlooking the entire island.

"You know, we could stay here forever," she said. "Live in the jungle, survive off fruit and berries."

"At this daily rate? You might need a job to fund it."

"And ruin these nails?" she laughed.

We fell quiet, watching the birds. I pulled her close.

"Baby, why is it so hard for us to just live?" she asked quietly. "Why can we not be free? Why does it matter who I want to be with?"

"I do not have an answer. People decide what is right in their minds and cling to it. They are quick to judge."

I paused.

"It is like they do not understand how much harm they cause when they truly believe they are doing good."

"But the Bible—"

"But the Bible what?" I said. "It teaches love and not to judge. Why do the most religious people spew the most hatred? I love and give freely, but I will be condemned because of who I choose to love. It is sad."

"I understand," she whispered. "And me having been one of them... it is sad. I cannot help that I fell in love—"

She stopped.

"Yeah. Most of us cannot," I said, kissing the back of her neck.

We sat still before heading back. On the cart ride toward the main house, my mind drifted.

I thought about every version of this conversation I had lived.
My grandmother turning her back on me.
The invites that never came.
The whispers.
The jokes.
The opinions on my existence.

Most straight people never question being straight. They just are. Same for most of us on this side.

I had read theories—brain wiring, developmental patterns—maybe. Maybe not. All I knew was that I had always felt different.

And that difference came with a war.

At first, the war was internal:

Why am I like this?

Then external:

Why can I not just be accepted?

No matter how much charity, how many people you help—some people only see who you love.

If you are lucky, you reach the "whatever" phase:

I am going to be me, and if you do not like it, that is your problem.

Too many never make it that far. That is why kids jump off bridges, disappear into tubs, swallow whole bottles of pills.

The internal fights—Will God still love me? Can I be forgiven?—never fully disappear. You bury them under work and success and money.

I buried mine like I buried most things.

Out here, on this island, with Elia's hand in mine, I could feel them starting to move.

And that scared me more than anything.

CHAPTER SEVENTEEN

THE Knock

Antoine

The knock came at 2:04 a.m.

Hard, impatient, the kind of knock that said someone already decided you were guilty.

I opened the door half-dressed, still wiping sleep from my eyes. Two detectives, one uniform behind them. No warrant. No explanation.

"Mr. Joseph, we just need you to come down and answer a few questions."

At that hour?

About what?

They didn't answer. They didn't have to. I threw on a shirt, grabbed my wallet, and followed them out of the building with that sick, sinking feeling in my gut. The elevator ride down was quiet enough to hear my pulse.

By the time I was cuffed to the metal table, I already knew this wasn't a misunderstanding—they had a plan.

"I did not rape anyone," I snapped, metal biting into my wrists. "It was consensual."

"That's not what she's saying, Antoine."

The detective kept that calm, patronizing voice like he wanted me to believe he was doing me a favor. "The SART exam showed tearing. That usually happens when someone is not prepared or forced. So why would that be?"

He just watched me.

No pen. No folder. No note-taking.

Just waiting for me to indict myself.

"Look, she likes it rough. I told you that three times already," I said, locking eyes. "I don't have to rape anybody. I can have damn near any woman I want. Why would I need to force someone?"

A slow head tilt.

A calculated pause.

"Why don't you go ahead and tell us what happened again," he said. "You want something to drink?"

"No, I do not want anything to drink. And I think it is time I call my lawyer."

There it was.

The first crack in his façade.

"Okay," he said, pushing his chair back. "If that's how you want to play."

"Play?" I leaned forward. "Detective, I don't know what kind of games you think I'm into, but I don't play with my life."

"Yeah. Well, your money won't get you out of this one."

He slammed the door behind him.

The sound echoed inside me.

I dropped my fists against the table—metal clattering, cuffs scraping skin. Hours passed in that room, stretching into something formless—four, eight, twelve. I stopped checking the clock.

All I could think was:

Shai is on a private island, phone off, while my life is beginning to burn.

She warned me.

A hundred times.

Tone it down.

Quit bringing randoms back.

You're a walking liability.

And I did exactly what she said I'd do.

I fucked up.

Her name was Alicia. We met three nights ago at Short Stop.

Tae and I had blown up at each other earlier—jealousy, messages, tension that lingered like smoke. I didn't want to sit in that energy. I needed noise. Noise meant no thinking.

I posted up at the bar, half-watching a game, half-scrolling through Intel-Ligent emails, Premmission data, investor pitches. My whole damn life fit in that iPad. Pressure everywhere.

"Excuse me?"

A voice behind me—sharp, impatient.

"Yes?" I said, not looking up.

"Can you slide down one seat so the three of us can sit together? You're kind of dead center."

I glanced up and realized she was right.

She was pretty. About five-six, petite, but her body sat right, mocha complexion, just beautiful. Early thirties—thirty-two if I had to guess. Big hair, bigger eyes, the kind of woman who knew the room watched her.

"No problem," I said, sliding down a stool.

She and her two friends filled the row. Engagement squeals erupted—rock on one hand, wedding band on the other. That left Alicia.

"What are we celebrating?" I asked.

"My friend got engaged!" she yelled.

"Well, that deserves another round. Four tequilas."

We went from shots to dancing, from dancing to laughing, from laughing to oversharing. East Coast roots, bad exes, cheap drinks—all of it blended into a night that felt harmless.

An hour in, her body language made it clear:

I pick you.

Breakfast after the bar.

A twenty-four-hour diner.

Greasy plates and confessions at two in the morning.

Then the hotel—my card, two-room suite. We barely left it all Sunday. Sex, food, sleep, repeat.

Nothing felt forced.

She kissed me first.

Pulled me close.

Told me what she wanted.

When I tried to leave, she grabbed my waistband.

"Give it to me one more time. This time, fuck me like it's yours."

No slur in her voice.

No sway in her stance.

Intentional.

I did exactly what she asked.

We ended the night clean. I gave her cab money. Told her to call if she needed anything. She didn't.

Two days later, I'm in a station accused of rape.

It had to be money.

If she'd asked, I would've helped.

The detective came back after God-knows-how-long.

"Let's go, Mr. Joseph."

As the detective uncuffed me and handed me off, Jim didn't even blink.

Perfect suit, perfect posture, perfect attorney expression — bored annoyance mixed with quiet superiority.

"I'll take him from here," Jim said, guiding me toward the exit like he owned the building.

The fluorescent lights buzzed as we walked down the hall.

"What the hell happened, Antoine?" he asked once we were out of earshot. "And where is Shai? She's not answering anything."

"She's off-grid. Vacation. No electronics," I muttered.

"Perfect timing," he said dryly. "Alright, start talking. Everything important. No edits."

We pushed through the station doors into the night air. His black SLR AMG waited at the curb, headlights washing the sidewalk in white.

"Get in," he said. "We're not doing this conversation hungry."

I slid into the passenger seat. As soon as we pulled away, I launched into the entire story — the bar, the hotel, the sex, the choking, the scratch marks, all of it. Jim listened without interrupting, jaw tightening once or twice but otherwise unreadable.

By the time I finished, we were pulling into the lot of a little pizzeria on the strip — his spot, apparently.

Inside, the smell of garlic and melted cheese hit me like a punch. Jim ordered without asking: pepperoni, cheesy bread, two Cokes. Like this was any other Tuesday.

Only then did he lean back and give me the breakdown.

She claimed:

- We hung out
- Fell asleep
- Woke up
- I "suddenly got rough"
- She tried to stop me
- I didn't stop
- She scratched me
- I kept going

Photos. Rape kit. Consistent story.

"And the scratches on you aren't helping," he added.

My stomach knotted.

"Shai is going to kill me," I whispered. "She said this would happen."

Jim nodded.

"Best case? We settle. NDA. Quiet. Worst case? A fight. But the optics are terrible. Tech money. A controversial CEO on a private island. Antoine, this could drag down the entire company."

I knew that.

I'd always known that.

We finished eating.

He drove me home with a list of rules:

Don't talk.

Don't text.

Don't move.

Don't breathe without calling him first.

When I walked into my condo, it felt like the air was heavier.

Same furniture.

Same art.

Different gravity.

The door clicked shut behind me, loud in the kind of silence I usually liked. Tonight it sounded like a lock on a cell.

I stood there for a second with my hand still on the knob, staring at my own place like it belonged to somebody else. Lights off, city bleeding through the floor-to-ceiling windows, everything neat and expensive and suddenly irrelevant.

I loosened my tie—ridiculous that I even wore one to the station, like a Windsor knot was going to impress anybody—and went straight to the liquor cabinet. I poured a double Hennessy, no ice, and took it to the couch.

My laptop sat open on the coffee table, half-buried under pitch decks and legal memos. I knew what I should do: wake it up, check Intel-Ligent emails, look at Premmission's burn, make sure no journalist had decided to earn a bonus by connecting dots they weren't supposed to see yet. Shai was off-grid; someone had to be the responsible adult.

I did not touch the laptop.

I sank into the couch, stared at the black TV screen, and swallowed half the glass in one go. It burned all the way down, a clean hurt that made sense.

I sat until the room blurred.

Then darkness.

CHAPTER EIGHTEEN

THE Morning After

Antoine

I woke up stiff and half-dressed on the couch, the room dim except for the city glow bleeding in through the glass. My head throbbed. My mouth felt like cotton. The half-empty bottle of Hennessy lay on its side next to me — cap still on, miracle of the night.

For a moment, I didn't know what time it was.

Or if it was the same day.

Then everything from the station slammed back into my skull at once.

In the interrogation room, everything felt like theater—the questions, the slammed door, the detective saying my money would not save me. Out here alone, it started feeling like math.

Allegation.

Black tech money.

Woman saying "choked," "wouldn't stop."

Put that in front of a jury, see what they do with it.

My phone buzzed on the cushion beside me. For a second my heart stopped, but it was just a calendar alert: Premmission status call—missed. Another buzz: three unread emails from legal, one from IR, two from a journalist I recognized by name.

Subject line:

Comment requested: Intel-Ligent executive questioned in connection with alleged assault.

No name in the snippet. Not yet.

My stomach knotted.

I didn't open it. Instead, I did what I do best when I don't want to feel anything.

I drank.

Another swallow. Then another. I sat there until the lines of the room went soft and the TV screen blurred into a dark rectangle floating in space. At some point the glass slipped out of my hand and clinked against the hardwood. I heard it, thought, I should pick that up, and then everything went black, again.

When I woke up, the condo was dark.

My neck hurt. My lower back screamed from sleeping twisted on the couch. The lamp in the corner threw a dim triangle of light across the floor where the Hennessy bottle lay on its side, cap miraculously still on.

Right now, a bottle felt safer than a woman.

It was a little after ten p.m. My mouth was dry; my skin felt sticky. I needed a shower and about twelve hours of sleep. I was going to get neither.

I sat up slowly, rubbing my face, and caught a glimpse of myself in the black reflection of the TV: shirt wrinkled, tie crooked, eyes dull and ringed in red. For once, I looked exactly like what I was—tired and guilty of something I wasn't ready to name.

I pushed myself up and headed for the bathroom, kicking my shoes off on the way. In the mirror, under real light, it was worse. Faint nail marks dragged along my collarbone and shoulder. They'd photographed those at the station. Neat little lines that could be read however anyone wanted to read them.

Fun.

Violence.

Evidence.

I turned the shower on hot. Steam started to ghost across the glass.

My phone lit up on the counter.

Tae.

Of course.

For a second I considered letting it ring out. I didn't have the energy to be anybody's boyfriend tonight, not even unofficially. Then the guilt kicked in—over her, over the texts, over the whole mess—and I grabbed it.

"Hey," she said when I answered.

"Hey," I replied, leaning against the sink, watching myself talk. I could already hear the weight in her voice. We had been off since the argument about the messages on my phone. Now I had a whole new pile of sins she didn't even know about. There was no version where I could tell her the truth right now.

"What are you doing?" she asked.

"Nothing much. I was about to take a shower and go to bed. What about you?" I asked, testing the water with one hand, trying to make my voice sound like any other night.

"I'm lying here thinking about you."

That cracked something in me—comfort and guilt at the same time, two hands in the same spot.

"Oh yeah?" I tried to smile, more for me than her. "What are you thinking about?"

"I just miss you, and I'm sorry," she said. "I know we haven't been talking that long, but I do like you. Finally someone I really like. I'm not into getting my heart broken. That's why I won't commit to you."

The irony almost made me laugh. Almost.

"Look, Tae, I'm not perfect. I make mistakes; everybody does," I said, staring myself down in the mirror. I barely recognized the man looking back. "That doesn't mean I don't like you or I don't want to be with you. I've seen a lot of women, and none of them are like you. I want you to give me a chance—the same way I want to give you one."

And that was true.

It just wasn't the whole truth.

"I understand. I feel the same way," she said quietly. "I just wanted to make sure we were on the same page. I haven't really slept in four days. I just needed to hear your voice. Take a shower and call me back. I'll be up."

Four days.

She hadn't slept because of us.

I hadn't slept because I couldn't stop replaying the last thirty seconds of a rough night with the sound turned all the way up.

"Ok, baby. Give me twenty minutes. I'll call you right back," I said.

We hung up.

For a second I stood there with the phone still in my hand, listening to the water hit tile, feeling the weight of everything sitting in my chest. Then I stepped into the shower and let it run hot over my head, like maybe temperature could wash off the station, the accusation, the detective's stare.

I scrubbed harder than I needed to.

The metal table.

The word "rape" sitting between us.

The way he said tearing.

I could feel my own hands at Alicia's neck, the way hers had clawed at my shoulders. The part where she said, "Harder," was loud. The part where she stopped talking was louder.

"Stop," I said out loud, to myself, to the memory.

Water drowned the word. It didn't drown the thought.

By the time I got out, the bathroom was a fogged jungle. I toweled off, pulled on clean boxers and a T-shirt, and went back into the bedroom. It felt smaller too. Like the walls had moved in while I was gone.

I made another drink out of habit more than desire—Hennessy on the rocks this time, like the ice made it more reasonable—and climbed into bed. Tae would take my mind off things. She always did. She was light. Soft. Normal. A decent woman who thought I might be her shot at something real.

That was the worst part.

She had no idea who she was talking to tonight.

I picked up my phone to call her and saw a new text from an unknown number sitting above her name.

"You know what you did", Antoine.

No punctuation. No emoji. No "LOL" to soften it. Just black letters on a green bubble.

My chest tightened. For a second, the room shrank, the way it had when they first said the word "charge" at the station.

I stared at the message, thumb hovering over the screen.

Delete it.

Block the number.

Forward it to Jim.

Pretend it never showed up.

Before I could decide, another bubble appeared under it, same number.

"You won't outrun this."

A slow chill rolled down my spine. I tapped the info icon. No name, no photo, just a ten-digit number with a local area code. I hit "Call" before I could talk myself out of it and listened.

One ring.

Two.

Three.

Then: "The number you have dialed is no longer in service."

Of course it wasn't.

Spoofed. Burner. Or somebody smart enough not to pick up. Either way, it meant one thing: this wasn't just in a police report anymore. Someone else out there had decided they were my judge and jury.

My first instinct was to screenshot it and send it to Jim. Let him sort out what it meant. Let him tell me whether it was dangerous or just noise.

I started to open the thread with his name, then stopped.

The more I put in writing, the more there was to subpoena.

I set the phone down face-first on the nightstand instead. Out of sight. Not out of mind.

For a long minute I just lay there, staring at the ceiling, feeling my pulse in my throat. Shai would have known exactly what to do—who to call, what to lock down, how to frame the narrative before anyone else could—but she was probably on a beach right now, laughing at something 614 said, with her phone tossed in her suitcase in a villa somewhere.

I was alone. And for once, I had to admit I'd done that to myself.

I picked the phone back up, swiped away from the unknown number, and hit Tae's name.

"Hey you," she answered on the second ring, voice softer now, calmer. "That was a quick shower."

"Yeah, I needed it," I said, settling deeper into the pillows. "Tell me something good."

She started talking—about work, about a client who'd driven her crazy, about her sister's new boyfriend she didn't trust, about a show she'd binged the night before. Normal things. The kind of everyday drama regular people cared about.

I listened.

Or at least I let her think I did.

Her voice moved in the background while my mind bounced between the station, Alicia's face, the detective's flat eyes, Jim's warning, the anonymous texts. I tossed in the right noises in the right places—"for real?", "that's wild," "you're crazy"—and she laughed on cue.

"See, this is why I like you," she said at one point. "You get it. You don't judge me."

If only she knew.

"I got you," I said quietly.

We talked until her voice loosened and her breathing slowed, like she was finally winding down after four nights of not sleeping. I felt my own body relaxing in spite of myself, the combination of hot water, liquor, and another human voice taking the edge off my nerves.

"Ok, I'm going to let you sleep," she finally said. "You sound tired."

"I am," I admitted.

"I'm serious about giving this a real shot," she added, voice small. "I know you have options, but... I don't want to be just a moment."

You're not, I wanted to say.

You're just in the wrong man's story.

"Me neither," I said instead. "We'll talk tomorrow, alright?"

"Promise?"

"I promise."

We hung up.

The room went quiet again, except for the low hum of the AC and my own thoughts trying to fight their way back to the surface. I rolled over, faced away from the nightstand, and shut my eyes like darkness could mute everything I'd heard in the last twenty-four hours.

Tomorrow would be a new day.

At least, that's what I told myself.

Deep down, I knew better.

CHAPTER NINETEEN

THE Email

Mikey

Almost got it.

I say it out loud as the last line of code completes and my terminal scrolls like a slot machine. I lean back, rub my nose, and reach for the small glass vial on my desk.

One bump.

Then another.

I really need to give this up.

The drip hits the back of my throat. I grimace, grab a Coke from the mini-fridge, and wash it down. When I sit back in front of the monitors, one of my alert windows is blinking red in the corner.

Of course.

Shai has been gone four days, and I have barely started processing the intel I already have for her. The FBI is on my back about some bottom-feeding social media scammer running soft porn identity-theft rings off cloned Facebook accounts. Government work pays, but it is rarely glamorous.

I have been doing this a long time. I remember my first computer: black screen, green letters, something that looked like it came out of a science museum. The more complex they became, the more I wanted to break them open. Most things in life were easy enough to figure out or discard.

But computers?

They were a universe.

You can create whatever you want, manifest it, move millions, ruin people, save people, all without leaving your chair. Times have changed, but the power has only increased.

I click over to the flashing alert.

One of my people at the station has pushed me an update: Antoine released yesterday on a four-hundred-thousand-dollar bond, into the custody of his attorney, Jim Cellazo.

Great.

I will compartmentalize that for later.

I clear the alert pane and my eyes land on another icon buried in the corner of my secure inbox—one I have been pretending not to see since before Shai left.

Subject line: YOU WANT TO READ THIS.

This is not the FBI line. Not my usual dark-net contacts. This one came in through her: routed into the Intel-Ligent / Premmission enclave, mirrored to me when she pinged right before wheels-up.

Check it out and do some research. Let me know what you find, but not until I return from my vacation.

That was the instruction.

Antoine is out on bond for a rape allegation. Premmission is burning cash.

Waiting suddenly feels like a luxury we do not have.

"Sorry, boss," I mutter, and open it.

"I wish I could tell you that your investment went to a purely noble cause, but I would be lying if I did.

This compound you funded was originally prototyped as a therapeutic. The goal was simple on paper: to help patients with severe trauma by disrupting and overwriting specific memories. The serum, once injected, circulates rapidly and temporarily disrupts oxygen flow to the critical memory regions of the brain. The disruption lasts seconds, but in that window, we can induce a surge, a controlled 'short,' in targeted

pathways.
During that surge, memories can be weakened or fully erased. New memories may be imprinted through a tightly structured stimulus protocol. In early tests, many subjects did not simply have their traumatic memories dulled. They lost the old memories almost entirely. Smell, taste, visual cues, audio prompts — nothing brought them back. The new memories dominated."

"In the beginning, this was positioned as clinical. PTSD, extreme grief, violent crime survivors. But once certain investors understood what the compound could do, the tone of the meetings changed.
I have sat across from some of the most influential people you can imagine. I have watched their eyebrows rise at the thought of being able to literally rewrite a person's narrative. The military is now circling, trying to position themselves for control of the patents. Officially, their concern is that this 'must not fall into the wrong hands.' That is true. What is also true is that they want it in theirs.
We do not yet know the long-term side effects. We know that once a treatment cycle starts, interrupting it is catastrophic. Partial runs have produced severe paranoia, profound memory gaps, delusional episodes, and violent outbursts. There is no halfway with this drug."

"I am familiar with your company. You may not remember me, but I bumped into you at Intel-Ligent years ago. I am the one who originally brought this concept to Antoine and convinced him to invest.
Recently, I sat in a meeting with Antoine and a silent investor. I truly cannot recall his name; he stayed in the shadows and let Antoine speak. They pushed hard to accelerate the second wave of trials to next month, provided we could 'shore up' funding. We are nowhere near ready for human testing, but when I tried to say that, I was told it was 'no longer my place to recommend.' I began to wonder if I had made a terrible mistake."

"I am reaching out because some of the samples have been stolen. We had a serious internal breach. They are trying to keep it quiet, but with those samples, parallel manufacturing is possible. Bootleg production in uncontrolled environments is almost guaranteed.
It pains me to say this, but Antoine may be involved. If he is not directly involved, he may know who is. He is too close to the money, too close to certain external parties, and his behavior has changed."

"Please keep your eyes open. If you see anything, tell no one. This is the kind of secret people kill to protect.
Do not attempt to trace this email. You will find nothing."

"Shit," I mutter.

Shai... Toine really pulled you into something this time. Your name is stapled to this project.

I flick my eyes to the header data out of habit. The relay chain is mostly scrubbed, but there—one tiny artifact in the routing path. A familiar pattern in the way the packets hopped: timing, padding, the exact jitter on the route.

Not enough for attribution. Enough to know someone reused a path they shouldn't have.

Duplicate footprint.

I have seen something like that before on a completely different job, years back. Same rhythm, different melody.

I tag the hash and route pattern into a little encrypted "LATER" folder, a place where ghosts of unsolved patterns go to wait.

Later, I tell myself, once I finish Antoine, once Shai is home, once the Premmission fire is contained.

I take another bump without thinking, then stop myself mid-reach.

Later has a way of never coming when you are coked, tired, and trying to hold up three collapsing roofs at once.

I delete the email from the secure drive, then pull the physical SSD from the small tower under my desk. Wiping isn't enough—not when the hardware itself has started to remember. I carry it to the steel drum in the corner.

My "incinerator" isn't pretty, but it works. Within minutes, plastic and silicon curl and melt into nothing recognizable.

Add that to my list of things Shai is going to hate when she gets back.

I light a Marlboro, inhale deeply, and start pinging my tech-leggers across the black-market channels. Somebody out there will have heard whispers about stolen neuropharma, military interest, or new synthetic memory work. If there is a leak, the underground picks up the scent long before the press ever does.

I send my beacons out through people I trust: small circles with big reach.

If nobody knows now, somebody will know soon.

The fastest way to keep a secret is to scatter the path. A maze of intermediaries makes it very hard to find the ghost at the center.

That has always been me.

I have been on the wrong side of the law since before I was old enough to vote.

I fell into anonymous hacker crews early. Sometimes it was politics, sometimes it was curiosity, sometimes it was boredom and ego. I narrowly avoided a federal sweep in 1999 when they busted up a hotel conference room full of kids who thought IRC handles made them invisible. I was late that day.

Wrong day to be on time, as it turned out.

They made up for it in 2000.

I got flagged for running with GoatSec—Goatse Security, at least one version of it. I was never "patched in" full time, but I tracked with them and a few other groups. It was not the association that got me caught though. It was something far more basic.

I made a rookie mistake.

I hit a mainframe using an unsecured domain, overconfident, sloppy. Twelve years of ghosting law enforcement, and the thing that finally tags me is bad opsec on a Tuesday.

They did not manage to convict me on half the charges they tried to stack, but they got enough leverage. Instead of disappearing me into a cage, one particular federal agent decided I would be more useful as a tool. His personal "go-to" for the things he could not officially request.

I did not snitch.

I did not sit in court pointing fingers.

I opened doors. I built access. I got paid. When the work did not conflict with law enforcement, I ran my own operations on the side. It was a truce of convenience.

By 2007, I was done playing freelancer for other people's agendas. I decided I wanted something that looked legitimate on paper.

California felt right.

I started scanning for a target: a young company in tech, something with momentum, but early enough that their security posture would be soft. I needed a place where I could both prove a point and offer a solution.

I read about an up-and-coming OS. New architecture, aggressive roadmap, big talk from a bunch of college nerds who had just secured real venture capital. The company's name?

Intel-Ligent.

That would do.

I went to work.

Their security slowed me down, which I appreciated. I bypassed two layers of perimeter defenses, then burrowed through their internal firewalls. It was not trivial, which meant someone had at least tried to do this properly. Once I had control, I quietly backed up their core data to one of my anonymized "lost in cyberspace" vaults, where nothing has a straightforward origin.

Then I dropped the hammer.

I deployed a custom payload: Trojan-style, but very aggressive. Across the office, every monitor began to "melt," screen output warping and sliding as if the glass itself was collapsing.

Complete outage.

I waited an hour.

Nothing came back up.

I had just single-handedly taken down a company and erased their running systems. For most people, that is a disaster. For me, it was proof of concept.

After sixty minutes, I pushed a simple graphic to every dead screen: a yellow smiley face.

Then I called the CEO.

"Intel-Ligent, this is Shai," she said, voice calm, no panic.

"How did I do it?" I asked, skipping the introduction.

"How did you do it," she corrected, completely unfazed. "You should be asking yourself how many people will try something like that when we are a multibillion-dollar company. You have my attention. Fix it. Then come to the office tomorrow."

She hung up.

I liked her immediately.

The next day, I went in once. Only once.

I told her I work better from home, that anonymity is not a preference in my world; it is a survival requirement. I would protect her and Intel-Ligent, but I needed to stay off the grid.

She listened, expression hidden behind oversized sunglasses, chair turned halfway toward the skyline.

Then she called security.

She had them escort me out of the building while talking about pressing charges. To anyone watching, it looked like she was done with me. As they walked me toward the elevator, I turned back.

She was watching.

Our eyes locked.

I knew right then that the conversation was not over.

A few days later, I sent her a message and asked to meet in neutral territory. We met at a small coffee shop. No suits, no boardroom, no legal counsel.

I explained how I broke her system. Why I did it. What it proved. I told her exactly what kind of ghost she could have on her side instead of against her. She asked smart questions, poked holes, laughed at the hacks of mine that had made the headlines.

I showed her three glaring issues still sitting in her infrastructure.

And I showed her how to fix them.

She offered me the role of Head of Software Security on the spot. She made it clear that almost no one would know who I am. Only her, and her COO, on a need-to-know basis.

We scheduled a follow-up at her place that Friday.

She did not give me the address.

Of course, I already had it.

I showed up at ten a.m. sharp. The door opened before I could knock. Antoine had not arrived yet.

Her apartment was small, downtown, bare. Practical to the point of denial.

"You know you cannot live like this," I said, scanning the room.

"What is wrong with it? It works for me," she answered, sitting at a tiny two-seat table in the kitchen. "Coffee is in the pot."

"For starters, you are the CEO of a fast-rising tech company. Your stock is climbing by the hour. You are worth at least seven figures, and you have zero physical security. No access control. No guard. Nothing." I shook my head. "You need protection."

Right on cue, the front door opened and Antoine walked in.

With a key.

"He has a key," I said under my breath.

"Antoine, this is MK. He is our new Head of Software Security," Shai said formally.

We shook hands. His grip was firm, his smile a little too confident. He had the aura of a man who had attached himself to a rocket and believed he was the one making it fly.

"Nice to meet you. Welcome aboard," he said, pouring orange juice like he owned the kitchen.

I watched him: the way he moved, the way he scanned the room, the way he looked at Shai — familiar, casual, like someone who had earned the right to be comfortable in her space.

I'll admit this much: for all his flaws, Antoine has never been a threat to her.

Impulsive? Yes.

Too confident for his own good? Absolutely.

But his loyalty to Shai has always been solid, even when his judgment wasn't.

Over the years, Shai told me stories about him — not the gossip, but the real things: the childhood moments, the ride-or-die history, the kind of bond you don't build as an adult. If anything changed, it wasn't his intentions. Life just makes people heavier, sharper, sometimes careless.

But he was never the enemy.

Not in my eyes.

My introduction that day was brief. I left, and Shai promised to come by my place later.

On the way home, I stopped at a contact's place and bought two hardened phones. At the time, they were state-of-the-art: encrypted, difficult to trace, expensive. That was 2007. It feels like the Stone Age now.

Shai came by that night.

I made us drinks, and we talked tech for hours. Architecture, exploits, countermeasures. She knew a lot. She also knew how much she did not know. Teaching her, sharpening her instincts, was fun. It made me better too. She forced me to push my own talent instead of coasting.

That became our pattern.

She would come by, or patch me into a meeting, or send over a file she did not trust. I upgraded her security at home, then rebuilt it entirely. Where she lives now, nobody has a key. Nobody just "comes upstairs." Every visitor is logged, cleared, controlled.

Fifteen years later, that has not changed.

She made me sharper.

I made her safer.

I am her ghost. I like it that way.

I take another bump and slide back into the present.

Antoine's situation flickers across my mind. The rape case. The bond. The headlines that will come if this gains traction. For Intel-Ligent, any scandal tied to an executive or key partner is not just "bad press." It is regulatory attention, investor panic, the kind of scrutiny that rips up floorboards.

I open a new secure workspace and start pulling case data.

Police reports.

Complaint narrative.

Timeline.

I do not hack law enforcement systems. I do not need to. I have a friend at Cellazo's firm, buried deep enough to see things and smart enough to know what to send and what to burn.

I send a single line through our back channel:

Need everything you can safely share on the Antoine matter. No names in writing. Just patterns.

She will know what I mean.

This case will have to disappear, one way or another. Between Premmission, stolen samples, and now this, too many fault lines are forming under Shai's feet.

My job is to know where the cracks are before the floor gives out.

Sometimes I see the fracture line early—like that duplicate footprint sitting in my LATER folder—and I tell myself I will circle back.

Then the phone rings.

The coke wears off.

Another fire starts.

And that is how ghosts miss the one thing that could have saved everyone.

CHAPTER TWENTY

THE Cost

Antoine

"Come on, Jim… what are you saying right now?"

I sit forward in Jim's leather chair, elbows braced on my knees, every muscle in my back tight. His office usually gives me confidence — mahogany walls, floor-to-ceiling windows, polished stone, the quiet hum of money.

Today it feels too small, like it's closing around my throat.

Jim closes the folder slowly, like a doctor about to give the kind of news that changes everything.

"Antoine," he says quietly, "she's not settling. She's moving ahead with the full charges."

My stomach drops so hard I forget to breathe.

"I pushed for a gag order," he continues. "We got the preliminary one approved, but I can't guarantee how long it holds once the official filing hits. Best-case scenario? You have hours. Worst-case?"
His shoulders lift once.
"Minutes."

"A day," I repeat, my voice cracking. "A damn day?"

"On a good wind," he confirms. "And Antoine… this isn't a case you can buy your way out of. Not neatly."

I drag my hands down my face and exhale through my fingers.
My mind shoots straight to Shai.

She trusted me to keep everything steady until she came back.

And here I am, sitting knee-deep in a wildfire holding a water bottle.

"Just tell me what I'm facing," I mutter.

Jim's expression shifts — not pity, just gravity. The kind surgeons get when they have to tell a family someone didn't make it.

"You're looking at prison time if this goes sideways," he says. "And career destruction either way. If anyone connects this to Intel-Ligent or Premmission?"

He exhales hard.

"We're looking at a corporate catastrophe."

My throat tightens until I can barely swallow.

"You should have listened when Shai told you to slow down," he adds. Not judgment. Just fact.

I stand — too fast. The room tilts for half a second. My pulse is loud in my ears.

"I'll try to reach her," I say, even though I know damn well Elia is the only one who could pry her phone from her hand. "Just... get the order signed."

Jim stands too, his face unreadable.

"Antoine... this is going to take more than paperwork."

But I'm already out the door.

I need air before I break.

The parking garage is dim and cool — concrete, echoes, the steady buzz of fluorescent lights. I lean against a pillar before my knees give out.

My mother answers on the first ring.

"Antoine," she says slowly — warm, measured, the way she gets when she's expecting truth instead of excuses. "How you holding up, baby?"

Something inside me bends.

My mother has always been three things:

A praying woman.

A brilliant woman.

A woman who can end an argument with either scripture or statistics — whatever shuts you up faster.

"I'm alright, Ma," I lie. "Just... holding things down while Shai's out."

"Mhm." I can see her in my mind, nodding once, eyebrows raised. "As much fuss as I gave that girl," she says, "she steadies you. Now tell me what has my son pacing."

She always knows.

I swallow once. Then again.

"Ma," I whisper, "I need you here."

Silence.

Not shock — calculation.

The kind that happens before thunderstorms.

"Antoine," she says gently, "what has happened? What's going on?"

"I'm... being charged."

"Charged?" Still calm. Still composed. "With what?"

The word is acid.

"Rape."

Her inhale slices through the phone — sharp, but controlled. She doesn't scream. She doesn't gasp. She switches into the tone she uses when the world tries her child and she decides she needs facts, not theatrics.

"Rape is a grave word, Antoine."

"I know."

"Is it true?"

"Ma, no!" My voice cracks. "I would never — it was consensual. Everything. Every moment. She—"

I stop before my voice breaks.

She breathes in slowly, grounding herself.

She's always done that — even when I was a kid and broke the neighbor's window and lied until she caught my reflection in the glass.

"Does Shai know?" she asks.

"No," I mutter. "She's unreachable. No devices. She trusted me to keep things steady and I—"

My voice splinters.

"I failed her, Ma."

Pages rustle softly — her prayer journal, or her Bible, the two books she treats the same.

"Book my flight," she says finally.

"You don't fly."

"I don't care." Her voice hardens. "When my son is in trouble, I go where my son is. God gave me legs before He gave me fear."

My throat closes.

"I love you, Ma."

"I love you too," she says. "And Antoine… the Lord does not put weight on your back without first strengthening your bones. Remember that."

"I hear you."

"And baby?"

"Yes, Ma?"

"You tell the truth at all times — especially to yourself."

Her words echo long after the line goes dead.

I slide my phone into my pocket, reach for my keys — and freeze as the screen lights up again.

Unknown number.

One line.

Money will not make this go away.

The world tilts.

My fingers go numb.

My stomach churns.

Someone knows. Someone is watching. Someone wants pressure — not answers.

I delete it instantly, heart pounding.

That reflex alone tells me everything:

This isn't random.

Someone is pulling strings.

And they want me rattled before Shai comes home.

I dial Tae.

"Hey baby," she answers — warm, soft, unaware her life is about to tilt.

"Where you at?" I rush. "I need to see you. Now."

"What's wrong? Antoine—"

"I'll tell you in person. I'm already on the way."

I hang up because "rape accusation" is not something I can say twice in one hour without something inside me breaking.

Tae's street is usually quiet — a sleepy neighborhood with manicured hedges and old couples who water plants at sunrise.

Not tonight.

Cameras swarm the sidewalk like roaches after sugar.

The moment I open my door:

"ANTON—! Antoine, over here!"

"Did you assault her?"

"Do you deny the allegations?"

"Is Intel-Ligent preparing a statement?"

"Where's Ms. Mercer?"

"Antoine! Why won't you answer the rape allegations?"

"Is Shai abandoning you?"

"Do you deny the charges?"

"Are you cooperating with investigators?"

Flashes explode so violently I stumble backward.

A mic hits my jacket.

Someone grabs my arm.

"I have no comment!" I bark, shoving through the cluster.

Tae's door flies open. She gasps.

"Antoine, what the hell is— have you been drinking?"

"Yes, I had— Tae, please, just get inside."

She pulls me in and locks all three bolts, hands shaking.

Her living room smells like lavender spray and melted candles. It feels safe — too safe for the storm that walked in with me.

She looks at me with glassy eyes.

"Antoine, what's going on?" she asks, voice tight. "Why are there cameras outside my house? What did happened?"

I pace, hands shaking. I can't breathe right.

She reaches for my arm.

"Baby... talk to me. You're scaring me."

"I messed up," I whisper, still pacing.

She swallows. "Okay. How bad? Are you in trouble with the company? With Shai? With—"

"It's worse than that."

She stops moving. Her face changes.

"Worse how?" she asks slowly. "Antoine... what happened?"

I drag both hands over my head.

"I shouldn't have gone out that night. After our argument."

Her lips part. A small breath escapes her.

"You... what happened after you left Antoine?"

I nod, ashamed. "A group of girls. We partied. We— I shouldn't have been there."

Her chin trembles. "Okay... and?"

"One of them..."

I can't get the words out.

I have to force them through.

"Antoine," she whispers, barely audible, "what happened?"

My chest tightens so hard I think I might black out.

I shake my head, but she steps closer, waiting, bracing.

"Just tell me," she says softly. "Whatever it is... just tell me."

The word fights me, claws its way up, burns like acid.

"Rape."

Silence hits the room like a physical blow.

Her face collapses.

Her breath stutters.

She takes two steps back as if the word itself shoved her.

"Rape?" she whispers. "You...?"

"Tae, I didn't. I swear—"

"No," she pauses before she start crying, "No, Antoine — no — not you—"

"Tae, please—"

"Leave," she whispers.

"Tae—"

"Leave."

She stares at me like I've spoken a language she's never heard before.

Her chest rises once.

Twice.

Then the betrayal hits.

"Antoine..." Her voice shakes. "No. No—tell me you didn't—tell me you didn't go out and—"

I try to step toward her.

"Tae—"

She puts a hand up, palm trembling.

"Don't. Don't touch me. Just answer me straight." Her breath slips out in a whisper that sounds like it hurts. "You went home with her?"

The guilt slices through my ribs.

"Yes," I say, barely audible.

Her whole face breaks.

She presses her hands to her mouth, shaking her head fast, like she can undo the words by refusing to let them land.

"You told me..." Her voice fractures. "You told me I could trust you. You told me you weren't out here moving like that."

"I wasn't—Tae, we weren't exclusive, we were still figuring out—"

She cuts me off with a strangled sound — half laugh, half sob.

"Oh my God... Antoine. I told you I don't want my heart broken. I told you that the second night we talked." Her fists curl at her sides. "And you — you left our argument and went straight to another woman?"

Her voice rises, but it's not yelling.

It's grief heated into disbelief.

"How could you do that to me?" she whispers. "How could you look at me the way you did and then turn around and—"

She swallows hard.

"You slept with her."

I reach for her again.

She steps back like the air between us is dangerous.

"You don't get to hold me right now," she says, voice trembling. "You don't get comfort from me. Not this time."

Her breath stutters.

Her eyes well again — big, wet, broken.

"And now she's accusing you of—"

She stops.

Her throat closes.

"It was consensual," she whispers.

"It was. Tae, I swear to God—"

"But she says it wasn't," she chokes out. "Do you know what that does to me? Do you know what it feels like to even hear that next to your name?"

She pushes my chest — not to hurt me, but because her body needs release from the pressure building inside it.

"You embarrassed me," she cries. "You embarrassed yourself. And now you want me to stand here and act like I'm not drowning in this?"

She stares at me like she's replaying the last twenty-four hours in fast-forward.

Then her expression shatters.

"Antoine..." Her voice thins. "Wait—did you know this when you talked to me last night?"

My heart drops.

Tae steps back, hand trembling over her mouth.

"You called me... apologizing, saying you couldn't sleep, saying you were just stressed—"

Her breath breaks.

"And you didn't tell me this? You let me pour my heart out, tell you I missed you, and you were sitting on something like—"

"Tae, I didn't know the whole—"

"You knew enough!" she cries, voice cracking. "You knew something was wrong. You knew you were in trouble. You knew you'd slept with someone else. And you let me sit there sounding stupid, telling you how much I missed you."

Her hands ball into fists.

"You lied to me last night by what you didn't say."

She pushes my chest once — not hard, but with everything inside her trying to escape.

"Do you have any idea how humiliating that feels?" she whispers. "To know you talked to me like everything was fine, and you were already halfway in hell?"

Tears spill down her face, fast and hot.

"I trusted you, Antoine. I—I actually trusted you. And you gave me silence instead of truth."

Her knees wobble.

Her voice softens into heartbreak.

"How could you let me be that close to you last night... when this was already happening?"

Her knees weaken.

Her fists hit my chest, soft, devastated, collapsing mid-impact.

I catch her before she sinks to the floor.

She sobs into me — shaking, trembling, covering her face like she wants to disappear.

I hold her until her breath stops hitching and her knees stop quivering.

When she finally pulls back, her voice is barely a whisper.

"Antoine... I love how you make me feel. That's the worst part. But I can't carry this. I can't stand next to you while—while this is happening."

Her tears drip off her chin.

"Please," she says. "Just go. I need some time to figure this out."

My heart craters.

I nod slowly.

I wipe a tear from her cheek with the back of my hand.

She flinches — not from fear, but from heartbreak so sharp it recoils.

I gently place a bottle of water beside her.

Make sure she's steady.

Breathing.

I rest my hand on her shoulder for one brief, apologetic second.

Then I turn.

Open the door.

And leave her behind — not because I wanted to, but because she asked me to.

I barely make it onto the porch before the mob closes in again.

"Antoine! Do you deny the allegations?"

"Is there physical evidence?"

"Is your company distancing itself from you?"

Flashes explode like gunfire — disorienting, violent.

I force my way through, shove into my car, slam the door—

A fist hits the window.

A camera scrapes the paint.

Someone screams my name so loudly it rings in the cabin.

I peel off so fast the tires squeal.

Halfway down the block, the adrenaline collapses.

My hands shake violently.

I pull over, chest heaving, forehead pressed against the steering wheel.

This isn't just a scandal.

This is a setup.

A coordinated strike.

It's too fast, too crowded, too detailed.

This is someone who knows exactly where my weak points are.

Someone who wants to break me before Shai ever gets home.

And the worst part?

A part of me — the part that's survived every storm until now — knows this isn't the end.

It's the opening shot.

CHAPTER TWENTY-ONE

CONNECTING the Dots

Mikey

"Hey Joyce. Thanks for getting back to me on short notice," I said the second I picked up. My eyes were burning from staring at code for too long, but urgency is better than caffeine. My brain snaps sharp when something feels off.

Joyce coughed into the receiver, that familiar rasp of menthol cigarettes and regret she wore like perfume. "Anything for my favorite guy. Make it quick. My son's wife is giving me that 'why is she like this?' look."

I allowed myself half a smirk. Joyce had lived nine lives—four of them shady—and she carried them all in her voice. "What you got?"

She exhaled hard. I could practically see the smoke cloud creeping out of her kitchen window. "Alright, the girl's name out in the open is Alicia Harper. Flew in for a bachelorette weekend. Basic girls-trip circus. They met Antoine at the Shortstop. Witnesses said she was leaning on him when they left. He basically carried her to the car."

I typed fast; my screens painted blue across my glasses. "Her statement?" I asked.

"She told officers they hooked up, fell asleep, woke up, and when she tried to leave, he got 'rough.' Claims he forced himself on her."

I waited for the rest. Joyce loved the dramatic pause.

"Rape kit shows some tearing. A few bruises on the inner thighs. Light marks on her neck."

"Marks consistent with what?" I asked.

"That's the million-dollar question. Could be consensual rough play. Could be what she's claiming. The point is—twelve jurors won't bother splitting hairs at first glance."

Joyce's tone softened, which meant she believed only about half of the story.

"I'm not lead on this," she added. "I'm stealing details before my lasagna gets cold."

"Your lasagna is always cold."

"You're not wrong." A sigh, tired and theatrical. "If she doesn't take a payout, he's screwed. Anyway, I'll stop by tomorrow for my cut. Old favor, don't forget."

She hung up before I could reply.

Classic Joyce—drop a grenade, demand pasta, disappear.

I leaned back in my chair, letting the silence settle around me. Something about this didn't smell organic. The story was too neat, too polished at the edges. In my world, neat equals orchestrated. Life is messy; plots are clean.

Time to dig.

I cracked a fresh Coke, wiped condensation onto my sweatpants, and pulled up the name:

Alicia Harper.

First stop: my standard sweep.

Government databases.

Healthcare systems.

Private data auctions.

Credit agency leaks.

One darknet database that technically doesn't exist unless you've bribed the right analyst.

Nothing older than five months.

That alone told me everything.

Five months = engineered identity.

Not stolen.

Not altered.

Built.

People treat identity like a name. It's not. It's a trail. Everyone leaves breadcrumbs—school registration, social media remnants, IP logs from old phones, DMV databases, tax addresses, digital photos tagged in someone else's cloud. Even ghosts leave shadows.

But Alicia Harper?

She appeared five months ago like someone flipped a switch.

I went deeper.

Medical records.

Community college transcripts.

Traffic tickets.

County-level arrest logs.

Anything that might fizz through old data caches.

And finally—there she was.

Harper Lewis — Trenton, New Jersey.

DOB: 5/25/1990.

Same face. Same jawline. Same faint scar above the eyebrow.

Now the trail lit up.

Juvenile shoplifting at fifteen.

Spotty attendance records across three high schools.

A half-finished medical assistant certification.

A handful of employment files attached to low-wage gigs in Camden, Asbury Park, Trenton.

Normal instability.

Normal survival.

Nothing that screamed "master manipulator," but nothing clean either.

Then the connections began to form.

Before the girls' weekend trip, Alicia had shared addresses—three separate times—with two other women:

Tiffany Shaw

Keisha Morgan

Both recognizable from Shortstop's bar footage.

I ran their faces through my recognition engine—my own build, faster and more honest than half the commercial tools used by government agencies—and tethered them to their real identities.

All three women popped up in archived employment rosters belonging to the same strip club in Atlantic City.

Club Mirage.

That alone wasn't unusual.

Three women working together? Happens in nightlife all the time.

But then I saw the timeline.

Mirage had new ownership eight months ago.

Not a typical acquisition.

A radical "rebrand."

The new owners changed the entire business model and forced out most of the old dancers, particularly the ones who didn't "fit the new aesthetic," which was code for "less melanated customer base."

Suddenly three women unemployed at the same time.

Suddenly all three leaving New Jersey shortly after.

Suddenly their digital trails start glitching.

Suddenly new identities begin forming.

That's not coincidence.

That's coordination.

And Alicia?

She was always the one listed as apartment leaseholder.

The one with the email accounts that tied the others together.

The one who moved first.

The one who changed her name first.

The ringleader.

The organizer.

The one with motive.

I kept digging.

No charges were ever filed against Mirage despite multiple internal disputes. But there were rumors—unstable paychecks, misplaced money, dancers whispering about the owners threatening them when they pushed back on unpaid wages.

I couldn't verify the theft rumor—not without subpoenas—but I could see the pattern:

They were desperate.

They were angry.

They were forced out.

They were running from something.

This was motive territory, not proof.

But motive always sits on the front porch of truth.

"What would drive them to target a man like Antoine?" I murmured.

The answer was always the same:

Money.

Leverage and money.

I turned back to Alicia's family tree.

Nothing there screamed "master blackmailer," but there were enough fractures to understand why someone might try to reinvent themselves.

Maternal side:

Patricia Lewis — two evictions, sporadic employment, outstanding utility balances. Nothing malicious. Just poverty.

Paternal side:

Gerald Peace — deceased at 30, car crash. Clean record.

Extended paternal relatives: minimal online presence, scattered through Trenton and Burlington County.

Siblings:
Jonathan and Michael Lewis — 17-year-old twins, truancy reports, school suspensions. Typical teenage chaos.

A family hanging together by threads, not rope.

I leaned back again, letting my brain map connections like constellations. This wasn't a random girl with a drinking problem. This was someone who had rebuilt her digital existence five months ago with remarkable precision—and pulled two women into the same clean slate.

That takes planning.
Or pressure.
Or both.

Now I had to see if the night itself matched the story.

I pulled Antoine's timeline:
Shortstop video logs.
Uber timestamps.
Hotel key-card data.
Room service receipts.
His credit transactions.
Her phone's GPS pings—scraped legally, if you're creative with interpretation.

The sequence looked consensual.
Too natural to be fabricated.
Her laughs, his arm around her waist, her leaning on him, both of them stumbling together.
It didn't look like someone afraid.

But the morning-after behavior?
She moved like someone expecting a payout.
Routine.
Efficient.

Her Lyft pickup.
Her airport arrival.
Her phone going dark for exactly six hours—standard if someone meets a handler or receives instructions. Not proof. Just pattern.

I rubbed my face.

"What the hell did you get yourself into, Toine... and what did you drag Shai into with you?"

I felt the itch behind my eyes—stress, adrenaline, the whisper of the vial on my desk. I took a bump, swallowed the drip with Coke, and refocused sharply.

I packaged everything into a clean report.
Encrypted every file.
Walled it behind a security layer even Shai couldn't bypass unless she pulled my dead-man protocol.

And I tagged the packet for Cellazo's office only.
Per Shai's standing orders:
No leaks.
No early warnings.
No unnecessary noise.

When she gets back from her blackout, she can deal with the fallout.
Until then, the only thing that makes sense is keeping her insulated.

I sat back, staring at the screens, letting the hum of the processors settle around me. Outside, the city looked deceptively calm, lights steady against the darkness, unaware of how close everything was to snapping.

This wasn't random.
This wasn't impulsive.
This wasn't a drunk girl making a bad decision.

This was a placement.
A performance.

A coordinated move on a chessboard Antoine didn't even know he was standing on.

And for the first time all week, I felt something unfamiliar press into my spine:

This wasn't just Antoine's problem anymore.

Someone was moving pieces around Shai, too.

My system dimmed, logs wrapping themselves for the night, when a lone alert blinked to life—small, out of place, almost polite.

One line pulsed on the screen:

"New connection identified."

My eyebrows lifted.

"Well hello there... what are you?"

CHAPTER TWENTY-TWO

614

The waves were the first thing I heard—slow, steady, persistent enough to draw me from sleep but gentle enough to make me want to stay under. For a moment I kept my eyes closed and just breathed. Warm air. Salt. Fresh linen. Her.

Shai slept curled toward me, one arm tucked under the pillow, the other resting across her stomach like she was guarding herself from a dream she'd never admit to having. Her breathing was deep, even. The kind of sleep that comes from trust, not exhaustion.

I propped myself on an elbow and watched her. Really watched her.

Her skin glowed under the early morning light filtering through the open wall, soft and golden where the sun touched it. Her lips were slightly parted. A loose curl had fallen across her forehead. She looked younger, unburdened—if someone had walked in right then, they'd never believe she was a CEO who carried a billion-dollar world on her back.

Something in my chest tightened at the sight. I didn't use to study people like this. Didn't memorize them. Didn't trace their features like I was afraid they'd shift the second I looked away. But she made stillness feel intimate, like every quiet second meant something.

I leaned down, kissed her cheek, and inhaled the faint trace of her cologne—warm, woody, familiar. It landed low in my stomach, a twist of want and something I didn't want to name yet. Something that unnerved me because of how easy it felt.

Shai barely stirred. Figures.

She sleeps like the entire ocean is her personal sound machine.

I brushed the sheets away from her hips, tracing a line with the back of my fingers down her stomach. The soft rise of goosebumps followed me. Her breath stuttered. A quiet hum broke out of her throat.

I slipped between her thighs before she fully woke, tasting her slowly, deliberately, letting my tongue move with a rhythm that made her body arch before her mind caught up. She moaned low and soft, fingers threading through my hair, guiding me with a confidence that always lit something dangerous in me.

She came quietly—shaking, breath caught, thighs trembling around me like she was trying not to wake the island.

Then?

She knocked right back out.

My mouth dropped open.

"Seriously?" I whispered to myself.

You mean to tell me I wake you up with a whole blessing from God's personal VIP section and you're just... unconscious again?

I slid the satin sheet back over her and shook my head at the audacity. Then I padded into the bathroom.

The shower filled with steam fast. Heat rushed over my shoulders, down my back, loosening all the tension that had been building since before we arrived. Two days. Just two days on this island, and this woman had my body betraying me like it had its own agenda.

I leaned on the tile and let my mind drift—to the way she pushed me against the shower wall last night, her fingers sliding inside me with that deliberate pressure that always hit the spot; the way she pinned my wrists above my head; the weight of her body keeping me still while she kissed the underside of my jaw.

My fingers drifted lower on instinct.

No.

Nope.

Absolutely not.

I snapped back and caught myself with my palm against the glass.

This woman had me losing track of what was real and what I just needed. It was dizzying, how fast she slipped under my skin. Back home, I could compartmentalize. I had structure, boundaries, reality. Here? The island made everything feel possible. Dangerous. Safe. All at once.

The water grew too hot. I shut it off, wrapped myself in a towel, and grabbed the oversized light-blue button-up she wore the night before. It swallowed my frame and smelled like her.

I didn't stand a chance.

I headed out to the hammock with my book. The ocean breeze rocked me gently until my eyes grew heavy again. I let myself drift.

A few minutes later—maybe twenty, maybe thirty—I felt her climbing into the hammock with the confidence of a woman who believed it was built for two.

"Hey," she whispered, sliding in beside me.

"Hey," I murmured sleepily.

"What you got going on?" she asked, pressing her body into mine, arms sliding around my waist.

"What do I have going on?" I teased, raising an eyebrow.

She made a face. "Don't act like I'm stupid."

I laughed and reached for my book. She snatched my glasses before I could get them on.

"Nope. Leave them on," she said. "They make you look studious."

"Do they now?"

"Read to me."

I opened the book and read the passage aloud. Her head rested against my chest, eyes closed, her fingers tracing lazy circles over the bare skin at my hip where her shirt had ridden up. Every time the story got intense, she'd hum softly under her breath, reacting without thinking.

When I finished, she exhaled and murmured, "So that's what I need to do to get you to listen? Command you?"

"You think that's what it takes?" I turned my head toward her.

She smirked. "Absolutely not. But being a little submissive doesn't hurt."

"I can be submissive, Shai. Question is—can you?"

"Absolutely not."

We both laughed.

"This is our last day here," I said quietly, shifting to straddle her gently. "I want it to be memorable."

She swallowed hard. "I can do memorable."

I unbuttoned the first button of the shirt—the only thing I had on—slowly, watching her eyes follow my hands.

Then the next button.

Then the next.

Her lips parted.

"Baby?" she whispered.

"Yes?"

"Don't freak out, but there's a—"

Before she could finish, I jumped up like I'd been electrocuted.

The hammock bucked wildly. Shai rolled clean off and hit the sand.

I sprinted into the ocean and performed a full baptism—rinsing, splashing, cussing, kicking water like I was fighting for my life.

Shai was doubled over on the sand, laughing so hard she couldn't breathe.

"You found that funny?" I yelled, wiping water from my face.

She tried to answer but could barely talk. "The spider wasn't even—ON you!"

I bolted toward her and tackled her into the sand, gently but with enough force to make my point. She squealed and grabbed handfuls of sand to throw at me.

We lay there after a while, laughter fading into comfortable silence. The sky stretched endless and blue above us, the breeze warm and soft against our skin.

"It's 7:30," she finally said, catching her breath. "Last day. Come here."

"So... game on?" I teased.

"No game," she insisted, sitting up.

"Oh no, baby. No game? Alright."

I stood, brushed sand off my legs, and walked toward the house.

"Elia? No game!"

"Okay, baby. No game," I repeated, fully lying. "Breakfast is ready."

A beat.

She narrowed her eyes and followed me.

And that's when Part C began.

***

BREAKFAST ON THE VERANDA

Breakfast was spread beautifully on the veranda—fresh fruit, eggs, pastries, smoked salmon, juices arranged like a magazine shoot. Warm air drifted through the open space, bringing hints of sea salt.

We ate mostly in silence. Not awkward. Full.

Shai reached for my hand across the table.

"Walk with me."

We stepped onto the sand barefoot. The morning tide brushed against our ankles, cool and playful. I felt her hand slip around my waist—not claiming, just anchoring.

We walked slow. The kind of pace people use when they don't want a moment to end.

"You thinking about work?" she asked softly.

"Not today."

"You always think about work."

I bumped her shoulder. "You always think you know everything."

"Don't I?" she smirked.

We walked farther, toward a part of the beach where the rocks softened the waves into gentler patterns. The world felt smaller there, quieter, like the island was giving us a corner to breathe in.

"Tomorrow we go back," she said quietly.

"Yeah... we do."

The words settled between us, heavy and real.

"I wish we had longer," she admitted. Not dramatic. Just true.

I looked at her—sun catching her jawline, hair moving softly in the breeze, eyes softer than I'd ever seen them.

"Me too," I said.

And my voice cracked in a way I couldn't hide.

She stepped closer, fingers brushing mine. "Whatever happens when we leave... just know these last few days have been everything."

My chest tightened. I swallowed hard.

"You're starting to sound emotional," I teased weakly.

"Don't get used to it," she warned, but her voice had that fragile thread running through it.

We kept walking—sometimes talking, sometimes just listening to waves crash against the reef.

The island glowed. We glowed. And somewhere deep down, I felt it:

This ends tomorrow.

This bubble.

This version of us.

This world where love wasn't complicated or forbidden or dangerous.

A breeze passed over my skin, and for the first time since we'd arrived, I shivered.

I wasn't ready.

Not for the island to end.

Not for real life to start again.

Not for whatever waited for us on the other side of paradise.

For the first time, I knew something with absolute certainty:

I didn't want this to be temporary.

Not anymore.

CHAPTER TWENTY-THREE

616

The sun was dropping low, turning the whole sky a warm orange that made the water look like it was lit from underneath. Elia curled against my chest, her head tucked just under my chin, and for a moment it felt like the whole damn world had paused just for us.

"Baby, I had the best time with you this week," she whispered. "You have no idea how good it felt to just... laugh. And—" She paused, catching her breath, eyes flicking away as emotion tightened her throat. "And have someone."

I kissed the top of her head. "You had me. Every minute."

Her body melted into me, and I held her tighter, knowing this stillness wasn't real life—it was borrowed time. She clung like she was afraid the ocean breeze might take me from her. And for the first time in a long time, I didn't want to be anywhere else.

She shifted, looking up at me. "After tomorrow... back to the grind."

"What's your next wave of chaos?" I asked, twirling a strand of her hair around my finger.

"Couple red carpet events. Press junkets. Then the premiere next month." She inhaled deeply. "God, I wish you could come with me."

"You know there's nothing I want more," I murmured. "Seeing you up there... Jordan Peele film or not... you're meant for this."

She smiled, soft and warm. "I can't wait for you to see it."

Something about that smile—the vulnerability in it, the hope—lodged itself deeper than I wanted to admit. It wasn't just happiness. It was a woman imagining a future with me standing somewhere in it.

For hours, we stayed there on the beach—talking about everything and nothing. A future together. Kids, maybe. What happiness could look like when things weren't so tangled. We avoided Anthony. That name alone could sour the air.

Elia's voice trembled when she talked about freedom. Mine did too, quietly. We were painting a life neither of us could claim yet, but God, it felt good to pretend.

By late afternoon, we wandered back to the villa to pack. The quiet between us was tender, almost reverent. She folded clothes with the easy softness of someone pretending to be calm. I checked my watch too many times, pretending not to.

Every move she made felt final in a way I couldn't shake—like she was packing away the version of herself I only got here on this island.

I needed tonight to leave a mark on her. Something she could carry back into the chaos.

By the time dinner approached, everything was in place.

The staff had followed my instructions perfectly: a path of pink and red rose petals down the steps, leading to a strip of red carpet I'd had flown in. Lanterns lined the walkway, flickering in the wind. Cameras were ready—fake paparazzi, just to give her the feeling she deserved without the invasion that normally came with fame.

I sat waiting in my vintage Brioni tux—red jacket sharp, Canali shoes polished so clean the light danced off them. Jameson warmed my chest while nerves prickled under my skin. Not anxiety—anticipation.

She deserved a world that applauded her without tearing her apart.

And then she appeared.

Top of the steps. Backlit by candlelight.

A vision that stopped my damn heart.

The gown fit her like it was sewn onto her skin—the iconic black "Safety Pin" Versace dress, thigh slit, hip split, diamonds catching the firelight. Her hair framed her face like she was stepping straight out of a dream.

Her eyes met mine. Tears welled instantly.

I stood, grabbed my handkerchief, and met her halfway.

"You look... beyond anything I could've imagined," I said, wiping the corner of her eye carefully.

"I love you so much," she whispered, voice breaking.

"No crying on my carpet," I teased, taking her hand. "Come on, Cinderella."

We walked the makeshift red carpet together, pausing under the flashes as if it were real. She squeezed my hand every time the lights went off, her breath trembling, overwhelmed. My security team collected the cameras at the end—no evidence of our world for anyone else.

Waiting for us was a white horse drawn carriage.

She stumbled getting in—those heels were no joke—and we both burst out laughing.

"If I knew you couldn't walk in them, I would've gone shorter," I joked.

"You've seen my work," she shot back. "I can handle as many inches as you can throw."

I raised a brow. "You sure about that?"

"Try me." She replied with a smirk.

The carriage rolled through the quiet parts of the island, breeze cooling, stars stretching out like a blanket overhead. She leaned into me, head on my shoulder, and I pulled her close enough to feel her heartbeat settle into mine.

Her heartbeat.

I didn't know then how much meaning that word was about to hold.

When we reached dinner, the scene was exactly what I wanted: lanterns, candlelit table, champagne chilled and ready. I wrapped a shawl around her shoulders and guided her to her seat.

"Everything tonight is breathtaking," she said softly. "How could I not fall deeper in love?"

"You are my royalty," I said. "Treating you less than a queen would be disrespect."

She swallowed, nerves flickering behind her eyes. "What's next for us, Shai?"

The waiter placed our appetizers down, giving me a moment to choose my words carefully.

"We have to be smart," I said. "Your career is about to take a leap. The divorce isn't final. And I can't pull you into my world publicly—not yet."

Her shoulders fell.

"Elia... the last 9 months changed everything for me," she whispered. "They say when you know, you just know."

"I know," I answered honestly. "And I feel the same. But we need strategy. We play chess. Not checkers."

She looked at me with raw vulnerability. "Promise me we'll get through this."

"I promise," I said, squeezing her hand. "And if it all collapses, we leave. Start fresh somewhere else."

Her lips trembled. "I trust you."

The moment felt right.

I reached into my jacket, pulled out the small velvet box, and pushed it toward her.

Her breath hitched. "Shai..."

I slid the diamond band onto her right hand. "This ring is my promise." My voice wavered despite me trying to steady it. "Inside is the rhythm of my heartbeat. A reminder that every beat is for you."

Her tears fell freely now.

"There's more," I whispered.

I opened the second box—onyx and black diamonds, sleek and dark. "One night while you were asleep, I recorded your heartbeat. I wanted to carry the sound with me."

She took the ring, hand trembling, and slid it onto my left ring finger.

"The Vena Amoris," she whispered. "Straight to the heart."

The words hit harder than she knew.

Because even though neither of us said it out loud...

we were binding ourselves to something we couldn't walk away from. A promise that would follow us into cities, into danger, into heartbreak, into whatever the world demands from them.

Emotion punched through me so fierce I had to look away for a moment. "I adore you."

"I adore you too."

We held each other until the world steadied beneath us again.

"Okay," I finally said, exhaling. "Enough tears. Let's eat before the food gets cold."

She laughed—a shaky, soft, beautiful sound. "I'm overwhelmed, Shai. In the best way."

"That was the point."

Dinner flowed into dancing. Dancing into laughter. Laughter into quiet confessions under the moon. By the time the sun started rising, we were tangled together on the beach, refusing sleep like it was an enemy.

But dawn always wins.

And reality doesn't care about romance.

We packed our bags and held onto each other all the way to the jet, both pretending we weren't counting down the minutes before life crashed back in.

Tomorrow…
everything changes.

CHAPTER TWENTY-FOUR

616

I finally powered my phones back on once we were settled in the air. The cabin lights were dim, the soft hum of the engines blending with the faint clink of glasses from the galley. The vacation bubble had burst—the woman I loved was asleep behind me, curled into the blankets, drooling on a pillow in the most peaceful way possible.

For a second, I just watched her... chest rising and falling, lashes resting on her cheeks, hair spilling over the edge of the cushion. Her mouth was relaxed, lips slightly parted, the kind of sleep people only get when their nervous system finally believes it's safe. It made me angry at the world for a second—angry that I was about to let reality yank that peace away from her.

I hated that this moment had an expiration timer.

We had roughly three hours before landing.

Three hours before real life clawed its way back in.

Three hours before the world demanded I stop being hers and start being CEO again.

I exhaled and reached for the first device—the line connected to MK. One unread message sat at the top, timestamped two days ago.

"REACH OUT TO ME BEFORE ANYTHING ELSE."

My stomach tightened. MK didn't speak in dramatic headlines. If he wrote that, something was wrong. He was my firewall—the one who filtered what reached my ears. If he bypassed every other thought to write that line, it meant the building was already burning.

I hit call immediately.

"Hey MK," I said, trying to lighten the mood with sarcasm I didn't feel. "Don't tell me I'm bankrupt and homeless. I just bought new swim trunks."

"Shai..."

His voice didn't match the joke. Too flat. Too direct.

"A hell of a lot worse than that. Where are you right now?"

My hand closed into a fist.

"Three hours out. What's going on?"

A long pause. I heard keys clacking on his end, the unmistakable noise of MK in crisis mode. Screens, feeds, legal docs, public statements—he was probably juggling all of it while talking to me.

"My friend... you're about to walk into a media shitstorm."

My pulse jumped, pounding through my throat.

"What the hell does that mean, MK? You know Elia is on this plane."

"You're gonna have to divert," he said bluntly. "Either land somewhere different, or get off first and let your crew take her somewhere else. You need attention on you, not her."

My fingers curled into my palms. "MK. Why?"

He exhaled like the weight of the entire city was sitting on his chest.

"Your boy finally did it. The past few days, it's everywhere. He's been accused of rape. And unless the girl takes a payout—which it does not look like—he's cooked. Press is camped out waiting for the CEO to show her face."

The world blurred for a second. I stared straight ahead, not really seeing the sleek cabin in front of me anymore—just headlines.

TECH CEO'S PROTÉGÉ ACCUSED OF RAPE.

INTEL-LIGENT FOUNDER'S INNER CIRCLE UNDER FIRE.

WHO DID SHE PROTECT, AND WHEN?

Antoine wouldn't rape anyone. I don't believe that for a second. I think to myself.

"Fuck... fuck, fuck!"

My voice ricocheted off the cabin walls. I shot straight up in my seat, loud enough to wake Elia.

My mind sprinted ahead of my body—

stock impact,
shareholder calls,
the board's patience snapping,
intel disclosures,
Premmission,
NDAs,
Discovery,
Elia being photographed beside me,
Anthony's insanity,
everything all at once.

This wasn't just about Antoine. This was about every decision I'd made that tethered him to my name.

"Where the hell is his publicist? Has he talked to Jim?" I snapped.

"Jim bailed him out. Antoine's mom flew in. He's been laying low waiting for you. But that's not all." MK's voice grew lower, harsher. "There's... other shit we need to discuss. Stuff about the lab work and that experimental drug. I didn't want to dump it on you while you were away, but you need to prepare."

My fingers pressed into the bridge of my nose. That old familiar headache pooled behind my eyes—the one that showed up during board battles, not vacations.

"This was supposed to be simple," I muttered. "One vacation. One week. One break."

"Yeah. Well." MK sighed. "You picked the wrong week to be unreachable."

I forced myself to breathe slow, steady, even though my insides were vibrating. The jet suddenly felt smaller, the ceiling lower. The ocean, the rings, the promises from last night—all of it felt like a movie I'd stepped out of too fast.

"Alright. If Elia stays on the plane, I need my full team waiting at the landing strip. Have them escort her to a different airport. I'll draw the attention."

"I already started," he said. "Just tell me where you land."

Of course he did. That's why he was MK.

I swallowed.

This was not how we were supposed to return home.

"Should I call Antoine?" I asked, even though I already knew the answer wouldn't help me.

"He's a mess," MK said instantly. "Scared. Not thinking straight. Wait until you get grounded and centered."

Grounded and centered. I couldn't remember the last time I'd been either.

"Alright," I said quietly. "Thanks for the warning."

We hung up. The line went dead. The silence rang louder than the engines.

Elia was sitting up now, still half-asleep, eyes soft with concern. The blanket had slipped down to her waist, exposing the curve of her shoulder, the faint tan line from the straps of the dress she'd worn last night.

"Hey baby... you okay?" she whispered, voice thick with sleep.

I shook my head. "No. Antoine got into something. Something big. There's going to be heavy media presence when we land."

Her hand flew to her mouth. "Oh my God. Baby... is he alright?"

"I have no idea yet." My voice cracked before I could stop it. "I'm arranging for you to stay on this plane. Security is going to take you to a different airport. I'll draw the attention."

The words felt surgical. Cold. Tactical. CEO mode swallowing the woman who'd been barefoot on a beach twelve hours ago.

Without hesitation—without fear—her fingers slid into my hair, gentle and grounding.

"Whatever you need," she murmured.

I looked at her, really looked at her, and the ache in my chest sharpened. The island glow was still on her skin; the ring on her finger still sparkled like a promise I barely deserved. She didn't flinch. Didn't ask what this meant for her image. Didn't make it about her at all.

"Elia... he's accused of rape," I said. "Allegedly. But the girl... she doesn't want money, from what MK's hearing. That's bad. I haven't even checked headlines yet. I'm trying to figure out if I should call him."

Her brows pinched together. "Shai... he does not seem like someone who would do that. You know him. You have to hear him out."

The rational part of me knew that.

The CEO part of me knew the opposite.

The woman who'd grown up with Antoine knew exactly how stupid and reckless he could be when ego and opportunity collided.

"I need to protect you first," I said. "The media will tear into anyone around me. The shareholders are going to want answers. This might be his final strike. He's brilliant—but reckless as hell."

She grabbed my face gently, palms warm against my skin, grounding me the way only she could.

"Listen," she whispered. "You're his best friend. All he really has besides his mother. You can't abandon him now. Help him. Then handle everything else."

Then she lifted my hand and placed it against her chest—fingers brushing the ring I gave her last night.

Her heartbeat thudded against my palm, steady and brave. For a second, the noise in my head dimmed. The cabin, the miles, the press waiting on the ground—none of it mattered. Just that rhythm. Mine on her hand. Hers under my fingers.

"Close your eyes," she said softly. "Feel my heartbeat. Breathe. You've got this. Take care of him. I'll meet you at home when it's safe."

Home.

She said it like it already belonged to both of us.

Her voice steadied something inside me I didn't realize had tilted. I'd been holding myself together with strategy and contingencies for so long that letting someone else anchor me felt foreign. Dangerous. Addictive.

I kissed her cheek, grateful in a way words couldn't touch.

"Just get back to me."

"I will." She stood slowly, stretching, the oversized robe slipping at her shoulder. "We've got two hours. Reach out to Toine. I'll check the news and see how loud the storm is."

As she walked toward the cabin, the ring glinting against her skin, something warm washed through me—love, fear, duty, gratitude, all tangled into one impossible knot. She was walking away physically, but everything about her screamed I'm still here with you.

"You're incredible," I murmured.

She smiled over her shoulder. "We'll weather this storm."

Then she disappeared behind the divider.

The cabin felt different the second she was gone—colder, sharper. It was just me, the low hum of the jet, the faint scent of her cologne on my hands... my phone...

my responsibility...

my fear...

and the courage I needed to finally dial Antoine's number.

I stared at his contact for a long moment, thumb hovering over the screen. Memories flashed in quick cuts—us broke and loud and stupid, us celebrating wins, him talking big about changing the world, me vouching for him in rooms full of people who didn't think he belonged there.

If he did this...

If he didn't...

Either way, the fallout was mine to manage.

I took one last breath, felt the ghost of Elia's heartbeat against my palm, and hit call.

CHAPTER TWENTY-FIVE

THE Silence Breaks

Antoine

"Antoine, has Tae reached back out to you yet?" my mother called from the kitchen.

"No Ma'am. I think I lost her," I said, sitting on the kitchen counter, staring at nothing.

Truth was... it wasn't just Tae I felt slipping.

It was everything.

My name, my reputation, my future.

One mistake had cracked the whole damn foundation, and I was waiting for the building to fall on top of me.

"Well, I'm sure she'll come around once all this—"

"Hold on, Ma. Shai's calling," I said, sliding off the counter and rushing into my bedroom to answer.

"Hello?"

"Toine... what's going on, bro?" Shai's voice was calm, but the edge underneath it was unmistakable. The CEO edge. The one she used when investors were circling like vultures.

"Hold on," I said, closing my door. "Shai, it was consensual. I swear on my mother. She wanted it rough — biting, scratching, all of it. Then next thing I know, the police are at my door. Bad enough I cheated on Tae... we were arguing, she left... I went out, met some girls, ended up with one. We hooked up. That's it. I swear, Shai, I didn't rape her."

"Okay," Shai said. "I hear Jim is on it, right?"

"Yeah, but it's looking real bad. She's not buying out."

I heard her inhale — slow and controlled.

A calculation, not a gasp.

Shai never panicked. She predicted outcomes.

"Alright. I'm a few hours away. Call Jim. Tell him we meet as soon as I land. I've got to handle something first."

"Okay... and Shai— I'm sorry. I really tried not to let you down."

There was a pause.

Barely a second.

But it was heavy enough to sit on my chest.

"Toine," she finally said, tone shifting into surgical calm, "listen to me carefully."

My stomach dropped.

"Given the severity of the allegations and the media exposure, I need you to step back from operations."

The words hit like a stomach punch. Expected, but still brutal.

"But listen," she continued, softer now, edges rounded, "this is not a judgment. This is standard crisis protocol. HR will issue a formal administrative leave — with pay — pending legal review. It protects the company, and it protects you. I am not cutting you off."

Relief shot through me so fast my knees almost gave out.

Leave... with pay.

Still trusted.

Still in the fold.

She went on:

"We built this company together. I'm not going to throw you to the wolves. But I can't let the board blindside us, and I can't walk into that room with nothing in place. This buys us time. Do you understand?"

I swallowed hard. "Yeah. Yeah, I understand. Thank you."

But she didn't hang up.

Not yet.

A softer breath came through the line — Shai slipping out of CEO mode like shedding a coat.

"Toine... don't hang up yet," she said quietly. "Let me talk to you as your right hand, as your closest friend."

My breath stalled.

Shai didn't switch modes unless it mattered.

"Are you safe right now?" she asked. Not like a boss. Like someone who'd seen me through every version of myself.

"Yeah," I muttered. "I'm home, my mom is here."

"Good. Is your mind steady?"

"...I'm trying."

She hummed, low and knowing. "Listen. No matter how bad this looks, you are not standing in this alone. I know your flaws. I know your impulsive ass better than anybody. And I also know you're not a monster. So breathe. Stop panicking. Handle your truth."

My eyes burned for a second, unexpected and unwelcome.

"Shai..."

"No," she said softly but firmly. "Hear me. You've had my back more times than I can count. So I'm not letting you crash out now. But you need to stay clear-headed. No running. No disappearing. No shame spirals."

A shaky laugh slipped out of me. "You really know me too well."

"Of course I do." Then her voice sharpened, just enough to cut through the fog in my head. "And Antoine?"

"Yeah?"

"Put the Hennessy down."

I froze.

Dead to rights.

"Shai—"

"No. You can drink once all of this is done. Not before. You need to be clear-headed. You need to be steady. Man up. It's real this time."

"Understood," I said, standing up, straightening my shoulders, pulling myself back into my body.

"Good," she murmured, tone easing again. "Call Jim. I'll see you when I land."

Then she hung up.

I stared at the blank screen for a long second.

The world still felt like it was caving in, but Shai's voice had cut through the panic like a lifeline.

Back in the kitchen, Ma looked up immediately.

"What did she say?"

"She... put me on leave," I said, exhaling. "Administrative leave. With pay."

Ma nodded. "Fair. That's fair, Antoine. Ain't nothing wrong with that."

"Yeah." I rubbed my hands over my face. "I should call Jim. She's meeting him tonight."

I slipped into my office and dialed Jim.

"Hey Antoine," he answered in a half-laugh. "How's my favorite client accused of a felony?"

"Cut the shit," I snapped. "Shai wants to meet tonight."

"I'll be up," he said. "Call me when you're on the way."

I hung up — and Tae's name flashed across the screen.

I stared at it.

My thumb hovered.

The weight in my chest doubled.

"Hey," I said when I answered, but she didn't give me a chance.

"Antoine, please stop calling me. I asked for space."

"Tae... I messed up. I cheated. But I did NOT assault that girl. I swear to God. I love you. Please come meet my mom. See the real me."

"Antoine... cheating is already betrayal. And now there are paparazzi outside my house. This is too much."

Her voice cracked.

That alone broke something in me.

"I know. I'm losing everything, Tae. I can't lose you too."

"You should've thought about that before sleeping with someone else," she said, voice breaking again. "You dragged me into a scandal I didn't deserve. Stop calling me."

The line went dead.

The silence afterward felt like cement.

Thick. Heavy. Suffocating.

For a long moment, I just sat there, breathing, existing, trying not to drown.

Memories stabbed at me — her smile, her forgiveness, the nights she softened me in ways nothing else could.

And now she couldn't even bear to hear my voice.

Eventually I stood, forcing my spine straight.

Sometimes you fake strength first and pray it sinks in later.

The hot shower helped.

Water running over my face, washing away nothing but giving the illusion of control.

When I stepped out, my phone buzzed — my barber confirming he was outside.

Routine.

Familiarity.

Normalcy.

Men survive off that when everything else is falling apart.

I stared in the mirror before opening the door.

The man looking back at me wasn't the same.

Stress had built shadows under my eyes.

Shame had carved something sharp into my expression.

But storms shape men.

And this one — I was determined — wouldn't break me.

Even if it tried like hell.

CHAPTER TWENTY-SIX

616

I couldn't believe Antoine put me in this position.

Not just personally—professionally. My reputation. My company. Everything I'd spent decades building. All on the line because he couldn't keep himself out of chaos for one night.

It wasn't fair to be furious and protective at the same time, but that's exactly where I landed.

He'd been my closest friend for over thirty years.

He knew the versions of me I'd buried.

And now he might be the thing that threatened everything I'd built.

By the time I pulled into Jim's office parking lot, my brain felt too full—too loud—like everything inside me was firing at once. The peace of the island hadn't even cooled on my skin yet, and here I was, walking straight into a wildfire.

Antoine was pacing outside the entrance, six steps one way, six steps back, like he was trying to outrun regret.

"What's going on, bro?" I asked, pulling him into a hug.

He clung a second longer than he meant to.

"Just trying to figure out what happens now," he murmured.

I stepped back just enough to catch his eyes.

"Look at me," I said quietly. He did.

"You are Antoine Joseph. Act like it."

He blinked, thrown for a moment.

"I need you to straighten up in public. No pacing. No looking broken. No letting anyone see you cracked. The media's already circling — don't give them a headline with your posture."

His shoulders tightened, instinctive, grounding.

"If you are innocent," I added, voice low and even, "then you need to look it with every step you take. You understand me?"

He nodded. Hard.

"Good," I said, squeezing his shoulder. "Now let's go."

Inside, Jim already had three tumblers of top-shelf scotch poured. Preparing for impact before I even spoke.

"It'd be better if I actually had something to make this go away, Shai," he said.

"Look, Jim—money is not an issue. What does she want?"

"That's the problem," he replied. "She doesn't want anything... right now."

My jaw clenched.

Women who didn't want money wanted fire.

"Then set the meeting," I said. "Get your team on it. Is she officially pressing charges?"

"As of right now? Yes. Antoine's out on bail. But Shai... the evidence is ugly. And a jury won't care about nuance."

Antoine's shoulders sagged.

"Let me talk to her," he offered, voice cracking.

Jim nearly choked. "Absolutely not. We need leverage—something she doesn't want public."

I turned to Antoine, voice sharpening into something surgical.

"Toine... did you rape this woman?"

The room froze.

"And don't fucking lie to me."

Jim raised both hands. "I can't be present—"

"Then cover your ears," I snapped. My eyes never left Antoine. "Answer me."

His throat worked, eyes shaking but honest.

"Shai... I did not rape her. I swear on my mother. I didn't."

I stared at him for a full beat.

Letting thirty years of history answer for him.

Finally, I exhaled.

"Alright. I believe you."

My voice didn't waver.

"I know you, Antoine. You don't have this in you. I'd bet my company on that."

Relief hit him so hard his knees nearly buckled.

I stood. "Okay. Then I'll handle it."

I left before the walls collapsed on me.

Outside, the air felt colder, sharper.

Damn it, Toine.

My phone buzzed.

Elia.

"Hey baby," she said softly.

"Hey love."

My voice didn't sound like mine.

"Are you okay? Where are you?"

"Downstairs. Waiting on my driver. I just... need a drink. Need air."

"I'm coming down."

"Elia—"

She hung up.

A moment later, the elevator opened. She stepped out, composed, focused, worried in that quiet, steady way that cut straight into my chest. She slid into the car and grabbed my hand without asking.

"Are you holding up?"

"I'm managing," I exhaled. "Barely. Toine really did it this time."

"Where to?" the driver asked.

"Just drive," I said, closing the partition.

Elia squeezed my hand. "Talk to me."

“It’s bad. Really bad. She doesn’t want money. And I had to suspend him. HR wants blood. The shareholders will want a scalp. They’ll want mine if this hits wrong.”

“You can’t carry all of this,” she said. “That’s what your team is for.”

“It’s different when it’s my company,” I murmured.

My phone buzzed — Mikey.

Get here. Now.

I sighed. “I need to drop you home. I’ve got a stop.”

“Why can’t I come?” she asked softly.

I didn’t give her the PR-safe answer.

I gave her the truth.

“You calm me down,” I said quietly. “And I don’t want to walk into Mikey’s space wired like this.”

I looked at her. She wasn’t asking to be included —

she was asking not to let me carry this alone.

I exhaled and nodded once.

“Alright.”

I texted Mikey:

Heads up, I’m ringing company.

Twenty minutes later, we arrived.

Mikey buzzed us in immediately.

The door swung open and he blinked at Elia before dropping into a dramatic bow and kissing her hand.

“So this is the famous Elia. Shai, you didn’t tell me she was stunning.”

“Mikey,” I said, giving him a look that meant not now.

He got it immediately.

He smirked and led us inside.

Neon code flickered across multiple monitors — his digital war room.

"Alright," he said, cracking his knuckles. "Let's get into it."

He dimmed the room lights with a tap, letting the glow from his monitors take over. Encrypted email chains, redacted attachments, and server logs filled the screens.

"Let me start with the email," he said. "The anonymous one I got before you left."

He enlarged the first attachment.

"This person knows internal patterns," Mikey continued. "They listed missing dosage logs, mismatched badge timestamps, unauthorized cold-storage pulls, and a lab entry that doesn't match any employee signature. Whoever sent this knows your systems."

"Can you trace them?" I asked.

"Not yet. Someone's actively blocking me. But I'm working through the firewall shadows. Give me a few days, we have more pressing issues."

He closed that monitor.

"Alright," he said. "The Antoine situation."

He switched screens.

"Here's what I have on her real identity."

He dragged up an old ID photo.

"Real name: Harper Lewis, Trenton. New identity built five months ago — from scratch. That's not reinvention for convenience. That's someone hitting a reset button."

Two more photos appeared.

"These two — Tiffany Shaw and Keisha Morgan — both connected to her. All three danced at Club Mirage in Atlantic City."

Mikey tapped open a timeline.

"Eight months ago, the club switched to new management. New owners. New aesthetic. New clientele. They fired almost the entire roster — including all three of them."

He pulled up a payment trace.

"Before that? Harper was using her dancing money to slowly pay back a debt tied to a failed robbery attempt at Mirage. Tens of thousands. Apparently her and her accomplices tried to hit the place up before ownership changed and was caught. Though they walked away empty handed, it still came at a price."

He zoomed in.

"When she wiped her identity five months ago, her debt wiped with it. Not forgiven. Not paid. Shifted. And debts don't just evaporate, Shai—they get reassigned."

A chill rolled through me.

"Exactly, but to who?" I asked.

"That's what I'm finding out," Mikey said. "But the timing is too tight to ignore. She gets a clean identity. Her debt shifts hands. She leaves the East Coast. Pops up here. And within days, she's positioned right next to Antoine."

"Meaning, this was intentional?" Elia whispered.

Mikey leaned back.

"Exactly. She didn't 'choose' him. Someone pointed her at him."

The room stilled.

"And I'm one trace away from knowing who benefits," he finished. "Once I get that, the whole thing opens up."

I stepped closer.

"Mikey..."

He held my gaze, calm and deadly certain.

"Don't worry, Shai. I'm already ten steps ahead. You don't call me Huck for nothing."

I smirked faintly. "And I'm Olivia Pope. You've got thirty-six hours."

Mikey's mouth curved — small, dangerous.

"It's handled," he said.

And for the first time since landing, I felt the ground steady beneath me.

CHAPTER TWENTY-SEVEN

616

"Mikey, where are you? I'm en route to meet her lawyers," I texted as I grabbed my suitcase and headed for the door.

My hands were steady, but my chest wasn't. I felt every heartbeat in places that shouldn't register pulse — my throat, my stomach, my palms. My mind kept looping through every possible outcome—none of them clean, none of them survivable without scars.

"Jim's prepped. Don't stress."

Mikey's reply hit instantly, like he'd been waiting in the shadows with his phone already unlocked.

"Good luck, baby," Elia called from behind me.

Her voice did something warm to the cracks forming in my spine. She crossed the room with those soft, deliberate steps that always made me feel seen before I said a word. She placed her hands on my face — thumbs brushing the hinge of my jaw the way she did whenever she sensed the shift inside me. The shift from woman to CEO. From lover to strategist. From soft to steel.

"You've got this," she whispered. "I believe in you. I love you."

I kissed her — slow, grounding, a breath I didn't know I needed. It loosened something under my ribs for half a second. A mercy. A moment of oxygen.

"I love you too," I murmured. "I'll be back soon."

Walking away from her felt like peeling off armor I couldn't afford to lose.

Downstairs, the car was already waiting—along with Antoine.

He looked like hell. Not the usual stressed-out, hungover hell, but the kind that sinks bone-deep.

Eyes red.
Shoulders tight.
Face puffy from crying or not sleeping — maybe both.
He looked smaller than he ever had in our thirty-plus years of friendship.

"You holding up?" I asked, sliding into the back seat beside him.

"As well as anyone about to be labeled a rapist," he muttered, staring out the window. "Ma's at the house waiting."

I hated that he was right. Even innocence didn't save you from the headline. The accusation alone was a prison.

"We'll get through it," I said, lying through my teeth with practiced confidence. "It's a negotiation. If we're lucky, we end this today. If not... we're in for a fight."

He nodded but didn't look at me. His jaw clenched. His knee bounced. His breathing was too fast, too shallow.

For a moment, I saw the kid I grew up with — scared, angry, out of his depth — and then I saw the man everyone else would see if he didn't get himself together.

"Toine," I said quietly, "look at me."

He did. Barely.

"Antoine," I said firmly, leaning in just enough. "Confidence."

He blinked at me.

"I told you — I'll handle it. I got you," I said, voice low, steady. "But you've got to meet me halfway. Shoulders back. Breathe. You walk in there looking guilty, they'll treat you like you are. You're innocent — so act like it."

He inhaled sharply, straightened his back, and lifted his chin. A flicker of the man I knew started to surface.

"Yeah," he murmured. "Alright. I'm good."

"Better," I corrected. He nodded once, a shaky exhale leaving him.

"Good. That's the Antoine Joseph I know." I said, tapping his knee. "Now let's go."

***

THE MEETING

The office parking lot was blessedly empty — the media was distracted by a bombing overseas. Behind the tinted glass of the car, the world felt muted, like someone had turned down the volume on a disaster long enough for me to breathe.

Jim met us at the door, suit immaculate, expression composed in that lawyer way where confidence and dread always hold hands.

"Shai, Toine — we're walking in with leverage," he said as he pulled the heavy glass door open. "Her story's unstable. There will be concessions, but she's the one standing on thin ice."

Antoine stayed outside as I stepped into the conference room with Jim.

The air was cold. Purposefully cold — the kind that kept people alert and uncomfortable.

Lynn Clover sat across the table, posture rigid, stare sharp enough to pierce metal. She had a reputation for dismantling men on the stand with surgical brutality. She didn't blink when I walked in.

"Let's begin," Jim said, sliding into his seat. "What's the number to make this go away?"

"This isn't about money," Lynn snapped back. "If this were your child—"

Jim cut her off cleanly. "Given the new information we've uncovered, charges dropped, compensation, NDA — or we file a countersuit for defamation and damages. Your choice."

He slid a folder forward. I opened mine.

The first page knocked the wind out of me.

Alicia Harper didn't exist.

Harper Lewis did.

New identity.

Multiple states.

A disappearing act that only made sense with backing.

A $75,000 debt cleared 5 months before she ever met Antoine, the exact same time her new identity began.

A setup.

Clear as day.

Jim leaned back, fingers steepled. "Someone paid to turn her into 'Alicia.' Someone invested in her being in that room with Antoine."

Lynn flipped pages with growing agitation, her anger cooling into something more cautious.

"This is circumstantial," she argued, but her voice faltered.

Jim wasn't done.

Another document slid across the table.

"We have one of the friend's notarized statement. She was offered five grand to 'cooperate.' Your client didn't disclose that."

Silence detonated across the opposing table.

John Curro finally leaned forward. "So what are you proposing?"

"My client was set up," Jim said simply. "Charges get dropped today, we sign an NDA, and you give me a number that covers your time."

They excused themselves.

The second the door shut, air exploded out of my lungs.

"Mikey's insane," I muttered. "I don't know how he pulled all this together."

"There's more," Jim said quietly, pulling a sealed envelope from his briefcase. He hesitated before handing it to me.

"Mikey told me not to open this," he admitted. "He said to give it to you and to only use it if everything else fell apart."

My stomach tightened.

I ripped it open.

A DNA test.

99% paternal match.

Between me and Harper Lewis.

The room tilted.

The floor vanished.

My heart stopped.

"Jim... what the hell is this?" I said causing Jim to snatch the paper from my hands.

He scanned the page, his face draining of all color.

"Shai... I don't understand this," he whispered. "This test says you and Harper share a father."

The words hit harder because he wasn't trying to interpret anything beyond the paper.

He was just reading the truth out loud — raw, clinical, impossible.

I felt the floor tilt beneath me.

"She's my sister?" I whispered, the word scraping out of my throat like it didn't belong to me.

Jim exhaled slowly, shaken. "It appears so. How... or why... this even surfaced now— I have no idea."

The word felt like it didn't belong to me.

Before Jim could respond, the attorneys returned.

"Our client will settle for $250,000," Lynn said stiffly.

"Fifty," Jim countered.

"Pay the two-fifty," I said abruptly, standing and grabbing the DNA paper off the table before anyone else had a chance to see it. "Finalize it."

"Shiloh—" Jim began.

"I said finalize it."

I walked out before my body has the chance to to catch up with my heart.

***

AFTERMATH

I stepped into the hallway — and froze.

There she was.

Alicia.

Harper.

Whatever her name had been before someone rewrote her life.

She lifted her eyes.

And in that split second...

I saw him.

My father.

In the tilt of her jaw.

The tension around her mouth.

The weary resilience in her stare.

A shadow of him echoed in her face.

No.

No, no, no—

I brushed past her, expression stone-cold as something shattered quietly inside me.

She didn't speak.

She didn't reach for me.

But her eyes followed me...

Not with guilt.

Not with victory.

With something like recognition.

For the first time in my life —

I felt exposed.

Like someone had peeled back my entire world and found the softest part.

This wasn't just a scandal.

This wasn't just a setup.

This was blood.

And somebody knew exactly which artery to cut.

***

BACK HOME

"Hey, baby—what's going on?" Elia asked as soon as I answered.

"It's done," I said quietly. "We settled."

"I thought she didn't want money. What changed?"

"She didn't have a case," I lied smoothly. "Shady past. We dug. That's all."

The lie burned.

"Are you coming home?"

"I'm on my way."

I hung up and dialed Mikey immediately.

"Mikey—what the fuck, bro?"

His voice was maddeningly calm. "Had to contain it before it leaked. Someone's orchestrating this, Shai. Until we know who—stay quiet."

"I paid the two-fifty. It shuts things down—for now. But I need you on this full-time."

"Already am," he said. Then hung up.

Antoine called next.

"Shai... you left. What happened? Did she drop it?"

"It's over," I said flatly. "Jim will bring you out the back. Go with him. We'll talk later."

I disconnected before he could ask anything else.

When I walked in the door, Elia wrapped her arms around me instantly. My body didn't even know how to respond — I'd been rigid for so many hours that warmth felt foreign.

"Are you okay?" she whispered. "What happened?"

"I don't even know." I headed toward the bedroom, unbuttoning my shirt with trembling fingers. "Apparently... this girl is my sister."

Elia froze. "Your... sister?"

"One of my father's kids. My mom only had me."

I walked into the bathroom. The tile grounded me. Barely.

Elia followed, rubbing slow circles on my back.

"A random woman accuses Antoine, turns out to be your sister, gets exposed for a fake identity—and someone clears her $75,000 debt right before the accusation? That definitely doesn't sound random, Shai."

"That's exactly what's bothering me," I whispered. "Nothing fits. Nothing adds up. Is someone targeting me?"

Elia exhaled softly, the kind of breath meant to calm both of us. She pulled me closer, guiding me toward the bed with slow, sure hands.

"Come here," she murmured.

I let myself fold into her, collapse really — the first time all day my body stopped fighting gravity. My head hit her chest and, for a few seconds, I just listened. Her heartbeat wasn't fast, wasn't nervous. It was steady. Strong. Like she was lending me the rhythm I couldn't find myself.

Her fingers slid into my hair, stroking through the tension there, untangling knots that had nothing to do with curls. My shoulders sagged. My breath finally — finally — slowed.

"You've been carrying the whole world today," she whispered against my temple. "Let it come down for a minute."

I swallowed, throat tight. "How was your day?" I asked quietly. It came out rough, tired, but real. I needed to hear her voice talk about something that wasn't burning down my life.

Elia hesitated, her thumb brushing the back of my neck like she was checking my emotional pulse before she answered. "Um... it was okay," she said softly. Her tone wasn't abrupt — it was careful, almost asking permission to share her own weight. "I met with my divorce attorneys. I meet his team this week."

She kept stroking my hair, grounding both of us. "I don't want anything but what's owed. I'm not fighting over assets or dragging this out. I just... want it over." Her voice cracked a little. "I want my freedom clean."

I opened my eyes, exhaling into her shirt. "I know," I murmured. "Soon."

She tightened her arms around me, like she was holding together everything I couldn't keep from unraveling.

And for the first time all day, I let my body rest.

Not because the chaos was gone — but because she made it survivable.

Just long enough to remember what safety felt like.

CHAPTER TWENTY-EIGHT

614

"Hello?" I said as I walked into my apartment, toeing off my shoes. The door clicking shut behind me felt louder than usual, like the sound belonged in a different world. I didn't realize how tightly I'd been holding my breath until the quiet hit me — flat, open, undemanding.

My nerves were still humming from the last twenty-four hours. Shai had held it together, but barely. And the emotional residue clung to me like mist that wouldn't shake off. My shoulders felt heavier than they should've; my mind kept flicking toward her, even now.

"Hey girl, what's going on?" Natalee answered, her voice bright and familiar — grounding me in a way that made my chest loosen by a fraction.

"Nothing much. Same ole," I sighed, sinking into the couch. The cushions caught me like they knew I needed it. For the first time all day, my spine actually relaxed. "How's everything with you?"

"Trent's at training camp. I was hoping we could have a girls' night — we're overdue."

I could practically see her rolling her eyes, her hair tied up, pacing her kitchen with that speakerphone confidence.

"Yes, definitely."

"Good, because the girls said I'm the only one who can drag you out the house," she cackled.

Of course they did. I hadn't been the most... available. Not lately. Not with my life split between my apartment and Shai's universe — a universe that had its own gravity, its own rules, its own storms.

"Alright. What time? Same place?"

"Eight. You got an hour. Move."

"Okay, okay — I'll get dressed."

"We've got catching up to do," she added, the edge of her voice softening in a way only old friends do.

When the call ended, I just sat there for a moment, the phone still warm in my hand.

I hadn't realized how much I'd pulled away from everyone — how I'd let my world shrink into work, survival, and Shai. There was a time when girls' nights were effortless. Now the thought of walking into a room and pretending everything was normal made my stomach flutter.

Not in fear.

In anticipation.

For the first time... I wanted to show up as the woman I'd become, not the one everyone remembered.

I wanted to say her name out loud.

I stared at my closet door, already knowing the truth — all my good stuff, all the things that made me feel like a woman who still had some control over her life, were across the hall. In her space. In her world.

With a groan, I stood up and headed to her unit.

The moment I opened her door, warmth hit me — spices, laughter, home.

"Hola, Elia," Rosa called from the kitchen, not even turning around. She always knew when I walked in, like intuition whispered my footsteps to her.

"Hey, beautiful. You making enchiladas without me?"

"My special ones," she bragged, tapping the pan and mixing spices with the confidence of a woman who'd perfected her craft long before I was born. "You want?"

"I will later. I'm running late." I glanced toward the hallway, but something in me hesitated. "They're gonna have questions, Rosa..."

She wiped her hands, looked at me for a long moment, and lifted her chin like she was passing down scripture.

"Elia, you must be true to yourself before you can be true to anyone else."

Her voice carried that layered wisdom — the kind that came from surviving hard loves, hard losses, and choosing softness anyway.

It hit deeper than it should've.

She stepped closer and squeezed my hand, her thumb drawing a slow circle like she could feel the knot sitting in my chest.

"You glow different now," she said. "Not just because of her... but because you stopped dimming yourself."

The words slipped right under my ribs before I could block them. Rosa always saw too much — but never in a way that made me want to hide.

Only in a way that made me want to breathe deeper.

"Thank you," I murmured. "I didn't realize how much I needed to hear that."

I gave her a small smile and walked toward the bedroom.

I opened the closet door.

Empty.

My little section — gone.

"What the...?" I whispered, stepping inside. "Rosa!"

A tiny spike of panic hit me. Had Shai moved my things? Did something happen?

She shuffled in, smirking like she'd been waiting behind the door for my exact reaction. "Why you not in your closet?"

"What closet?"

She grabbed my hand, warm and steady, and led me down the hall to the spare room. When she opened the door and I hit the light switch — the entire room came alive.

Shoes rotated outward in smooth synchrony.
Lights warmed to a soft glow.
Clothing racks slid forward like a high-end boutique greeting its favorite client.
The floor beneath me seemed to breathe.

Every color-coded section gleamed under golden lighting.
And in the center, behind pristine glass, sat a jewelry case arranged like a museum exhibit.

My jaw dropped so hard it almost clicked.

I stepped farther inside, letting the room wrap around me.
The air even smelled different — clean, cool, like luxury stores in New York where everything costs more than rent. The leather of the shoes gave off a faint richness, the fabric sections released soft hints of perfume Shai favored, and the warm lighting made every color look intentional.

It wasn't just a closet.
It was a map of the life she saw me in.

A life where I wasn't visiting.
A life where I existed here — with her — unapologetically.

I grabbed my phone instantly.

"SHAI!"

"What's wrong?" she answered breathlessly, like she'd sprinted off a treadmill.

"This closet — what did you do?"

"What closet?" she tried, but the lie dissolved instantly. "Hold on, I'm coming up."

I hung up and just... stared.

This wasn't a closet.
It was intention.
Architecture shaped into affection.
A silent confession built into walls.

A place that said: I want you here. Not visiting. Here.

"Hey baby," she said a moment later, stepping inside. She took one look at my face and burst into a grin. "Rosa beat me to the surprise. THANKS, ROSA!"

"Sorry, Shai!" Rosa called, absolutely not sorry.

I turned to Shai. "Why? I have two closets in my apartment."

She shrugged — shy. Shai Mercer, billion-dollar mind, ruthless negotiator, global CEO... shy.

It softened me instantly.

"I wanted you to have your own space here," she said quietly. "You're here more than you're not. It just felt right."

"You rebuilt an entire closet and half of room," I said, still stunned.

"It wasn't being used, so we just opened the room up a bit. Nothing too much." she smiled, walking toward me. "Anything for you."

I opened the center case. Diamonds caught the light and threw it back in colors I didn't know existed.

"All this too?"

"I want my woman to have the best of everything."

"Oh, I'm your woman?" I teased, half-breathless.

"Unless you want to give the title to somebody else."

Her smirk alone could've knocked me down.

"I don't," I whispered, kissing her. "And thank you. Really. This... it's beautiful."

"I know you appreciate it," she murmured.

I exhaled, letting the truth settle between us.

"So... I'm meeting the girls tonight."

"And?" she asked, narrowing her eyes slightly — the protective tilt.

"I'm telling them."

Her jaw tightened. A flicker of protectiveness crossed her expression — calculation, risk assessment, fear of exposure.
But also… softness.

"Elia… that affects me too. It's not just—"

"Shai, it's my friends," I said gently. "I'm not calling TMZ. I'm tired of pretending. And…"
I touched her chest, right above the heartbeat that always steadied mine.
"You're my truth. I want to own that."

Her shoulders eased. Something tender replaced the tension.

"Okay," she breathed. "If you're sure, I support you."

"It's 7:15. I've got about an hour."

"Let me get out of your way then," she said, brushing a finger along my jaw before stepping out.

I moved fast — shower, lotion, perfume.
Hair up in a messy, side-swept up-do.
Red-and-white romper that hugged me just right.
Six-inch denim stilettos that made my legs feel like a sin.
Light hoops, studs, bangles, simple gold watch.

Each step made me feel more like myself, more in control of the world spinning under my feet.

As I switched bags, I called out, "What are you doing tonight?"

"Probably going out with Toine and some of the crew. I still haven't talked to him about… everything."

"You should go," I said, stepping toward her. "Get out the house. Clear your mind."

She paused mid-sentence, her eyes drifting down my body — lingering on the heels.

"You know I love when you walk in heels."

I smirked. "I know you do."

She lingered for a moment, her eyes tracing the curve of my leg, the line of my shoulders, the way the romper hugged my waist. Not in a possessive way — in that slow, appreciative way she only used when she was trying to memorize me before I walked out the door.

"Be safe," she murmured, almost under her breath.

"I will," I promised, brushing my thumb across her cheek.

Walking away felt different now — like stepping out of a chapter we were actively writing together.

One quick kiss — warm, grounding — and I grabbed my purse.

"Text me when you head out," I told her. "Go have some fun, babe."

The door closed behind me with a soft click that felt like the start of something.

For the first time in a long time...

I felt ready.

Ready to walk into a room as myself.

Ready to let my friends see truth instead of fragments.

Ready to step into a life I wasn't hiding from.

A life with her in it.

CHAPTER TWENTY-NINE

616

The door clicked shut behind Elia, and the silence that followed wasn't empty — it was heavy. Weighted. Like the apartment exhaled for both of us the moment she left. I stood there for a beat, palm still resting on the doorframe, letting the quiet settle into my bones.

From the kitchen, Rosa's voice drifted out through the soft clatter of pans.

"You're pacing."

I blinked. I hadn't even realized I'd been moving.

"Am I?" My voice came out rougher than I intended.

She didn't look up from the enchiladas she was assembling, but her tone carried that familiar, unshakeable certainty. "Yes. Like a lion with something stuck in its paw."

I huffed out something between a laugh and a curse. "It's been a day."

"It's been many days," she corrected, sprinkling cheese with the ease of someone who had seen a thousand storms and never once let them steal her grace.

I walked toward the kitchen island but didn't sit. Couldn't sit. My body was wired, restless, like I was waiting for the next blow.

Rosa finally turned, wiped her hands on a towel, and nodded toward a stool. "Sit, mija."

This time, I did.

Her eyes searched my face, quietly taking stock of every silent fracture. "Your shoulders are too high," she murmured. "Your jaw is locked. And your eyes..."

She softened. "Your eyes look like you haven't rested in months."

I dragged a hand over my face. "Someone is moving pieces around me, Rosa. Someone knows exactly where to hit. I keep trying to stay ten steps ahead and somehow I'm the one getting blindsided."

She stepped closer and placed her hand on my cheek — the way she used to when I was twenty-something and thought the world would crumble if I wasn't holding it together.

"Shai," she said gently, "you have survived worse storms than this."

"I don't know about that," I whispered.

"I do."

She tapped her fingers lightly against my temple. "You are too smart. Too strong. That is why they strike at your heart instead of your head."

The words landed so precisely I had to swallow hard before responding.

"This feels... personal."

"It is," she said simply. "But not because of what you built. Because of who you love."

My breath hitched. "Elia?"

Rosa gave me a knowing smile — soft, maternal, devastating in its accuracy.

"You glow, mija. Even when you try not to. Love makes you bright. Bright things are easy to spot... and easier to attack."

I stared down at my hands, flexing them slowly. "I don't want her caught in this mess."

"Then stand firm," Rosa said. "Face this storm so she never has to."

A beat passed — stretched, quiet, necessary.

She stepped closer and studied my face with that quiet precision she'd mastered long before I ever became somebody important.

"And Antoine?" she asked softly. "He has always been reckless with his own life... but never with yours. Do not forget that."

"He messed up," I said, rubbing the back of my neck. "And I know he's scared. But I'm tired, Rosa. Tired of cleaning up messes. Tired of trying to be ten steps ahead of people who shouldn't even be on the board."

Her brow creased — the kind of worry that came from knowing me too well.

She let out a quiet breath. "He'll find his footing. Sometimes a man has to lose it all to understand the price he paid to build what he had."

My throat tightened. "I'm trying," I murmured. "But I'm angry too. There's just... a lot I can't even process yet. And I can't even articulate half of it."

Rosa didn't push. She never did.

Her expression softened into something understanding and ancient, like she'd held countless secrets for countless people and learned exactly which ones were too heavy to touch.

She reached out and rested a hand over mine.

"You lead too much alone," she whispered. "You take everyone's fear and carry it in your own chest. That is not strength, mija. That is loneliness wearing armor."

I inhaled slowly, the words hitting bone-deep.

She tapped two fingers lightly against my sternum. "You carry too much in here. When the heart is overloaded, every problem feels like the end of the world."

I exhaled shakily. The knot behind my ribs loosened by a thread.

Then her hand cupped my chin — firm, warm, grounding. "Be careful with your heart, mija. You pretend it is steel, but it is softer than you think."

I closed my eyes, letting the truth of it settle without shattering.

"There's something coming," I whispered. "I can feel it. Someone's moving pieces around me, and I don't know the play yet."

Rosa rested her palm on mine. "Then stay steady. Storms reveal who you are — and who they are."

She turned back to the stove, humming softly, as if she hadn't just held my entire spirit together with her bare hands.

"Go wash up," she said gently. "You need clarity before anything else."

I nodded, letting her words anchor me the way only Rosa ever could.

CHAPTER THIRTY

616

I sat on the couch for a moment, weighing my options, before finally pushing myself up to shower and dress. The apartment felt heavier than usual—still, quiet, like the walls were waiting to hear what move I'd make next. Under the hot water, I tried to keep my mind from replaying the chaos of the last few days. Antoine, my own brother, caught in a mess he never saw coming. Someone was setting up a board around me, and I had to believe Antoine was just a pawn on the wrong square.

Steam fogged the glass, wrapping around me as if trying to smother the thoughts I had no interest in dealing with yet. I pressed my hands to the tile and let the heat bite into my skin, grounding myself. It barely helped.

As I dried off, I grabbed my phone and dialed Mikey.

"Hey, Shai. How is everything?" he asked. His voice was calm, but I could hear the fatigue—the low hum of a man who had been working nonstop.

"The usual," I sighed. "How is the investigation moving?"

"I made some progress," he said. "The project Antoine invested in collapsed. The FDA shut it down, and investors are furious. A lot of money evaporated. I am digging to see who all the investors were. Someone might have figured out your involvement was only on paper and used Antoine as the weak point."

"So they hit two targets with one shot," I muttered, pulling on my shirt. "Sink Antoine, and stain my name and the company."

"That is exactly where my head is," he said. "The challenge is that some investors hide behind dummy corporations, trusts, or borrowed identities. I have most of them traced, but there are three I cannot pin down yet. They're ghosts. I will keep going."

"Good. And where is Alicia?"

"Miami area," he answered. "Laying low. I have eyes on her."

"Thanks, Mikey," I murmured. "I mean that. I would be lost without you."

He exhaled like he wanted to say more but chose restraint. "Stay safe, alright?"

"I will," I said quietly, ending the call.

I stood still for a second, staring at the floor. My reflection in the hall mirror looked calm, composed—even confident. But my chest was tight. My mind was racing. My pulse was doing double-time under my skin.

I texted Elia to let her know I was heading to Novacane Sports Bar in LA and that we'd regroup later. She said she was glad I was getting out and hoped things would smooth over between Antoine and me.

I hoped so too.

Driving down the strip, the city lights blurred through the window—streaks of white and red flashing across my peripheral vision. I muted the noise in my head and focused on my breathing. Tonight needed to be calm. Uneventful. Quiet.

For once.

***

Elia

"Hey ladies!" I called as I walked toward the table, weaving through the crowd.

"Girl, where have you been?" they shouted back, all standing to hug me at once, practically pulling me into the booth.

"You all know me. Working myself into the ground," I said, sinking into my seat with a sigh of relief. Their energy was like a reset button—loud, warm, familiar. I felt a tug in my chest. I hadn't realized how much I missed being... me. Just Elia. No cameras. No pressure. No chaos.

"We saw you at the premiere," Austin said. "Tickets already purchased for this weekend."

"Good," I smiled. "This one means a lot to me."

"It should. Critics are calling it your best," Melissa said proudly.

"Maybe we should all go together," Natalee added. "Girls' night number two."

"Nat, you will go anywhere with drinks involved," Melissa said, making us all laugh.

"What are y'all implying?" Natalee's eyes widened dramatically, hand over chest.

"Nothing, sis. You just enjoy the devil's juice," Austin teased.

"I will remember that when y'all are crying on the phone and need me to bring the wine. No loyalty," Natalee said, finishing her drink with attitude.

"We love you," I said, laughing, as the waitress set a cosmo in front of me.

We settled into the usual banter—work drama, relationship updates, and a quick recap of everything I'd missed. Little by little, my shoulders started to drop. My mind loosened. I sipped my drink and let myself exist in a moment that wasn't tied to a crisis or a secret.

God, I had missed this.

Then my phone vibrated.

Before I even looked, Austin caught the shift in my expression—the way my mouth softened, the way I tried (and failed) to hide the smile tugging at me.

"Oh no. What is that grin?" she said. "Spill it."

Melissa leaned in across the table. "Yes ma'am. It has been months. You have been M.I.A., working, living in silence, not seen out in public with anyone. Which means... you are hiding something."

"There is not much to talk about," I said, though heat was already rising to my cheeks.

"It is that lesbian, isn't it?" Melissa said, and the whole table froze for half a second.

"Elia... are you carpet-munching?" Austin whispered dramatically.

"Come on, y'all," Natalee said, smacking Austin's arm. "Give her space."

"No, it is fine," I said, lifting my glass.

My pulse stayed steady.

My voice didn't shake.

And suddenly... I realized I didn't want it to.

"I am done hiding. Yes. It is her. Her name is Shai. She is the sweetest, most loving, most thoughtful person I have ever met. And I am in love with her."

Silence.

But not the bad kind.

The heavy kind.

The kind where everyone is recalibrating everything they thought they knew.

Natalee was the first to move—reaching for my hand with a softness only she had.

"Well, we always knew you were a little freak, so does this shock anyone?" Austin said.

"Hell no," Melissa added. "Shots."

"Really?" I laughed, disbelief melting into relief.

"Honey, I have never seen you glow like this," Melissa said. "If she has you this happy, then... I mean, I do not get it, but okay."

Then Natalee leaned in like she was telling state secrets. "I have been waiting to ask... how is the sex? Because she looks like she eats good—"

"Nat!" Melissa hollered, nearly choking on her drink.

"What? I am curious."

We dissolved into laughter. Real laughter. The kind that shakes your shoulders and unclenches your spine.

"She is... fine," I said, shrugging, though every nerve in my body wanted to roll its eyes at the understatement.

"Well then cheers," Melissa said, lifting her glass. "A new love life and a new movie."

We toasted, warmth sliding into my bones.

Austin wasn't done.

"We are not stopping here. Elia's birthday is coming."

"Shai probably has something extravagant planned," Natalee said knowingly.

"Does she have a friend?" Melissa teased.

"No," I shot back smiling.

"So are you going public with her?" Melissa asked.

"I have not decided," I admitted. "There is too much going on. My divorce, her business, the media, everything. She is very low-key, and I do not want to drag her into my world."

"There is nothing wrong with a group of people hanging out," Melissa said. "Invite her. Let us meet her."

The suggestion hit me harder than I expected.

It was simple — but it felt like a step.

A big one.

One I wasn't scared of anymore.

I stepped outside, cool night air hitting my skin, and called her.

"Hey baby," I said softly.

"What is up beautiful?"

"Just drinks and food," I said. "I miss you."

"Do you need me to come get you?" she asked immediately.

"No. I am good. What are you doing?"

"Watching the game with the guys. It feels like old times."

"Why do you not come meet us?"

She hesitated. I heard it. Felt it.

"Baby... I do not think—"

"Shai, it is a group of adults at a lounge. Please. I want you here."

A beat.

Then she exhaled. "Alright. I will talk to the guys. Maybe the Room Hollywood. Friendly crowd."

"Good," I said, smiling.

We hung up, and I headed back inside, calling for the check.

"Alright ladies," I said. "We are meeting the others at the Room."

"Say less," Natalee said, standing.

We headed to the garage, still laughing, still loud, still wrapped in warmth.

Tonight was going to change everything.

CHAPTER THIRTY-ONE

616

"Was that the missus?" Antoine called out when I stepped back into the section, his tone half-joking, half-prying.

"Yes. She and her girls are coming to meet us," I said, dropping into the seat beside him and lifting my glass again.

"Come on, Shai. This was supposed to be a guys' night out. Who is coming?" Antoine pressed, grinning like he already knew the answer.

"Brother, you need to be worried about Tae and not about who is walking through that door," I replied, giving him a pointed look.

"That is a lost cause," he muttered, eyes flicking away toward the bar like it hurt him to admit it.

"Nothing is ever a lost cause," Teddy chimed in. Teddy was the steady heartbeat of our circle — a producer who'd survived fame, industry politics, and a decade-long marriage. He didn't raise his voice often, but when he did, you listened. "You just have to want it badly enough to fight for it."

"Amen to that," DC added, lifting his glass. He'd spent years running from commitment until his wife finally walked. Now he was rebuilding his career from the ground up, writing scripts like his life depended on it. "If she's worth it, keep fighting. There's nothing out here but money-hungry women. A good woman is hard to come by."

"Truth," I agreed, raising mine. "She likes Elia. Maybe we let Elia talk to her first."

"I doubt it will work," Antoine said quietly. "I messed up. Even with the charges gone, I still cheated. I knew from day one cheating was the one thing Tae would not tolerate." He stood abruptly. "I'm going to get some shots."

He moved like a man trying to outrun a thought. Like if he stayed seated too long, reality would catch him by the collar. Antoine always did that—acted first, processed later. And normally, I could manage it. Tonight, I didn't feel like managing anything. I felt like watching carefully and counting exits.

"DC, you got my five grand?" I asked, glancing at the score on the TV.

"Shai, the game is not even over. Are you really stressing me over five thousand?" DC said, voice cracking like he already knew the answer.

"Yes. Don't make bets you can't cover. No shorts," I said flatly.

"I told you not to bet with him," Teddy laughed. "And no, I'm not loaning you anything."

"Man, forget all of y'all," DC snapped before storming away.

"Don't try to sneak out the back either," I called after him.

"He's going to cry in the car," Teddy said, and we all broke into laughter just as Antoine returned with a tray of shots.

We threw them back, settled the tab, and headed out. The drive to the lounge was quick, the kind of night where music spilled out of every car window, and the city felt awake in a way that fed you.

But my mind didn't feed on music.

My mind fed on patterns.

Headlights in the rearview. Cars that stayed too long. Men on corners who looked like they weren't there for the nightlife. I hated that my life had turned me into someone who noticed those things first. I missed being able to walk into a room and only care about the playlist.

We arrived before the girls and secured a section on the back wall. The lounge was packed — heat, perfume, bodies, music. Alive. The bass hit my chest in steady punches. The lights swung low, cutting faces into shadows and flashes.

I watched Antoine try to settle into the vibe, but his body wouldn't let him. His knee bounced. His jaw worked. His eyes kept skating across the room like he was looking for the moment his life went wrong.

Then I saw her.

Elia wove through the crowd with her girls, cheeks flushed from laughter, hair curled loosely around her shoulders. She spotted me instantly.

Something in me unclenched.

"Goodness, it is crowded in here," she said, stepping into the section.

"Hello, love— I mean Elia. Fancy meeting you here," I corrected myself quickly.

"Hi, my love— I mean Shai," she teased back, lips curving.

That smile did something dangerous to me. Made me forget for a second that I was still sitting in the aftermath of a storm.

"Ladies, this is Shai," she said, turning to her crew. "Shai, these are my girls: Melissa, Austin, and you know Nat."

"Hello, ladies. It's finally a pleasure," I said, greeting each one. "This is Teddy. This is Antoine, my brother. And... here comes DC."

Once drinks hit the table — champagne, tequila, and a few cocktails — the energy shot up another level. The music got louder. The laughter got looser. And for a minute, I let myself pretend this was normal.

"So, Shai..." Melissa said, crossing her legs and eyeing me. "What exactly are your intentions with my best friend?"

I glanced at Elia, who hid a smile behind her glass. "I'm not sure how to answer that."

"Oh no," Antoine blurted suddenly, standing up so quickly his drink sloshed onto the floor. "Chantae is here."

"Toine, wait," I said, steadying him. "If you rush over there, you'll scare her off. Give her a second to get settled."

"I need to talk to her," he said, voice low and tight.

"You will. Let her breathe first." I handed him a beer. "After a while, we'll send a round of drinks to her table and gauge her response."

He exhaled, nodding reluctantly.

"Ladies, what do I need to do to get my woman back?" he asked, turning toward Elia's group like they were a panel of experts.

"That depends," Austin said. "How long were you together, and what did you do to make her leave?"

"A couple of months. And... I'm sure you saw the headlines," Antoine said, lowering his head.

"Oh, that was you," Melissa said, leaning back. "Well in that case? Nothing. You had her name in the media. That's a lot."

"Make her jealous," Natalee suggested, dead serious.

"No, Nat," all three women said in unison.

Natalee rolled her eyes. "I'm just saying, it works sometimes."

"Come on, Nat. Let's do the 'Hey girl, how you been?' routine," Elia said, dragging her up.

"We'll be back," Natalee called as they disappeared.

"Toine, you dragged my woman into your mess," I muttered under my breath.

"Oh, 'your woman?'" Melissa echoed, eyes narrowing at me playfully.

"I'm heading to the restroom," I said quickly before she could dissect that slip.

"You better run," she laughed.

Walking toward the back hallway, I scanned the room the way I'd been trained to — patterns, posture, anomalies. Two men at a corner table stood out immediately. Their eyes tracked movement, not music.

Their clothes weren't flashy enough for the setting. Too deliberate. Too clean.

When I passed, they pretended to talk. One stood.

Followed.

My pulse tightened. Not panic — focus.

Inside the restroom, I reached for my phone — and cursed under my breath. Still on the damn table.

I stepped into a stall and listened.

The door opened. Closed.

Footsteps. A pause. Too long.

My heartbeat was loud in my ears now, matching the bass outside like the building and my body were synchronized.

I held still, breath shallow, listening the way Mikey trained me to — for weight shifts, for fabric movement, for intention.

When I pushed open the stall, a young woman was touching up her lip gloss in the mirror while her friend brushed past me toward the toilet.

I exhaled, grounding myself.

Maybe nerves.

Or maybe instincts tightening for a reason.

I washed my hands and returned to the section, forcing my face back into something neutral before anyone could read what my body had just done.

"Where is Antoine?" I asked Elia as I slid in beside her.

"He's talking to Chantae. It looks like he's crying," she said, sipping her drink.

"Good job, ladies," Nat toasted as she looked up.

"I don't know about all that," I murmured, watching Chantae's body language — present, but on guard. She wasn't leaning in. She wasn't shutting him out either. She was listening. Measuring. Letting him work for every inch.

Two more hours drifted by in a blur of drinks, music, and the kind of laughter that makes the night feel soft around the edges. Chantae eventually wandered closer with her friends, settling near Elia. Antoine lit up like a damn lantern.

Elia and I kept our distance in public — stolen glances, quiet touches hidden from the room. Austin and DC left early; Melissa and Nat danced until they couldn't stand straight.

When they finally hugged us and climbed into their Uber, the night air outside was warm and thick.

"Toine, let's go," I said, pulling him from the spot he'd rooted himself in.

"I'm going to call you," he told Chantae, earnest as a puppy.

"Don't call me. I'll call you," she said, giggling as she walked away.

"I love you, more than you know!" he yelled after her.

She waved without turning around.

"Let's go, lover boy," I said, guiding him out.

We walked Elia to the car waiting at the curb. The driver opened the door.

"Babe, I'm taking Antoine home. I'll meet you back at the house," I told her.

"Are you sure? You drank a lot tonight, and I don't feel comfortable with you driving," she said, leaning out the window.

"I switched to water hours ago. I'm fine," I said, holding her gaze. "I love you."

"I love you more," she murmured before the door closed.

I didn't know then that it would be one of the last times she said that to me.

CHAPTER THIRTY-TWO

THE Breach

Mikey

Mikey hadn't slept in two days.

Not the jittery, half-awake kind of not sleeping either. The real kind. The kind where your body gives up asking and your brain just keeps running laps around the same dark track.

Seven calls.

No answer.

He stared at Shai's contact on the secure phone, thumb hovering, then pulled it back like the glass might bite him.

She wasn't ignoring him. That wasn't her style.

She was just out.

Which was worse.

He exhaled slowly and rolled his chair back from the desk. The apartment was quiet in that thin, brittle way that made every sound feel suspicious — the hum of his fridge, the faint buzz of the power strip under the desk, the distant siren threading through the city outside his window.

Secure email?

No.

Shai wouldn't touch it until morning. She'd insisted on blackout protocol — no exceptions. The one time he'd argued with her about it. The one time he'd said just in case and she'd looked at him like he was tempting fate.

So he waited.

And while he waited, his eyes drifted back to the screen.

The thing that had been needling him for days now.

Not loud enough to demand attention while Antoine was burning. Loud enough to scream once the noise died down.

The duplicate footprint.

At first he'd thought it was a cache glitch. Then a shadowed session. Then maybe — just maybe — his own paranoia finally tipping over into delusion.

But paranoia didn't replicate permissions.

He pulled the logs back up and leaned forward, elbows on the desk, pupils shrinking as the data resolved.

There it was again.

His access key.

His permission scope.

His fingerprint — down to the pressure curve and micro-delay he'd trained into his own systems to spot impostors.

Except it wasn't him.

Someone else was moving through the architecture wearing his credentials like skin.

Not stealing.

Not copying.

Watching.

They hadn't shut him down.

They hadn't poisoned the system.

They hadn't even blocked him.

Which meant they wanted him right where he was.

Authorization wearing his face.

Mikey leaned back slowly, heart rate ticking up despite his best efforts. Whoever this was had enterprise-level reach. The kind you didn't buy. The kind you were granted — or inherited.

He glanced at the clock.

1:17 a.m.

Too quiet. Too late. Too perfect.

He grabbed the mirror from the edge of his desk and dumped a line without ceremony, straightening it out of habit more than desire. The razor scraped softly, a familiar sound that grounded him even as his nerves buzzed.

He told himself it helped him focus.

He knew it didn't.

The burn hit fast. Chemical. Sharp. His eyes watered, pulse spiking, thoughts snapping into painful clarity.

Okay.

If they were watching digitally, they'd already clocked his panic. If they were watching physically—

His gaze slid to the door.

He checked the tracker on his phone.

Shai's dot was moving. Slow. Normal. Not distressed.

Good.

He stood and pulled on his hoodie, pocketing the secure phone and the backup. His first instinct was to go to her. It always was. Muscle memory. Loyalty wired into bone.

Then his brain caught up.

Outside, he was an easy target.

Inside, at least the walls were familiar.

He stepped toward the door anyway, hand lifting toward the biometric panel — not a code, not something that could be shoulder-surfed or guessed. Retinal scan, depth-mapped, calibrated to him alone.

The panel lit softly.

He leaned in.

The door unlocked with a muted click.

He hadn't fully stepped out when the pressure came.

Cold steel pressed into the back of his neck, precise and practiced. Not shaking. Not rushed.

"Inside," a voice said quietly, close enough that he could feel breath against his ear.

The door was shoved inward as he was forced back across the threshold. His shoulder clipped the frame. The lock slid home behind them with a heavy finality that echoed too loud in the small apartment.

Mikey raised his hands slowly.

No sudden moves. No heroics.

"Gentlemen," he said, voice calm despite the thud in his chest. "This feels aggressive for a social call."

They guided him forward, gun never leaving his spine.

He let them.

Better to see the room. Better to understand the shape of the trap.

He dropped into his chair like this was just another meeting, another night where he wasn't three steps from getting killed. The chair creaked under his weight. He set his phone face down on the desk with deliberate care and pulled the baggie from his pocket like he was alone.

"So what is this about?" he asked mildly.

A figure stepped out from the corner.

Tailored suit. Perfect posture. The kind of calm that came from never having to check your surroundings twice.

"Hello, Michael," the man said.

Mikey smiled thinly. "Anthony Bennett. What a pleasant surprise. To what do I owe the honor?"

He poured powder onto the mirror, lined it cleanly. Ritual. Rhythm. Something he could still control.

"Can I offer you a drink? A line?" he asked, extending the rolled bill like they were old friends catching up.

"No, thank you," Anthony said, taking a seat opposite him and crossing his legs neatly, one ankle resting on his knee like he was at a country club.

"Suit yourself." Mikey took a line in each nostril. The burn flared, eyes watering, heart hammering. He swallowed it down and leaned back, chair rocking on two legs.

"You are a hard man to track down, Michael," Anthony said conversationally. "If I did not have someone almost as good as you on my payroll, you would still be a rumor. I admire people like you. A ghost in a digital world. No family. No attachments. No life... outside of Shai."

"Yeah," Mikey said lightly. "She's good people."

"I'm sure she is." Anthony adjusted his suit jacket, smoothing the fabric like he had all the time in the world. "But that is not why I am here."

He leaned forward, elbows resting on his knees.

"You accessed systems that did not belong to you," he continued calmly. "You left a trail."

Mikey shrugged. "Must be sloppy code. Happens."

Anthony straightened his cuffs, gold watch catching the light.

"You received an anonymous email. You pulled records. Names. Amounts. Patterns," he said. "You interfered with business. My business. And I take pride in good business."

Silence stretched.

"So," Anthony said softly, "what do we do about that?"

Mikey turned to his computer, fingers gliding over the keyboard like a pianist taking a final bow. A few keystrokes. A forced crash. The screen tore into colored lines and went black.

Anthony didn't flinch.

"I do not have time for games," he said, standing. "If I wanted what was on your computers, I would already have it."

"We both know how this ends," Mikey replied quietly. Beneath the drugs and bravado, a strange calm settled in. "I'm not an idiot."

"You're right," Anthony said. "There are always casualties of war, Michael. Unfortunately, you are one of them."

He turned toward the door.

"Hey, Anthony," Mikey called.

Anthony paused, hand on the handle, head turning just enough.

"How does it feel," Mikey asked, smiling crookedly, "to know another woman is fucking your wife better than you ever did?"

He laughed — loud, reckless — and dragged his face through the remaining line on the mirror like defiance itself could get him out alive.

Anthony's jaw flexed once.

The only crack.

"Make it quick," he said to the bodyguard. "And destroy everything. Including that phone."

The door closed.

Mikey leaned back, breath finally shaking loose.

Shai, he thought.

I tried.

The room went dark.

CHAPTER THIRTY-THREE

616

The city always lies at night.

It dresses itself up in neon and laughter and music that bleeds through walls, like the noise can convince you nothing bad ever happens here. Like there aren't people who wake up in alleys. Like there aren't men who make phone calls and end lives without raising their voice.

I used to believe the lie when I was younger.

Now I just move through it.

Antoine walked beside me toward my car with that loose, relieved stride men get when they think the worst part is over. Like the air itself had forgiven him. Like one good night with the right people could erase what the internet did to his name.

"Man... Shai, look at us," he said, grinning through tired eyes. "We made it."

I glanced at him, reading his face the way I'd been reading him since we were kids — the small crack under the smile, the overcompensation, the hope he didn't want to admit he still had.

"With everything we've been through," he continued, "everything you been through? God is good, yo."

"Yeah," I said, voice quieter than I meant. "He is."

We reached the parking lot. Gravel crunched under our shoes. A streetlight flickered over my car, casting long shadows that stretched and shrank like the world couldn't decide what shape it wanted to be.

I unlocked the car and slid into the driver's seat, exhaling as the leather met my back. The day had been too long. The week had been too long. My body was running on fumes and discipline.

Antoine buckled in, twisting his cap backward like he was resetting himself into "regular life."

"Chantae gonna call me," he said, staring at the water bottle he'd grabbed from the bar like it might predict the future.

"She's checking for you," I told him, starting the engine. "But don't do the most. Don't blow her up. Let her breathe."

He nodded. "I'm trying."

I pulled out slow, letting the car ease forward. The streets around us were still alive — Uber drivers circling, couples arguing outside taco trucks, the usual LA midnight chaos. But it was thinning. The kind of thinning that made everything look more vulnerable.

I kept one hand on the wheel and the other resting near the center console, mind still half in CEO mode — scanning mirrors, registering movement, doing the quiet math I always did even when I told myself I wasn't.

Antoine stared out the window for a moment, then looked over at me.

"I'm sorry," he said suddenly.

I didn't answer right away.

"Shai... I'm sorry," he repeated, voice heavier. "I shouldn't have put you in that position. None of this. Not the headlines. Not the lawyers. Not you having to walk into rooms and save me like I'm a damn child."

I exhaled through my nose. My jaw clenched and released.

"I told you already," I said, keeping my eyes on the road. "I got you."

He swallowed. "Even after finding out it was your sister the whole time? That's cold, bro."

My grip tightened on the steering wheel without permission.

"Life is cold," I said simply. "And I'll figure it out. I always do."

"You always do," he echoed, like it was prayer.

Silence settled for a beat. The kind that should have felt peaceful.

It didn't.

Something was wrong.

Not obvious wrong. Not "sirens in the distance" wrong. Something smaller. Something internal. Like my instincts were standing up in my chest, pushing the chair back.

I tried to ignore it.

Tried to tell myself it was exhaustion.

Tried to tell myself I was only tense because my world had been under a microscope all week.

But then I realized what it was.

My phone hadn't buzzed in a while.

That wasn't normal. Not for me.

Even when I'm "off," I'm still on. A text from security. A board email. Rosa asking what time I want dinner. Mikey sending something cryptic that makes me roll my eyes.

Nothing.

I glanced at the dash clock.

1:27 a.m.

My mind flicked to Elia. The way she'd looked earlier before she left for girls' night — glowing, confident, proud. The way she said she was done hiding. The way she kissed me like she wanted to anchor herself to something real.

I should've been home by now.

I should've been answering her "you safe?" text and telling her I was ten minutes out.

Instead I was here, driving Antoine home, doing what I always do — cleaning up, carrying, managing.

I reached for my phone on reflex.

The one I'd been using earlier was missing.

I patted my pockets once. Twice. Checked the cup holder. The side compartment. Nothing.

My chest tightened.

"Damn it, Toine," I muttered, eyes flicking down to the console. "Where is my other phone?"

Antoine leaned forward, lifting receipts and tapping around the passenger seat like it was a scavenger hunt. "I didn't see you with another phone."

I kept driving, scanning the road while my brain ran through possibilities.

I'd been in the section. I'd been at the bar. I'd been in the hallway.

I remembered the restroom. The lack of my phone in my hand. The quick flicker of unease that I'd shrugged off.

A memory flashed — two men in the lounge who didn't look like they belonged. Too clean. Too deliberate. Eyes tracking movement instead of music.

My stomach dipped.

"You sure you didn't pick it up?" I asked, voice tighter now.

Antoine lifted the edge of the floor mat. "Hold on... oh. Wait."

He reached into the front compartment and pulled out my other phone like he'd just found a spare key.

"There," he said. "This one?"

I snatched it, thumb hitting the screen before my brain could slow me down.

Seven missed calls.

All from Mikey.

My heart didn't speed up. It dropped.

The missed calls sat on the screen like warnings — timestamps stacked too close together, like he'd been calling in a hurry... then calling again because he didn't have another option.

Mikey didn't do that.

Mikey didn't panic-call.

Mikey didn't repeat himself.

He only did that when something had teeth.

"Who's blowing you up like that?" Antoine asked, craning his neck to see the screen.

"Don't worry about it," I said automatically, but my voice had gone sharp.

I clicked into the missed calls, scrolling, searching for context like context could save me. My thumb hovered over Mikey's name.

I hit call.

Straight to voicemail.

My stomach turned cold.

Again.

Voicemail.

No text. No encrypted ping. No "call me back now."

Just... silence.

A silence that didn't belong to him.

I pulled the phone to my ear anyway, like if I listened hard enough I could hear him breathing on the other side.

Nothing.

I ended the call and stared at the screen.

Seven missed calls.

No answer.

No follow up.

I clicked into voicemail.

One new message.

My thumb hovered over play.

Everything in me hesitated, not because I was scared of the content — but because some part of me already knew what it meant.

I hit play.

Static.

A rough inhale.

Then Mikey's voice—low, tight, like he was forcing calm through clenched teeth.

"Shai—"

The message cut off.

My blood went ice.

"What the hell..." I whispered.

Antoine shifted beside me. "What is it?"

I didn't answer.

I redialed.

Voicemail.

I tried again.

Voicemail.

I looked up at the road and suddenly it felt too open. Too dark. Too exposed. The streetlights weren't comforting anymore — they were stage lighting.

"Antoine," I said, voice dropping. "Lock your door."

He blinked. "What?"

"Lock your door," I repeated, sharper.

He did it without arguing, fingers fumbling with the lock like he finally heard the alarm in my tone.

I kept driving, eyes scanning mirrors. Cars behind us. Cars beside us. The one lingering too long at the light. The one that matched my speed a little too clean.

My breathing got shallow without permission.

I hated that.

I'd trained myself out of panic years ago.

But this wasn't panic.

This was pattern recognition.

My brain was stitching together a picture and my body was responding before the thought fully formed.

Mikey calling seven times.

Silence.

A cut voicemail.

Two men in a lounge.

A missing phone.

Someone was close.

I didn't know who. I didn't know how.

But they were close.

I should've called security.

I should've called my driver.

I should've rerouted.

But the road ahead was an intersection, and the car beside me was moving like it had somewhere to be.

I looked down for one second — one stupid CEO second — to hit Mikey's number again and switch to my secure line.

"Oh, shit, Shai, look out!" Antoine shouted.

I snapped my eyes up.

Headlights.

Too close.

Too fast.

The impact hit from my side like a bomb. Metal screamed. Time snapped in half.

The car lifted, spun, and the world turned into sound and glass and white light.

My body jerked hard against the seatbelt, pain slicing across my shoulder. The steering wheel yanked out of my hands. The airbag detonated into my face like a punch from God.

Everything went silent.

Not quiet — silent.

That monstrous, high-pitched ringing swallowed the world whole.

We spun again.

And again.

The streetlights smeared into long streaks like someone dragged paint across my vision.

Then we stopped.

My head lolled, neck screaming.

I blinked hard, trying to make my eyes work.

The windshield was spiderwebbed. The passenger window was gone. Cold air rushed in. My mouth tasted like blood and burned plastic.

I turned.

Antoine was slumped over, his head tilted at a wrong angle, blood dark on his temple.

"Toine..." I tried to say.

My tongue felt thick.

My hands didn't feel like mine.

I reached for him, fingers numb.

"Antoine," I forced out, louder this time — but the ringing swallowed it.

My door wrenched open.

Hands grabbed me.

Not helping hands.

Not emergency hands.

Rough hands.

My body scraped against broken glass as they dragged me out, my skin catching, slicing, burning.

I tried to fight.

My arms wouldn't work right.

My legs didn't know what to do.

The world tilted, nausea ripping through me like a wave.

I heard Antoine's name in my head like a chant.

I heard Mikey's cut voicemail.

I heard Elia's voice — text me when you head out.

Then something hard cracked against the side of my head and the ringing became everything.

The sky flipped.

The ground disappeared.

And the city's lie finally fell apart.

The world went black.

CHAPTER THIRTY-FOUR

616

I came back in pieces.

Sound first — an engine hum, steady and indifferent. Then the ringing in my left ear, high and shrill, like someone had jammed a whistle into bone and snapped it off. It didn't fade. It didn't pulse. It just stayed, making every thought feel like it had to push through wet cement.

My mouth tasted like pennies. My lips stuck when I tried to swallow. Pain followed next, patient and thorough — jaw, ribs, the side of my head where blood had dried in tacky streaks. I kept my eyes closed, not from fear, but strategy.

Listen first. Move second.

The car was rolling over something rough. Gravel. Dirt. Not freeway. Not city. The suspension shuddered in short, ugly bursts. Stones popped under the tires.

Two sets of breathing sat with me.

One to my left — slow, bored. The kind of breathing you do when you're on hour six of a job you've done a hundred times.

One in front — heavier, agitated. Adrenaline or anger or both.

My wrists were numb. I tested them without moving my arms — tiny flex, slight roll. No cuffs. But I wasn't free. My shoulders were pinned, my body angled wrong, like I'd been tossed into the back seat instead of placed there.

Antoine.

The memory hit like a fist: his blood, the passenger seat, my hand reaching—

I forced my mind to stop spiraling. Spiraling wasted time. Time was the only currency I had left.

The engine changed pitch. The car slowed. Gravel got louder, more distinct. A curve — the kind you take when you're driving into nowhere on purpose.

We stopped.

The engine idled. A door opened. Footsteps on gravel. Another door. Murmurs too low to catch. Then the engine cut, and silence dropped so hard it felt like weight on my chest.

My body tried to shift toward the door. A hand slammed down on my shoulder.

"Don't," a voice said, flat.

I swallowed blood and forced my voice into something usable. "Look," I said, measured. "I have money. Whoever is paying you, I'll double it. Triple it. You don't have to do this."

No response. Just someone exhaling like I was inconvenient.

The door beside me opened. Cold air punched in. Hands grabbed my arms and hauled me out before I could brace. My shoulder scraped the frame. Pain lit up my skull in white.

My feet hit dirt. My knees dipped. I caught myself.

A hood went over my head. The world vanished.

Smell took over — damp earth, pine sap, gasoline, and the metallic bite of my own blood. They shoved me forward. My shoes sank into soft ground, then found gravel, then something harder.

I counted steps. Eight. Twelve. Twenty.

They didn't talk.

People who talk are nervous. People who stay quiet are professionals.

My hands were yanked behind me. Something bit into my wrists — zip ties. Cheap. Fast. Disposable. My shoulders tightened against the burn.

A chair scraped. Metal legs on rock. They forced me down. The chair was cold, hard, unforgiving. My ribs screamed when my body settled.

The hood came off in a rough jerk.

Moonlight slapped my eyes. For a second it was all blur — trees, smoke, shadow. Then my focus snapped into place.

Two freshly dug graves sat in front of me.

Raw dirt was piled at their heads like small ugly hills. The holes were wide enough to swallow a person whole. An empty chair sat beside mine, waiting like a threat made physical.

A chill crawled up my spine, slow and deliberate.

"What the fuck is this?" I demanded, testing the zip ties. They cut into my skin immediately. "Where is Antoine?"

No one answered.

A lighter flicked to my right. A brief flare of orange revealed a jawline and a cigarette, then darkness again.

I forced my breathing to stay measured. My mind, however, was sprinting.

Two graves. Two chairs.

This wasn't a kidnapping.

This was a message.

A performance.

Shapes moved in the tree line — at least three men, maybe four. No masks. No effort to hide. That meant they didn't plan on me describing anyone. That meant they didn't plan on me walking away.

"Now you're paying attention," a cultured voice said.

My blood went cold in one clean drop.

A figure stepped out of the shadows like the woods had opened for him.

Anthony Bennett.

Tailored coat. Crisp shirt. Shoes too clean for dirt. Hair perfect. Face calm, almost entertained — a man arriving late to a dinner party, irritated the appetizers were already served.

"It's a shame we had to meet under such extreme circumstances," he said, strolling closer as if he owned the air.

"Anthony," I said, flat. "What the fuck are you doing? Where is Antoine?"

He smiled, slow and patronizing. "Always worried about your boys. So loyal."

"I asked you a question."

Anthony paced in front of the graves like he was deciding which view he liked best. "You're bold," he said. "I'll give you that."

"Stop talking and answer me."

He stopped in front of the second grave and looked down into it. Then he looked at me, smile widening just enough to be ugly.

"You like the holes?" he asked.

My jaw clenched. "What are they for?"

Anthony's eyes slid over me, slow and predatory. "One is already spoken for," he said. "That's a debt."

My stomach turned. "Who?"

He smiled like he'd been waiting for me to ask. "Elia or Mikey, I haven't decided yet."

My chest tightened so hard it felt like my ribs might crack. "Where's Mikey?"

"Oh, Mikey," Anthony said softly. "The cokehead." He shrugged, casual. "Last I saw him, he was face-down in a pile of cocaine."

Something inside me snapped. "You motherfucker!"

I lunged as far as the chair and zip ties would allow. Hands yanked me back. A fist cracked across my face.

Light exploded behind my eyes. The clearing tilted. My ear rang even louder, like it was laughing at me.

"What a waste of talent," Anthony said, already bored.

He stepped closer until I could smell him — expensive cologne, antiseptic, control.

"See Shai, this was never just about you and my wife," he said, and the warmth he'd been pretending at drained clean away. "I had Antoine in my pocket. He helped finish the funding. Then your friend Mikey sent us money that didn't exist, and somehow the FDA discovered the side effects and shut everything down. Luckily for Antoine, he might be redeemable, if he's not dead."

He crouched in front of me, close enough that it felt intimate in the worst way.

"Tens of millions, Shai," he said calmly. "Do you know how many people I answer to for that kind of loss?"

My throat tightened. I forced my voice steady. "This is about money."

Anthony's smile twitched. "Finally. You're learning."

"I didn't sabotage your project," I said, slow. "I didn't pull your plug. Mikey can attest—"

Anthony cut me off without raising his voice. "Mikey's not attesting to shit."

He stood, dusted imaginary dirt from his coat, and nodded toward the graves again.

"And the second hole?" I asked, because I needed to hear him say it.

Anthony didn't blink. "That one is for you," he said. Plain. Certain. "If this doesn't go the way I want — if my wife doesn't come home the way she's supposed to — she'll be in the hole next to you."

My stomach dropped, heavy and immediate.

He leaned in slightly, voice low, personal, meant to sink hooks into bone. "And you'll know, right before the dirt hits your face, exactly why it happened."

Footsteps crunched behind him.

A second set. Something softer, uneven — someone being guided, dragged, handled.

My pulse went hard, brutal.

Then I heard her.

A muffled inhale. A small stumble. The sound of restrained panic trying not to become a scream.

"Elia?" My voice broke before I could stop it. "Elia!"

A hand slammed the back of my head. Pain flared sharp and bright. Stars burst across my vision.

"Shut up," someone hissed near my ear.

Elia's voice shook, sharp with panic. "Shai? Baby—what is going on?"

I swallowed blood. Forced my voice into control. "I don't know, love," I said hoarsely. "But don't panic. Breathe. Stay calm."

Anthony laughed softly, like I was adorable. "Listen to you."

They shoved her into the empty chair beside mine. Her shoulder brushed mine. She was trembling so hard I could feel it through contact.

Anthony stepped in front of her, head tilted, studying her like she was an object he'd misplaced, removing her blindfold.

"Anthony," Elia said, voice shaking but clear, "what are you doing?"

His expression softened — fake tenderness, a performance clean enough to fool strangers.

"You broke my heart," he said.

Elia's breath hitched. Tears slid down her cheeks.

"Please," she whispered. "Don't do this."

Anthony's eyes slid back to me, slow and predatory again.

"No," he said, calm as a verdict. "Shai did this to herself. Did you not?"

I forced myself to breathe. Forced my voice into steady lines even as the zip ties burned into my wrists.

"Look," I said, controlled. "I don't know what story you've built in your head, but we can work something out that doesn't end like this."

Anthony's expression hardened. Whatever warmth he'd been pretending at drained away.

"Oh, this was never just about you and my wife," he said again, like he enjoyed repeating it. "This is about actions and consequences."

I stared at him, refusing to give him fear.

Anthony reached into his coat and pulled out a syringe.

Clear liquid shimmered inside the barrel, catching a thin sliver of moonlight.

"I saved a few vials." he said conversationally. "Insurance."

"No," I said, voice low. "Don't."

Elia struggled harder. Two men stepped in, pinning her shoulders down like they'd rehearsed it.

"You don't have to do this," I said, hoarse now. "You know what that drug does. You know the risk."

"We've refined it," Anthony replied. "And I have the antidote."

He stepped closer to her, swabbing her skin with clinical precision.

"As long as she gets it on time, she'll be fine," he continued, and his eyes flicked to me. "Key words, Shai — I have the antidote."

"You are a sick piece of shit," Elia spat through clenched teeth. "I can never love you again."

Anthony leaned close to her ear, voice meant for her but designed to hurt me.

"Look at her," he said softly — to Elia, not me. "Because this is the last time you're going to remember that face."

Elia's eyes found mine in the darkness of the night, like love was its own light.

"Elia—" My throat closed.

Anthony didn't hesitate.

He drove the needle in.

Elia screamed.

The sound ripped through the clearing — raw, animal, unbearable.

"I love you, Shai!" she cried, voice breaking. "I will always love you—"

"I love you," I forced out, and my voice finally cracked open. "I'll be with you always. Remember that."

Her body went slack.

Like someone cut her strings.

Anthony stepped back, satisfied, like he'd just closed a deal.

"Now," he said calmly, "we're going to fix what you broke. She becomes proof that it works. We replicate it. We sell it on the black market. The investors stop asking questions."

"You're turning her into a lab rat," I snapped. "Your mother should've swallowed."

Anthony didn't react.

Not a flinch. Not a blink.

He only smiled, faint and indulgent, like I'd said something childish.

"That," he said evenly, "is why you were never meant to be in rooms like mine."

His men lifted Elia with practiced efficiency and carried her toward a black SUV idling at the edge of the clearing.

No ritual. No spectacle.

Just extraction.

I fought again, screaming her name until my throat tore, until a boot drove the air from my lungs and the world swam.

Anthony paused at the open door, glancing back at me.

"You don't get to play hero," he said quietly. "You don't get to rewrite my life."

He adjusted his jacket like he was smoothing out the last wrinkle in a plan.

"And you don't get to keep what isn't yours."

He turned to get into the SUV, then stopped — one last look, one last knife.

His gaze flicked to the graves.

Then back to me.

"This," he said, enunciating each word, "is what power looks like when it doesn't need permission. That second hole stays open until I get what I came for."

"Finish her," he said quietly to his henchman. "And make sure she clearly understands why she'll never be a man."

His gaze lingered just long enough to make sure the message landed.

Then he got into the SUV.

The door shut.

The engine rose.

Headlights flared through the trees once, then disappeared into the dark.

I was left zip-tied to a chair, staring at two open graves — one promised to a dead man, the other waiting on my next move — while the night breathed slow and even, like it already knew how this story ended.

CHAPTER THIRTY-FIVE

616

Time did not move forward. It folded.

Sound went first — not all of it, just the edges. Like someone turned the world down a few clicks too many. The forest stopped sounding like a forest and became air rushing through a tunnel.

My wrists burned. Then they didn't. Then they did again.

Hands grabbed me — rough, impatient, not careful. The chair tipped, scraped, fell. My shoulder slammed into the ground hard enough to punch the breath clean out of me.

I didn't scream. That surprised me. I waited for it — the reflex, the instinct — but it never came. My body moved without asking. Rolled. Curled. Took impact where it would hurt less. Muscle memory from a life where control mattered.

Zip ties snapped. Someone laughed.

A boot pressed into my ribs, grinding, testing. Something gave. I tasted blood.

My head hit dirt. Gravel bit into my cheek. Pine needles stuck to the wet of my face. The smell of the woods pressed in close — earth, sap, oil, sweat.

Hands again. Too many. Not rushed.

That was the part my brain rejected first. They weren't frantic. They weren't angry. They weren't improvising. This was routine.

That realization slid somewhere deep and locked itself away.

I left my body. Not all at once. Not dramatically. Just... stepped sideways.

Suddenly there was sand beneath my feet. Warm. Fine. Sun-bleached. The sound of the ocean replaced everything — steady, endless, forgiving. Waves rolling in slow, unbothered rhythms. Salt in the air. Heat kissing my skin instead of tearing at it.

Necker Island.

Elia was there. Barefoot. Laughing. Wind lifting her hair. That soft smile she only wore when no one was watching. The ring was still on my finger — warm from the sun, familiar against my skin.

My hands were steady there. In the clearing, they were not.

Something cracked across my face. Hard. My head snapped sideways. Pain flared, then dulled, like it had been wrapped in cotton.

I focused on the waves.

Too loud. Too close. Elia teasing me for flinching when the water rushed higher than expected. Pulling me back toward her, laughing, warm, alive.

Someone yanked my hair. My neck screamed. Fabric tore. Cold night air invaded places it didn't belong.

On the beach, Elia pressed her forehead to mine. I felt her heartbeat — steady, real — beneath my palm. The sun on my shoulders. The certainty of being held.

In the woods, hands pinned my shoulders.

My breath hitched.

No.

The word echoed far away, like it belonged to someone else.

I watched the tide pull back in my mind. Foam dissolving. The ring glinting once as my hand moved. Proof I existed. Proof we existed.

Laughter cut through the air. Not mine. Not hers.

Something struck my jaw again. Stars burst. My ears rang. The world narrowed to sensation without context — pressure, heat, the wrongness of being touched where I did not consent to exist.

I wasn't thinking anymore. I was cataloging. Weight. Smell. Texture. The exact moment pain tipped into numb.

This wasn't survival. This was endurance.

On the beach, Elia leaned into me, breath warm against my neck. The ocean never stopped moving. It never noticed pain. It never cared.

In the clearing, someone spoke. I didn't catch the words. The tone mattered more — casual, almost bored.

A hand clamped over my mouth.

Another blow landed low, stealing air, folding me inward.

I tasted dirt. I tasted copper.

I floated higher. Above the trees now. Looking down at a body that used to be mine. Small. Restrained. Surrounded.

Detached enough to notice how efficient they were. Detached enough to feel my name slipping away.

Time fractured again.

There was no before. There was no after.

Just this long, endless now where my body was something being handled, and my mind refused to stay inside it.

Then a sound cut through everything. Different. Final.

A sharp crack that did not belong to fists or boots or bodies.

A gunshot.

For one suspended second, even the forest seemed to inhale.

Pain bloomed white-hot — overwhelming, absolute. My vision collapsed inward, tunneling fast.

The last thing I felt was her heartbeat, radiating through the ring, along the vena amoris, straight into my heart.

Then nothing.

Black.

* * *

Acknowledgements

This book exists because I kept going.
Thank you to those who knew when to listen and when to let me finish.

About the Author

Zo Ramey writes contemporary fiction exploring power, identity, and intimacy. 614 is their debut novel. They live where stories demand to be told.

More at read614.com

Made in the USA
Coppell, TX
22 February 2026

72010899R00169